BAD

ALSO BY ALAN WALL

FICTION

Curved Light

Bless the Thief

Silent Conversations

Richard Dadd in Bedlam

The Lightning Cage

The School of the Night

China

Sylvie's Riddle

POETRY

Jacob

Chronicle

Lenses

Alexander Pope at Twickenham

Gilgamesh

Doctor

Placebo

ALAN WALL

BADMOUTH

Harbour

First published as a paperback original by
Harbour in 2014
Harbour Books (East) Ltd, PO Box 10594
Chelmsford, Essex CM1 9PB
info@harbourbooks.co.uk

A CIP record for this book is available
from the British Library

ISBN 978 190512822 8

Typeset in Great Britain by Antony Gray
Printed and bound in Finland by Bookwell

Contents

To My Mother Elizabeth
and to the Memory of My Father
Arthur Wall

*The world has become sad because a puppet
once was melancholy.*

Oscar Wilde, 'The Decay of Lying'

Acknowledgments

I would like to thank the following for their help:

Jeremy Beale, Ann Denham, David Elliott, Andrew Hedgecock, Steve Lloyd, Michael Moorcock, Jenny Newman, Emma Rees, Anthony Rudolf, Bernard Sharratt, Chris Simon, Chris Steare.

Harry Sprite and the Professor

1

The age of the vents is dead. When was the last time you saw a ventriloquist with a dummy on his knee, treating you to his wooden grin? They don't do them any more. That world went with the last variety shows, and they're dead too, as dead as the dusty *artistes* who once graced their bills. Theatres where crowds gathered night after night have been turned into cinemas or bingo halls or simply demolished. Now when people talk to a piece of wood it's out in the forest, bonding with native flora, asking for roots to sprout downwards through the damaged urban psyche. Some intellectual honcho embracing a tall pine in California, stripping off to feel rough bark against naked flesh; certainly not sharing acid repartee with a besuited stiff-backed dwarf at the Hackney Empire. A homunculus with a borrowed voice. Insolence's painted face and *rigor mortis* grin. Your other half, a cackling Hyde to your oh-so-gracious Dr Jekyll.

And that's the only reason I picked Harry up cheap. No one else wanted the little bugger. His face is dented from colliding with the inside of his dummy's case, collateral from the haphazard itineraries of one too many gyrating, late-night dypsos with him on their knee. (The ventriloquist has seldom made a virtue of sobriety. We are usually obliged to drink for two, remember.) Harry was orphaned when his last owner fell off the wagon and pawned him. And now I'm inclined to dispose of him myself, but he simply won't shut up and go. You can be sure of that much: he certainly won't go quietly. He'd start jabbering to his new possessor. About everything. I'd have to cut him up, and I don't think I could face the screams. Wood bleeds. Take it from me, it does. Sap leaks still from the ancient fetish. Tears and blood. Harry weeps and Harry bleeds, but he doesn't do either quietly. Harry doesn't do anything quietly. Even in sleep he cries out. Egyptian messages on the walls of our little pyramid of shadows here. And whenever he bleeds, he makes sure I do too. I have a collection of wounds to prove it. The scab and the cicatrix. He's a little tyrant. And his language is . . . well, you'll find out for yourself soon enough. If you think it's quiet now, that's because he's completely blacked-out in his box over there, his ebony coffin with the ivory inlays. His well-carved wooden head is back in the forest now, blowing this way and that, biting the wind's tail. But he never sleeps for long, our boy. Insomnia: something else Harry and I have in common. One more bond between the dead branch from the sacred wood and yours truly. I call him Harry and he calls me Mr Bones. Now what exactly do you make of that?

'Do you know you're talking out loud again? If it weren't for me, they'd be putting your jacket on back to front. Bones, Bones, Dry Old Bones. Let me out. Transport me from this dark over here to that one over there. EARN YOUR KEEP, MY KEEPER.' The voice is muffled, trapped inside its portable domicile, but understandable. There's a thumping sound now as he kicks the box lid: and I've never understood how those boneless legs of his can do that. Silk to the touch but limp, entirely lifeless, when he's out of his box. Nothing but crumpled sleeves with boots dangling on the end. But inside his little box . . . once in there he has a life all his own, whenever he chooses. There have been times, I'll confess to this, when I've even been jealous. Particularly when he calls out in his sleep. Such a variety of cries. How many creatures does he keep in there? Is it a circus? One night I'll gain entry to those dreams of his, inside that three-foot oblong where he holds his sabbath shake-downs, and observe his skeletons with painted faces for myself. The white horses and laughing tigers. Dragons with articulate tails.

'I know you're there, Mr Bones. I hear the sound your thoughts make when they collide with one other. Things that go bump in the night. Molecules. The room is heating up.'

There is almost nothing, you might note, which that dwarfish companion of mine has not read. I taught him to read, so that he could read to me. In the long dark hours of the night. None longer and none darker than mine. Dread's metronome. The terrible hours when the heart's clunk is louder than the clock's. Sometimes it's like being vomited over by a thesaurus. I think he has a special gift for absorbing print in the dark. Is that possible? His mind is made of wood, remember, like the paper on which these words are printed. Shall we spring him? No, let him sweat it out for a few minutes more. There'll be grief enough when he emerges, though he can always make me laugh if he has a mind to.

Does this curious situation have a history? And are you interested anyway? Ask him then. He'll tell you the lot. Harry doesn't do repression: everything that happens gets repeated, without apology, without legal representation, and apparently without emotion. A glittering mirror with a mouth. But Harry is unlike the mirror: he forgets nothing that once enters the shiny surface of his grin. And unlike the mirror he carries on smiling, sometimes using your face to do it, long after you yourself have stopped, and turned on the tears instead. For Harry, history is nothing but what's been dredged out and stored inside him, ready to be disgorged again at any time. History is fast food, memory's disposable protein. So let's get him out and listen to him as he starts disgorging once more. Are you sure you're ready?

2

Just look at that grin. Whatever happens in here, whatever happens out there, that grin never slips; whatever you tell him, whatever he replies. Even if you should strike him, or he should strike you back (it does happen, I'm afraid), even then the grin stays constant: I've been looking at you lot over the years, and a manic grin is surely the only intelligent response to your appalling behaviour – that's what Harry's grin seems to say, though it has many ways of saying it.

'On about my grin again, are you, Mr Bones? You've got an obsession, you have. An obsession with me and my attributes. You know what I put all this down to, don't you? Come on; get me sitting comfortably on your knee, and I'll tell you what I put it all down to again, shall I?'

I settle him down, smooth out his silky boneless legs, and take hold of the mechanism inside him. Now we're both comfortable. His head turns slowly towards me.

'So what do you put it all down to, Harry?'

'If I were a psychoanalyst you'd have to pay for this.'

'I feed you.'

'Only with resin, which you squirt into my veins with something that looks suspiciously like a hypodermic to me. You only do that so I won't squeak. Which means, you feed me for your own purposes, not mine. To ensure that all my parts move smoothly, without grating on your nerves.'

'You still haven't told me what it is you put my obsession down to.'

'I reckon you've ended up obsessed with me because of the way your obsession with all the others turned out. Or haven't you told them yet? You can be so coy, Mr Bones. Your audience surely deserves something in the way of explanation. If only as a courtesy.'

I did warn you, didn't I? Harry has no inhibitions, no morality; no feelings, I sometimes think, except for a sort of hilarity when faced with the emotional failures filling up my life. Or yours. Our lives, mind, not his. He tells me the only real trauma he ever suffered was when they cut him down beside the river eighty years ago. Cut him down, cut him up, carved and carpentered him, fitted him back together with a few metal rods inside, and then painted his garish features. He said that was so bad, everything else ever since has made him smile. The alder's death.

'Try getting pulled out of the womb,' I said once.

'At least they didn't take a saw to you, sir.'

'It was a Caesarean, so they did actually.'

He is fingering his face again. He does it without thinking sometimes. It's hard not to be moved, don't you think? His right arm opens out into a white glove, which fills with fingers, agile, dexterous fingers, remarkably like mine. Thin. Finely tapered. Not a labourer's hand. A scholar's perhaps? With great delicacy, and a kind of tactile sadness, he touches his little craters one by one.

'The Pavilion, Llandudno; Central Pier, Blackpool; the Glasgow Empire; the Winter Gardens; the Richmond; the Alhambra.'

'A wound in each place then, Harry.'

'A wound in each place, uncle. Occasionally in the dressing-room, or on the way to the stage, but usually in the pub later, or in some dingy boarding house, halfway down a bottle of whisky. So often they did what you do here each evening. Picked me up, dropped the mask at last, and talked; drank and talked, talked and drank. Told me their griefs, confessed their sins. Old Jack Tomkyns, Silas Freake, Tommy De La Mare and Dr Dibette – my owners before you found me in what was once a junk shop in Clerkenwell. These days it's a purveyor of prestigious antiques, of course.'

'Dr Dibette was the last?'

'Dr Dibette was the last, and I rather suspect the worst of the lot. Dirty-minded old bugger. If he'd ever told the police what he told me, his performances would have stopped long before he dropped dead in Mrs Remington's superior residential establishment in Hove (it's a DHSS dosshouse now). He would, I fear, have been detained at Her Majesty's Pleasure.'

'Not for the Royal Command Performance, though.'

'You're the only young man I've ever got inside – that's what he used to tell me, Mr Bones. I had to grit my teeth sometimes, to sit up there on his knee in front of those audiences. There were children down in the auditorium, you know, down in the darkness . . . and then you came along.'

'I must have made a pleasant change, surely.'

'For a while you did, yes. I thought, goodness, I've been adopted by an intellectual at last. Before you started.'

'Started with what, Harry?'

'Started with those confessions of yours.'

'Hardly the same as Dr Dibette's now, are they?'

'Well, they don't involve young boys, if that's what you mean, but I've found some of them almost as shocking. I may have a wooden heart, but you've managed to make it shake sometimes, almost as much as the wind did once. Don't cry, Mr Bones. I don't want my blue silk trousers stained with salt again. I'll start dreaming of the sea, if you weep. I've spent most of my life by the sea, after all. By the river I grew as a tree; but by the sea I worked as a dummy. For the better part of eighty years. Where the piers all set out into the briny and then turn back, defeated.'

3

'You have been out drinking, Mr Bones. I can smell it on your breath. If you must drown your sorrows, then why not do it here? It would be cheaper and you would have better company, surely. Someone at least who would *listen*. That poor lady in the Regal didn't listen for long, now did she, Bones? Told you she had to go and powder her nose and never came back. And you'd just bought her another drink, which you then had to down yourself, even though you were drinking whisky not gin. Are you afraid I'll be shocked? Why do you think I keep grinning, however acidly, if I'm so easily shocked? Jack, Silas, Tommy: they were all piss-artists. And Dr Dibette was a bona fide, Grade A, fully qualified soak. A professional. Breakfast for him was sour whisky, with an occasional double for dessert. His breath had the stench of the sepulchre about it, the dentist's own charnel-house, but I never stopped grinning. You're the one who blubs round here, remember, not me. Make sure I don't fall off your knee. Enough ditches in my battered face already. I don't want any more. In the limelight sometimes I looked like the trenches on the Western Front. Aren't you going to speak then, Mr Bones? Not a word? No messages for little Harry, left here to his own devices all evening?

'The next time you go down the pub, you'd be better off taking me with you, old son. That woman wouldn't have crept out so swiftly if you'd had me on your knee. The three of us would still be there now. Or here. She'd probably have come back with both of us later. Though she might well have wanted me in the bed alongside you, like that woman in Epping. Am I sleeping with you again tonight? I think I'd rather return to my little box, if you don't mind. It's more interesting in there, in the darkness without you. Distinguished visitors come to consult me as I tread the boards once more. Your presence would merely confuse things.'

4

DEAR UNCLE GRAHAM – When I wrote in my last letter that you needed help, I was not disparaging you. Many people need help at some point or another in their lives. I certainly have, more than once. And the condition I was describing is far from uncommon. I know that you take great delight in disparaging the terminology of modern psychology, but the combination of displacement and condensation is frequently found in dream activity. In your case it has taken a very specific form; that of visible and audible alterity. To be able to separate out so much that cannot be integrated is frequently the beginning of a psychosis. To the extent that you have turned it into a game, a ritual, an entertainment even, you have done something remarkable. I don't wish to stop you engaging in this, far from it, but I still wish you would attend to certain disturbing traits before they become unmanageable.

I have become friendly with a very intelligent psychologist, Dr Helsford. Would you at least let me effect an introduction?

With fondest regards,

ROBERT

5

'Bognor Regis. Scarborough. Bridlington. Whitby. Southend. Hastings. The man there had poisoned seagulls every year, they squawked so, filling his mind with distractions. Poisoned them and hung them from the ceiling of his pub. So our act – that was when I was with Silas, of course – had to take in the gulls, address them, sing them songs, even mistake one of the bigger ones for an albatross, and do a lot of gags about the Ancient Mariner. Penzance. Margate. Bangor and Rhyll. Make sure they bury me at sea, Mr Bones, or I'll never rest. Never never never never never. And stop dreaming about her, for heaven's sake, whoever she is. Another bimbo in a bar. Every time you go out boozing you come back with that dreamy look in your eyes. There are probably better lookers than her inside the box here. Shall I introduce you? We're all dolls, aren't we, Mr Bones, when all's said and done? That's why it's time you also stopped thinking about that tart in Epping; just another doll on just another knee. Even if she did end your distinguished life in education once and for all. Not to mention my life on the stage, which might have been slightly more significant, as a matter of fact. She has a lot to answer for, that belly-dancer. Remember our routine though, Bones? We did make them chuckle, even if they were puzzled for some of the time.'

'Where did you come from, Harry?'

'Out of the earth, Mr Bones, where all trees come from. I grew leaves. I lived by a river. I thought I might reach the sky one day. Put my head in the clouds. But the men came.'

'And what did the men do, Harry?'

'They cut me down with saws, Bones. Carried me away. Shaved and hammered and adzed me, then painted me. Painted my face till I looked like a dog's dinner. Caught your eye, didn't it, in that old junk shop in Clerkenwell all those years ago?'

'It did.'

'But then you like a painted face, don't you, Mr Bones? Look at that one down there in the darkness of the auditorium. Look, she's still there. In the third row. She must have her own personal shares in Max Factor, surely. You'd be covered in moondust by the time you'd finished canoodling with Little Miss Cosmetical there. But you wouldn't mind, would you, Bones? You like the face powder and the kohl, the lipstick and the perfume. You can already hear the cotton sheets rustling when you're surrounded by those scents. I tell you, folks, our hotel room smells like a Paris boudoir some nights. I have to hold my breath. One painted face isn't enough for the Professor here. Oh no.

'They loved it, didn't they, Bones? The more you mocked them, the more they liked it. Except for that one night . . . That really did turn nasty, didn't it?'

6

'Why did you ever teach me to read?'

'So you might understand the script.'

'Like Caliban then. You taught me language and my profit on it is I know how to curse. And it never had that effect on you, did it – being able to read? You've never understood your own script. All right then, I'll read to you, if only by way of gratitude. From that article in the newspaper you were sighing over earlier. News from the great out-doors has evidently darkened your features once more.'

He's right as usual. And now he starts to recite the article. What a memory. You don't need the details. Once more, darkness invisible becomes darkness visible. The usual story.

'Funny thing about papers, isn't it, Mr Bones?'

'What's that, Harry?'

'They're made out of wood like me. And you never do seem to learn anything much from either of us, do you? So many catastrophes. So many horrible disasters. Might as well talk to me: I can tell you all about the decline of the West, you know. I used to be a tree. I was covered in leaves, and frequently pollarded. I conversed with winds. Now I've got rouge on my cheeks and I converse with you instead, which is hardly an improvement, believe me. Instead of being rooted in the Lord's good earth, I've got your hand stuck up my rear end, turning me this way and that. So where's the justice in that then? I could get the social services on to you.'

'How so?'

'Because you're always putting your hand up my backside. Which is undoubtedly illegal with a non-consenting minor.'

'Are you a non-consenting minor, Harry?'

'All depends on how you look at it. In terms of dendrochronology, I'm getting on for my century now. The rings in the wood do rather age me. Which would mean you're abusing a senior citizen, you filthy academic pervert. But in terms of my identity, I'm a schoolboy, or hadn't you noted the silk pants, the blazer, the stripey tie so endearingly askew?'

'Do you want me to remove my hand then?'

'No. Because then I won't be able to move my mouth to ask you for some gread and gutter.'

'Speak properly when you're being spoken to.'

'All right then. Bread and butter, you miseragle old gastard.'

I warned you. He is sleeping now, on his side. The grin remains constant whether he sleeps or wakes. He has, I think, become a little more savage lately, if that is possible. He has, of course, encountered nothing to modify his bitter appraisals. But then what exactly have I encountered to modify mine? Given our mutual salty thirst for justice, what could ever slake it? The phone is ringing. Shall I answer it? I shall. Well, well, well. It is my nephew Robert. He has remembered, I suppose, that we two are now pretty much all that remains of the Fowey family, intellectually speaking. His father is one of the Plymouth Brethren, though still more intellectually endowed than his mother – my sister. Robert believes none of it, thankfully, and thinks we should meet. I suspect he's also trying to get me entangled with his friend the psychologist. Something else to look forward to, eh, Harry? (Robert has retained our dynastic name, for reasons I'm not sure I've ever fully understood. There are worse things, evidently, than being a Fowey.)

'You once looked forward to our success, Mr Bones, remember? Amazing Harry and the Prof. That was the name of our act, if you recall. And it wasn't bad, if the truth be told. In fact, it was extremely good. Except that you lost your nerve after our famous night in Epping. That woman on the front row who started asking the awkward questions – well, you do remember, obviously. And we've never done a show since, have we, Mr Bones?'

'Shut up, Harry.'

'Judy, wasn't it? She was so taken with our act that she had to accompany us to the hotel afterwards. As so many of them did, of course. And it was me she was after, if you care to recall, not you.'

'I remember.'

'And you never could forgive me for that, now could you? Or her.'

'You're staying in your box today. All day.'

'In the dark all day, master?'

'In the dark all day, my sprite.'

'I sometimes think that what Essex Judy said about you was true, you know.'

'Get inside. And stay there.'

7

'Grimsby. Southport. Bexhill. King's Lynn. Portsmouth. Bournemouth. Padstow.'

'Shut up, Harry. Leave your litany alone for one night, or at least travel through your past more quietly, if travel you must. It's like listening to some old Italian woman. Singing a Neapolitan song. Rattling her rosary.'

'Both praying for the dead then, Mr Bones. Knowing we must all join the dead 'ere long. Do you remember that night in Dover? One of my more sparkling performances, I always thought.

' "My friend here has made me promise not to reveal to you the fact that he is as upright and rigid as a unicorn. Close your ears, madame, down there in the second row. My friend has been in the manly position for some hours now. I should know. I have to sit on his knee. My God, it's awful. It's painful to behold. He should have had a girl dummy, I reckon; they might have come to some sort of arrangement. Money could have changed hands. I really can't help, you know, and I'd like to think he wouldn't want me to. Though you can never be sure these days. I once had to work with a perverted old soak by the name of Dr Dibette . . . but let's not spoil the evening with such sordid recollections. What I'd like to say is this . . . *and I'm leaning forward and whispering so he can't hear me* . . . if one of you ladies could see your way to giving him a hand, or something even better, he'd be most grateful. He's an interesting man. Very educated. A lovely talker. A professor, actually, who is the author of a book called *Ritual Voices in Antiquity*. Out by the dressing-room door then, after the show."

'Amazing how often it worked, wasn't it, Mr Bones? They would say they'd only come for the autograph, and you'd sometimes have the pick of two or three. Leave your choice till the last. I'd be signing their programmes for them – it's a wonder I didn't suffer from repetitive strain injury – the wanker's wrist, as I believe the legal profession call it these days. Or is it the wanker's writs? A lawyer's anagram. Then you'd suggest a drink, even a little meal. With me in my box, though they would all too often be asking for me to come out again. Which was understandable, I'd say. I've always improved your presence, though I wasn't always sure you were glad to see me reappear. The truth is that without me you're only half a man.'

8

I met my uncle for the last time after I had phoned to arrange a meeting. We ate in a small restaurant in Soho, of which he was fond. I was astonished how much he had aged. Only in his mid-fifties then, he seemed to me to have shrivelled since his early retirement from the university. This had followed the notorious events in Epping. Undoubtedly the most brilliant member of our family, if also the most troubled. But after the performance in Epping . . . well, that has passed into the public domain now, even if the truth of it never did. Not if my uncle is to be believed, anyway. Or the plaintiff, dear little Essex Judy. But his position as Professor of Ancient Religions was no longer tenable. He had an enemy in a position of power in the university, one of those men who need to exercise power twice a day, the way other people exercise their dogs. 'Man dressed in a little brief authority,' as my uncle would say. The endless flurry of missives and injunctions this man generated camouflaged, in my uncle's view, the void where his talent should have been. He made sure no compromise was possible. So Graham Fowey took early retirement, arranged speedily by the University of London, for whom my uncle's non-professorial notoriety had suddenly become something of a liability. Frankly, the whole business struck me then, and strikes me now, as not far off farcical. He retired to that curious flat of his, in the

Guinness Buildings off the Mile End Road. My cave, he always called it; my stony domicile where the old gods speak.

I still have the press-cuttings:

Professor's Dummy Accused of Indecent Assault

Professor Fowey and the Sex Toy

The Professor, the Ventriloquist and the Belly-Dancer

Most people in academic life had known nothing at the time of his new career as a vent, and had never heard of the act Amazing Harry and the Prof. I doubt if it occurred to anyone who saw it that the man up there with the dummy on his knee actually was a professor – and a very distinguished one too. His book, *Sacred Voices in Antiquity*, was published by the Clarendon Press at Oxford. He was eccentric, but no more eccentric than many people in academic life, and at least his eccentricity was accompanied by brilliance. Although much younger, I can be eccentric enough myself on certain days, but no one has ever suggested I should leave an academic post, even if they've not always been particularly zealous in awarding me one. But I could already see that behind the eccentricity lay something rapidly turning pathological. Uncle Graham dismissed my own ways of describing this. He found my terminology repellent. For him the diagnosis lay in the kind of ancient wisdom modernity had no means of approaching. His book is explicit about the matter. The single psyche is not large enough to contain all the forces acting upon it or generated within it. Ritual in antiquity was a way of separating some of these mighty forces out into exterior forms, and then acknowledging their potency in sacrifice or the mimicry of what had once been a sacrifice; what my uncle called the second life of liturgy. Here he is in *Sacred Voices in Antiquity*, p. 290:

> When Achilles talks to his patroness Athene, or Jesus talks to his Father on the cross, we are witnessing a ventriloquism which enunciates a truth. Truth is always a species of doubling: it is dialectical. Even the concept of the Trinity in Christian thought

establishes that all truth is relational. We must always come at ourselves from the other side. It is possible that Western civilisation has of late taken to ventriloquising a robotic machine called science, which never answers our protected psyches back with sufficient venom, but provides us instead with a confusing familiarity of equations and statistics.

I had heard stories about how he had started to take his dummy in to his lectures; how, in explaining the oracle's speech, in Delphi or anywhere else, he argued we were looking at priestly ventriloquism. That the throwing of voices, the disguising of voices, the discovery of alternate voices, became a part of the priestly arcana, and that no insincerity was involved in this. Indeed, according to the last article he ever published, the priestly trance that permitted the emergence of a different voicing of reality had subsequently transmuted into notions of trance, possession and ultimately spiritualism, and was also at the root of all our modern entertainment and drama. 'They have become their own vents' dummies,' my uncle once said about contemporary popular entertainers, 'but without the bite which comes when the wood begins to speak. They have forgotten that the whole point of the ventriloquial discourse is to be merciless. To scrape the conscience; to see the skull beneath the skin.' This had been the burden of the most problematical chapters in my uncle's undoubtedly problematical book. Uncle Graham would demonstrate his theories by engaging in a dialogue, both learned and funny, with the old vent's dummy he'd picked up on a whim.

The students loved it, apparently, and his seminars and lectures were soon over-subscribed. The authorities scratched their heads and bided their time, but if they were finding themselves confused as to what to do with Professor Graham Fowey, he resolved the matter for them five years ago, one November evening.

'I can't even return as a visiting lecturer, did you know that? My old alma mater won't let me give so much as an evening lecture. It wasn't as though she died, was it? And she wasn't raped either. If you can be raped by a ventriloquist's dummy in Epping these days, then presumably you can also be impregnated by a Greek god. Old Zeus must have many cases pending.'

'She said she was traumatised, Graham.'

'Then she was traumatised by an encounter with intelligence, and nothing more. All the rest she asked for – quite explicitly asked for. But the intelligence – that came as something of a shock, I suppose.'

'You mean she didn't realise how intelligent you were?'

'Didn't realise how intelligent he was. At least get your facts right, Robert.'

'He?'

'Harry. Before that it had been monologues or private conversations. I myself had no idea how cunning he could be, not before that night, even though we'd often found ourselves in such a situation. A hotel room; a woman; me and . . . '

'A piece of wood.'

He started to laugh then, my distinguished uncle. He laughed and laughed. His face, always skull-like, always emaciated (bad eating habits), took on a rictus, and I could see death inside it already, lurking there, rehearsing. How pale his blue eyes were; had they always been so pale? And what were the little cut-marks on his cheeks? They looked as though they had been made with a very sharp blade. Razored incisions.

'That's the mistake she made. Miss Elenor aka Judy French, shop-assistant of Epping and, come the evening, belly-dancer at the local Turkish restaurant. She thought Harry was just a piece of wood too.'

'Isn't he though?'

'Only if you're just a sequence of biochemical reactions, Robert.'

'But all the intelligence Harry displays really comes from you, Graham, doesn't it?'

'I wish that were true, Bob. I really do wish it were true, believe me. If that were true then all the conundrums surrounding ancient religion, and so much else, would be soluble in an afternoon. But they're not. I'm not convinced they'll ever be soluble. All our intelligence comes from others, initially. We all learn through mimesis. We flatter ourselves that we control the voices we ultimately release, but we don't. Once freed, they start to talk back. Once the spirit enters the wood, the tree regains its old life. But this time with a tongue instead of roots. A tongue grown from the old injustice of deforestation. I did not invent Harry, you must understand that. I simply encountered him. We reinvented one another. Now neither of us can escape.'

I realised that what my mother had often said to me might have been true: 'Your uncle may well be the last representative of a great tradition: the Fowey family's ancient history of periodic insanity. Some say that was why I married your father.' It doesn't really matter any more – that's what I thought at the time. I was wrong, I acknowledge that now. In writing out these notes I can finally acknowledge my mistake.

'You're the nearest thing I have to a living relative, now that my mother's gone.'

'There's my mother. Your sister.'

'She's certainly a relative, but living? Sorry I shouldn't really, should I?'

But I was already laughing. In following my father and joining the Plymouth Brethren, then raising me in it until the day I escaped, my mother had abandoned any claims on my affections.

'I wanted to make appropriate arrangements.'

'You want to leave your wealth to me?'

'My wealth? That sounds a bit grand, Robert, but I suppose I do have a bit put away. What I've spent on drink I've saved on food. Alcohol can be proteinaceous. And Harry is very frugal. So, unless you can think of a better recipient . . . '

9

DEAR ROBERT – I am only sorry you never saw Harry and me when we lectured together on the ancient religions. Then you might have taken the point of what we started to do, before the cant of our modern propriety contrived to shut us up.

Your mention of founding a small museum of puppetry with the money I will leave you rather intrigues me – it intrigues Harry too.

The Fowey Puppet Museum. Yes. Why not? All our names could live on in perpetuity, instead of being writ in water.

Shouldn't take too long, eh?

GRAHAM

DEAR GRAHAM – Thanks for the letter. I think I'm now committed to the scheme, though I sincerely hope it can't happen for a very long time indeed. Not too fussed about preserving our name in perpetuity, or anywhere else for that matter. Maybe all our names are writ in water from the start. Who cares anyway? At least we'll have clean reputations. Maybe one day someone will bear my child. If not, I could always buy myself a wooden dummy, and call him Robert Junior.

In fact I did see you and Harry lecture together one afternoon in London. I crept in to the lecture hall without telling you I was coming, in case you might have tried to deter me.

I found it extraordinary – and disturbing. [Pedagogy was never more properly theatrical than in these lectures of my uncle's, with Harry as interlocutor. This was philosophy. This was dialectics. To cede more than I actually felt proper to my uncle's growing pathology, I felt that Harry had finally come to speak for himself, with considerable eloquence.] The extent to which the energy of one psyche can be transferred to another object or system of belief, the extent to which the primal energies of any mind can become fetishised (what Freudians call cathexis), and perhaps might even need to be so to provide a release for the libidinal energies, touches on the work I am doing in the area between art, cognition and psychology, which I still hope to complete one day. I had been meaning to talk to you about it all, and hoped that you could meet the colleague I mentioned, the psychologist Helsford, but then that ridiculous business in Essex took place, you were forced into sudden retirement, and it all seemed too sensitive a topic to broach.

Maybe one day – but then again, maybe not. I'm growing superstitious about counting days.

Love (if you'll permit it),

ROBERT

10

'You weep so, Mr Bones. They made me from the alder tree, and the alder thrives by water. It doesn't split and it doesn't rot. That's why they used it for mill clogs and lock-gates on the canals. But so many tears, Mr Bones. You've become a real blubberhouse. If this goes on, you'll have me fearing for my varnishes.'

'I think I might be dying.'

'I know. You all are.'

'Sooner than expected.'

'Poor you.'

'My nephew saw us once, did you know that? He crept in to one of our lectures on ancient religions. Watched us performing our little number.'

'I know.'

'You saw him?'

'Yes.'

'Why didn't you tell me?'

'I thought it might unsettle you. You were easily unsettled in those days.'

'Not now then?'

'The term doesn't seem to apply any more. I don't think there's enough balance left between us to worry about unsettling anything. You can't really unsettle a seesaw. Let's watch television.'

'You know I hate television.'

'Not always. Let's watch the one about the man in Rochdale and the mail-order bride. You read the details out to me earlier. That one should provide us with a little amusement.'

So he sits on my knee, even lays his head against my breast, and we watch. This is billed as a documentary but is in fact a lengthy screening of the self-demeaning pageant of a humanity self-afflicted with distress. When not actually performing, it seems they're rehearsing for the performances that one day must lie ahead. The public grief; the self-examination.

All his English girlfriends had left him because they found him

26

self-absorbed, graceless, an inattentive lover, one moreover afflicted by nocturnal flatulence. Exasperated at the faithlessness and treachery of Western women, Rochdale Jim had gone to considerable lengths to acquire a mail-order bride from the Philippines. Two months after acquiring her own UK passport, this Asiatic beauty had left him too, remarking in her broken English on his self-absorption, gracelessness, inattentiveness as a lover, and the seemingly incessant noises he generated between the sheets during the hours of darkness.

He had decided there and then that he had best attend to his sexual needs in the same way he attended to the petrol tank beneath his car. Mostly, it could remain unnoticed, unthought of, but now and then a nozzle needed to be inserted into an appropriate aperture to deliver a gush, after which the refitting of the covering and (usually anyway) some form of payment would follow. Jim had started to frequent the kind of singles bar where you discover within a couple of minutes why everyone there is still single.

'Maybe you should get that address and try it, Mr Bones.'

'Maybe you should get back in your black box, Harry.'

'Fancy an evening in Epping then?'

'Watch it, son, or there'll be another dent in your face.'

'At least that stopped you crying for a bit. The air round these parts is suddenly less salty.'

11

It had only struck me after so many students said the same thing: 'You should be on the stage with that routine. You really should.'

I had studied, of course. Picked up all the books. Even found an old vent in Ilford who showed me a few tricks I'd never have got to hear about without him. ('It's a figure; not a dummy,' he insisted.) His knotted veiny hands had trembled as he brought his beloved dummy (Lord Cinders, as I recall) to life. All the same, it was thoroughly mechanical until one day, when Harry sat on my knee and seemed to turn his head towards me without my even considering it: 'I think we might be getting on, professor,' he said. I was taken aback. 'I do believe you are beginning to facilitate my further existence. Perhaps we should venture out in the evenings, and do a few shows. The vent's venture. I think you might perform quite creditably. And remember I've been vented by a few in my time: Jack, Silas, Tommy, Dr Dibette, the dirty old sod, but they were all pros. And I'd say you're up there with them these days. You have come through, sir.'

I was astounded. It was the first time he had spoken entirely in his own voice, finding his own solutions, quoting his own history. The first time he'd been him and not me. I tried out some of my theories on him. He was the finest inquisitor I'd ever known on the subject of the ventriloquial ritual, the central theme of my own book. He was so practical. 'Not from there, Mr Bones. The voice cannot be thrown so far, not even at Delphi. Remember that we are dependent on you for our power. That does not mean we are limited to saying what you want us to say, but it does mean we cannot surpass the physical limitations imposed on you. We have to work through human means, even for inhuman purposes, as is also the case with the fallen angels, according to Christian teaching. You remarked tellingly on the matter somewhere, in regard to beliefs about the devil in the Middle Ages; Chapter Four of your book, as I recall.'

'Did I show you that?'

'No. I must have found it for myself on your shelf over there.'

'You have become a great reader, Harry.'

'I'm teaching myself to write, too. I thought I might start a column in one of the newspapers.'

It is not unusual for a man to find himself wedded to a doll, which remains inert except for certain fixed purposes. This was pretty much the story of my one, utterly disastrous, marriage. No new life ever proceeded from it, thank God. And Alice cleared off six months after our honeymoon – *honeymoon*: whoever treacled up the planet with that noun obviously wasn't present during ours, however sticky it became. Harry has begun to point out to me how people repeat; they think they're escaping, but more often they're repeating, however far away they might have gone from the original location to engage in the act of repetition.

'Alice was a doll who lay on your bed, professor. And look at me now. Where have you put me?'

Harry lay on my bed too, legs akimbo. A lot shorter than Alice, and even she was never quite *that* wooden. Never wore so much rouge either, though she too favoured blue silk. But all the same, I took his point.

'There's a big difference though, prof. I can't oblige you with the physical side of things the way she did, but I am your intellectual equal. You know that, don't you? I never say anything which isn't at your own intellectual level. Because that's not possible, is it? What a lethal thing mimesis is. Now that we've started doing these dialogues on the ancient religions, I think we should try them out on your students. I think it might make your lectures a little more . . . enticing.'

It was Harry's idea, you see. It would never have occurred to me, never, but once we'd got going, it became evident how right he had been.

'A new pedagogical principle, Mr Bones. It should apply everywhere. We act out what we see; put our money where our ventriloquist's mouth is; do what we think. Imagine if they all had to do that. If all who prattle on about sonnets should be obliged to produce one to the requisite standard; if all who talk of popular culture were required to be both popular and cultured; if all who speak so confidently of the love of the martyr be obliged to offer themselves up for immolation during their lectures. Think of the new respect which would soon be visible in your students' faces.'

'How long have you been thinking about this, Harry?'

'Exactly as long as you have, Mr Bones.'

Later. A lifetime later.

'You did choose her, didn't you?'

'Who?'

'That wife of yours. I mean, you picked her out. You can't really blame her for being who she was. You went into the big department store and you made your choice. Over by the perfume and jewellery counters, as I recall. All glittery, with nice smells. Gold gleaming around wrists and necks. Kohl and blusher and powder and pearls. It's what you wanted, Mr Bones. Maybe what you still want. You paid your money and you took your choice. I'll have one of those, please. And then you sent her back to the manufacturers because she couldn't discuss Dante with you. But that's like sending a Ferrari back to Italy because you can't plough a field with it. It's like taking a toothbrush back to the chemist's because it couldn't cut the Sunday roast. The only companion who's ever satisfied your mental needs is me. Now why's that, do you think?'

'I can't imagine.'

12

'Should they not have grown weary by now of the card-trick and the swallowed knife? After Galileo and Newton and Einstein. Should they not have more respect for their own reason? The cobwebs of superstition, Mr Bones. I once saw a cat which had been eating cobwebs – some do – and its muzzle was bejewelled with gossamer. A black cat with a face full of diamonds from the cellar. That's like their minds, don't you think? How primitive strands of cobweb form minute nets of confusion over their much-vaunted rationality.'

'Where did you see that cat, Harry?'

'It might have been in the days I was still a tree. I don't have to tell you everything. It does strike me sometimes that you can be covetous of my perceptions, you know, as though you don't believe they're really my entitlement, what with me being your little geek in a box. The son you never had, all that's left of the splinters from the old dynastic tree. Sometimes, Mr Bones, you're not convinced I'm anything other than a piece of wood, are you? Like that nephew of yours.

'Watching us, they should never again believe the churchyard gibberers, and yet, and yet. Somehow they start to become convinced of my reality by the end, and they don't go home through the churchyard after all. Ask them how many believe in spirits.'

'You ask them, Harry.'

'You want me to check up on the visitations of angels? You want a painted piece of wood to make windows into men's souls, even though Queen Elizabeth herself refused to do it?

'Suspicion is a fog, Mr Bones, but then so is incredulity. Six of one and half a dozen of the other, that's what I say. We do so need some enchantment in our lives, and if we don't find it in one place, then we'll surely search for it in another. If not in the chapel then the personal ads. If not in the marriage bed then the brothel. But how we want to be taken out of our rational, organised, hygienic selves. We crave the dance of shadows at midnight in the woods, the rituals in the grove of Nemi. One priest cut down so another might flourish. Our psyches go there, even if they must leave their bodies at home. Or should I say your psyches? Are they the dupes of your illusionism or their own? You say, "Abracadabra," and they hand over their credulity to your wizardry. And you're not all that much of a wizard really, when it comes down to it. Ah, why did you ever do it, Mr Bones?'

'What?'

'Introduce me to the pages of the dictionary, those pages made from wood, just like me, taken from the side of the river, taken away from the language of the winds to be riddled in the language of men, then mired in it?'

'Glorified too, Harry.'

'Sometimes glorified, Bones. But more often mired, I'd say.'

13

'The freak and the mountebank are, I fear, our companions, Mr Bones.

The devil's familiars and the dance of the demons: this is our true location, surely, not the lecture hall and the pious public meeting. You taught me how the gods speak once.'

'Did I? How do the gods speak then, Harry?'

'Watch my lips closely and observe.'

How he smiles sometimes. How *contrived* he can appear. He waits for me to move his lips; I wait for him to move my hand. His painted eyes have a weird beauty – the way they reject nothing that comes their way. The god's smile is insouciant. Like something painted on an Egyptian tomb wall.

'I enjoyed those lectures, you know: the final series, I mean.'

'You gave half of them.'

'I thought we were getting very close to solving a part of the problem. Occasionally the theme became so strong I seemed to speak for ten or twenty minutes at a time. Not even sure your hand was moving any more; it seemed somehow . . . unnecessary. Let's see if we can recall . . . ah yes.

'We told the students that one of the tragedies of civilisation was being confined inside one self. That was it. Your big theme. That there was far too much data in life to be contained in just the one self: that's what we said. We turned and looked at one another then, and the students all laughed. The schizoid twins. The Gemini brothers. So from earliest times, we said, we have devised the means of escaping from one self into another. The priest dons a mask. Then he can wield the blade with which he kills the child. Without the mask he couldn't do it; without the mask he'd be merely himself. The airman dons his mask, climbs into his plane and flies across a foreign country. He presses the button that drops his metal messages from the plane's belly, and that kills many children too. But he is an airman, and he wears his mask to prove it. The old ritual has remained, though, underneath the transmutations: a dead child beneath the city's foundations will palliate the dreadful powers above.

'Now what came next? The shaman, I think. Where are your notes when I need them? The shaman puts on his mask and attains a different consciousness. In deep hypnosis the patient in a trance can speak with many voices, many identities. Mimesis again. The songwriter, the poet, the actor, speak as many selves, not merely one. You said the priests had learned their craft in antiquity, and when the pilgrims came in search of enlightenment to the *omphalos*, the oracle spoke. The sound might have come from the priest's belly, but by the time it was in the belly of the stone, it had changed its nature, just as the priest in the mask with a blade in his hand had changed his nature. He'd become hieratic; capable of the necessary sacrifice. Capable of seeing the brevity of life and the suddenness of death. Ah, the lovely blades, Bones.

'But now, you said – I remember you said this bit – now we have turned the sacred into spectacle; the enchanted has morphed into the phantasmagoria of film; ritual into showbiz. That was your argument, Mr Bones, and you said that we were still fascinated by the vent and the dummy on his knee because little fragments of the original ceremonies, the sacred ritual, still clung about them. We could still hear the echoes from inside the Omphalos. You still see the sacred figure in the lights conducting a sacrifice up there, if it's only a lethal operation on himself. Judy Garland imploding; Elvis Presley exploding. James Dean acting himself to death, as though he were the dancer in *The Rite of Spring*. You were very convincing, prof; the students fell silent. You said that with the vent and the dummy, the murderous ritual had been replaced by a murderous humour. The dummy was licensed to kill with merciless words, the way the Fool in *King Lear* is licensed to jest, and so mock the mightiest in the land. Then you listed how we seek to escape the one self; by schizophrenia, by drugs, by dance, by music, by sex, by art, or even by creating a voice that talks back to us, out of a piece of wood.'

'Even by marriage.'

'Most tragic of all the delusions.'

14

'You, madame, please pay attention when a piece of wood is talking to you. The last time that happened must have been this morning, when your husband said goodbye and went to work. You have almost as much rouge on your face as I have on mine. How would you like to sit on his knee then, have his hand caressing your controls? Would you? By your smile you seem to say so. You're nodding but I think I'd better warn you that a nod in this theatrical establishment constitutes a legally binding agreement. It's as good as a wink, which rhymes with drink, and my friend here, the professor, is gagging for both. He hasn't been shown a good time since our gig at Reigate, and that was nearly a month ago. He is . . . pining, frankly. I can't do anything for him. My affections do not that way tend. But you, with silk on your buttocks, and perfume on your neck and sweet deodorant squirted up your armpits, and God-knows-what elsewhere – if you should see fit to appear round by the dressing-room door after the show, my friend would doubtless be happy to give you one. Or more than one, if it comes to that. The night is young.

'How they laughed, Bones. All we ever did was to tell them the truth, and they laughed and laughed. Did they not?

'And the ladies. They always loved a bit of smut, down there in the dark of the theatre. It was as though a grinning pornographer had turned up in the British Museum, cracking gags. And you nearly always had one afterwards, didn't you? A little lap for your unicorn's horn to nestle in. I used to listen to them moaning and purring. What lies you told them all, Bones, and how they wanted to be lied to. In that, I suspect, you are no different from other men. You are exactly as other men, only more so.

'You were so much graver in the lectures. All we want to know is that the dead live, and that is what all art is for. Mimesis as resurrection. That's what you said, Mr Bones. You would look at me then, and say, "*Isn't* that so, Harry?" And I would turn slowly towards you and say, "All vents go nuts in the end. He thinks I'm real, don't you, son?" Oh how the students roared. Not one of them ever got the reference to Arthur Worsley, first vent you ever saw, was he not, professor? In Morecombe, if memory serves. Dear old Arthur. Never said a word. Let the dummy do all the talking for him. Which is what you appear to be doing tonight. I might as well get back inside my box. There's more in the way of conversation there. Not to mention physical affection.'

'They love enchantment, don't they, Mr Bones? Love to sit in the dark and see the magic shapes: the magician, the dummy coming to life, the phantasmagoria, the cinema, the rock stars cavorting. Dead trees resurrected. In its early days the phantasmagoria was obsessed by death, that's what you told them. Even staged inside tombs so that the ghostly shapes of the projections could seem like the dead arising. One of Madame Tussaud's early jobs, was it not, travelling round Britain staging phantasmagorias? Then she got started on the waxworks, which is the same thing really: recreating the dead so that they appear to be living. Meet Amazing Harry and the Prof then. Resurrection men, opening up the tombs and springing the cadavers. They made effigies out of the plenteous human waste of the French Revolution.

'And then the cinema took over where the phantasmagoria left off: we sit in the dark and watch as one wall comes to life with magical creatures. The wall of the tomb of life has become animated once more. The fruit on the Egyptian Pyramid wall is being eaten. One wall out of four; that's not a bad average where eternal extinction is involved. I liked it when you explained how the food provided for the Pyramids rotted so quickly. Priests had to keep coming and replacing it. So someone one day tried to make it permanent by painting it on the walls, and hey-presto, we have art. Food for the dead that won't rot. Or the Neolithic cavemen recreating images of the creatures they had slain, down in the womb of the earth, atoning for their slaughter. To ensure that that which dies shall be restored. As though the film *Shoah* atoned for the Shoah. All art refuses to acknowledge death. A lump of carbon on your knee becomes a living intelligence. The tree springs afresh from the earth. And Harry prattles once more.

'It was the phantasmagoria which first made men doubt their senses. The dead came back to life. Spirits spoke. And it was there before your eyes. You couldn't deny it; your own eyes told you the vision was real, and your own eyes confirmed that reality. (Strange how your comrades in humanity fashioned me without a frown, which could make some think I lack *gravitas*. Nothing could be further from the truth, of course: beneath my garish grin there is more intellectual activity than with the average man on the Clapham omnibus. Or the average man in the marriage bed, for that matter. Both obsolete modes of transport, if you ask me.)

'La Chapelle used his expertise in ventriloquism to demonstrate to the credulous their credulity. A dead man's voice was once more resurrected in the chapel. Then he would show how he had tricked the foolish monks. The illusion is stripped bare by the illusionist; the machinery of deception is revealed; the smoke and mirrors are foregrounded and disenchanted. Smoke and mirrors is a good description of the phantasmagoria, since that's exactly what it was half the time.

'The puppeteer was ever a mimic-man, no? But when the phantasmagoria got going in earnest in the early nineteenth century, the ventriloquists found new employment, which they made love to. They were the dead, the beloved dead, come back to converse with the beloved living. They were emperors and tyrants, queens and murderers, the temptress and the villain, the martyr and the whore. Now the voices came from the illusion and the illusion became real. If you believe in me then I exist: thus spake Tinkerbell, and Tinkerbell is of course right. If we all believe in something, then it must exist, because otherwise *we* don't. The ghost-shows; the spectral apparitions; the shadow dancers on the wall. We watch the shadows dancing and take it for reality. Well, we've progressed. We've now transferred the shadows from wall to electronic box and added colour. And every night we sit and take it for reality. We sit before it in an attitude of silence and prayer. Why do you never praise me for my zeal and assiduity, Bones? Can you really be asleep?'

16

A lump of dirty ice journeying silently and to no purpose among the stellar spaces. Then I wake briefly. Harry is snoring, very gently. And now I am a fly cocooned in spider silk, conscious but paralysed, awaiting the tremble along the web-line. The unmistakable approach. This is a bad-dream night. I get up out of bed and knock on Harry's box.

'Pour yourself a whisky, Mr Bones. If you need someone to sit with you then call the Social Services. I'm trying to get some fucking sleep.'

I sit with the whisky and stare out of the window. The little bastard. After all I've done for him. The blur of London's nocturnal lights stretches out over the old canal. And I remember once more my father's shoes.

'It was when your mother found the box of them, wasn't it? That's when she finally broke down.'

Harry has found his own way out of his box and climbed up on my knee. Don't ask me: I don't know how he does it either, but I think it might be whenever he senses there's a genuine necessity. Even a tree can bend in the wind. He picks up waves of distress; waves of melancholy. Cerebretonic wave-forms, as we'll doubtless be calling them later. (You'll have to trust me here.)

'So stoical she'd been, hadn't she, through all those months, those years of illness, and then she found that box of shoes underneath the bed. He hadn't been able to bring himself to throw them away, though they were all beyond repair. And with every crease in the old leather, every puncture in the sole, every lopsided sheering of the heel, his life, the slow and mighty struggle of it, seemed to be expressed somehow. And she broke down, didn't she, Mr Bones? And you stood in the doorway, unable to go to her and offer comfort. Why was that, Mr Bones, why couldn't you go and comfort your old mother in her terrible hour of need?'

'We didn't touch, Harry.'

'What never?'

'I think she'd kept it to an absolute minimum from the moment I was out of the womb. As little as possible. Whenever she did, it was usually in front of others, for their sake, not mine. It felt like punishment, not solidarity.'

Harry is caressing my face very gently with the mildest of touches; this is rare, and should probably be duly noted, as it has been.

'I think I might have been born in that room where the only child

37

sat brooding, staying clear of the mother who didn't ever want to touch him. I mean, I was out on the boards, of course, probably with that old deviant, Dr Dibette, but I sensed a new self getting born one day. Hello, I thought, another life beckons over yonder. I wonder where it is. I think that was you, Bones, giving birth like your old mum did, in the privacy of your boy's bedroom.'

His eyes open and close; his mouth works with rapidity; his hand reaches out towards my face again, as it does now, but so rarely, in the dark. His eyes are wide and manic as a duck's. And my heart goes out to him. He too once grew in the darkness before being cut down, carved and painted. Then he speaks again.

'You used to say, on stage that is, that the taps of her prattle were constantly turned on full, but that all their gold-plated gushing produced streams too shallow to drown a gnat. An endless flow, all the same, fizzing, bubbling, meandering. You never introduced us, you know. Never actually took me home. Were you ashamed of me?'

There is a tear on his cheek; rain on the alder's bark. What goes around comes around.

'I wasn't ashamed of you, Harry, never have been. I think I might have been afraid of what you might say.'

'I might have told the truth, you mean?'

'That's always been the big worry with you, hasn't it?'

'Like that night in Epping, you mean? One night of truth and a whole life wrecked. A glittering career abandoned. Well, two actually . . . '

17

. . . all right then. No secrets. Either from him or you.

We had got our act together. It had become fluent, engaging, compelling. I never knew what would happen before we went out there. He had become so astonishingly inventive. The bookings were starting to come in; we didn't have to chase them any more. In Brighton we had three encores.

'You have established, I believe, professor, that the first showing of the phantasmagoria in Britain was in 1801?'

'That's right. Chimeras created by means of magic lanterns. Insubstantial creatures made of light. Flitting photons really, precursors of the cinema.'

'And yet, how many millions have sat for how many millions of hours staring at flitting shadows on a wall? It's as though the flickering images cast in two dimensions are more real for those few hours in the darkened chapel of dreams than the brightly lit reality outside. Who would want to sit in the dark for hours looking up at something that isn't even real?'

We would pause then and turn slowly towards the audience, sitting out there, in the dark. They always laughed. Why, I've never been sure. Why *do* you people laugh, out of interest? Do you laugh every time you look in a mirror?

And one of those bookings was for Epping. One dismal November night. That didn't matter, of course. Once inside the pyramid, once the bright lights of the phantasmagoria were turned on, and all others turned down, there was no weather but the lightning inside their heads. This particular night, Harry had evidently been drinking: I could smell it on his breath.

'I thought we had a deal about this: no drinking until after the show.'

'I thought we did too, Mr Bones; your understanding was identical with mine in this regard. But it looks as though we'd better go out there and give them hell, all the same. I had thought I was drinking for you, as it happens. The whisky tasted . . . a little vicarious to me. Are you sure it's my breath you are smelling?'

Out we went. The patter came quickly and easily. The difficulty of cooking that Egyptian crocodile which once tried to swallow Harry, with no salt to add savour; his dreadful marriage to a Giselle-like marionette; his memories of life by the river as an alder; how he always kept smiling through, just like you used to do.

'Do you regret anything, Mr Bones?'

'Nothing.'

'*Non. Je ne regrette rien.* I have a lovely singing voice, don't I? So you really wouldn't do anything any different?'

'Nothing at all.'

'Not even that time when you fell off your bike and broke your arm? You'd ride around that corner at exactly the same speed, would you, on all that gravel, with the triple fracture looming up ahead? Or when the bent carpenter from Stockport cheated you out of thousands of pounds? Still slap him on the back and tell him what a fine fellow he was, would you, as the money disappeared day by day from your account? And that little tart in Leicester, the one who gave you something you really would rather not have been given. You'd still chat her up in the pub with the same alacrity, would you? In which case, there's only one conclusion one can come to, professor: you're an over-educated cretin.'

Then the voice started up from the front row.

Now, once the lights have been on for a while up there on the stage, it's very hard to focus on anyone in the dark down in the auditorium, and it was very rare indeed to have hecklers in the audience. Not unknown, but rare. The trick is to work out where they are coming from, what their number is – drunk, sober, friendly, malicious? Harry and I looked at one another for a moment.

'You ask her,' I said. This was an agreed strategy we'd worked out months before. The one thing none of them will ever do is to come up out of the dark and actually show themselves on stage. So we went for it.

'Would you perhaps like to join us up here?' Harry asked, and the audience roared. But we were to be surprised. She stood up and immediately walked across to the side-curtain. Thirty seconds later she was there with us. And what's more she was dressed as theatrically as we were. For this was Miss Elenor, who had just finished her stint at the Turkish restaurant, and who was still dolled-up in her gladrags.

'What precisely does your stage-act comprise, my dear?' Harry asked in his old impresario's voice. I thought he was showing remarkable presence of mind.

'I'm a belly-dancer,' was the reply. 'Like me to show you?'

'YES.' A roar from the crowd. It was too late now. The little band were on to it and started playing 'The Stripper' very low and enticing. So we continued as she danced, having little alternative now.

'Tell them, Mr Bones. Tell them what we have in common with . . . I'm sorry, my dear, I don't think I caught your name.'

'Miss Elenor,' she said, pulling a veil back and forth before her midriff.

'Ventriloquism. Go on, prof.'

'Well, as you will remember, Harry, it comes from the Greek word for stomach. It was believed that the sounds of the spirits could be thrown out of the area of the belly to another place. That's where we get the word from, originally.' By now Miss Elenor was putting herself through her paces. She seemed greatly involved with her own movements. So did the audience. I think it's fair to say that I had mixed feelings about all this.

'And Herod's stepdaughter . . . '

'Yes, she danced to please her stepfather, by removing veils one by one until there were no veils left. He promised her she could have whatever she wanted.'

'And what did she want, Mr Bones?'

'The head of John the Baptist.'

'Which she was given.'

'Which she was duly given.'

'What's his name again?' Miss Elenor had her hand on Harry's sleeve now. She was still moving suggestively.

'Harry.'

'Come for a dance, Harry.' He looked at me, my ancient boy, my alderman, with a look that suggested both panic and mischief at the same time. But it was too late. She pulled so hard that I had to let him go, or she could have caused him some lasting damage. And then she employed him as part of her dance. He had stopped being my companion for the evening (or for life), and had now become instead her erotic accoutrement. I remember choking back fury. And then she was done and taking her bows, while I sat on the chair in the middle of the stage. And I remember her kissing him on the lips and saying, 'Meeting anyone after, handsome?'

'You, my dear. In my hotel room. There are still a few things that remain for us to do together.' The voice emanated from him, not me, and the crowd once more yelled its approval at such preternatural ventriloquism. I swear I had nothing to do with any of it. It was like watching your son go on his first date.

An hour in the bar. Too many drinks.

'They loved it out there. Why don't we put the two acts together? We could have a real winner.'

We already had a winner, lady, before you ever came along. In case you hadn't noticed.

'My real name's Judy, by the way. What's yours?'

'Mr Bones. Mr Bones and Harry Sprite, the alder's son.'

'Why don't we get a bottle sent up to your hotel room, Mr Bones? I want to dance with Harry one more time. I think we might have a lot to talk about. Things to *discover* about one another. I'm a girl who likes to discover things.'

And so it was that the three of us found ourselves on the third floor in the hotel room that night in Epping. I ordered her the wine but I'd brought my own whisky with me, in Harry's little coffin. Harry was already on my knee while she sat on the floor before us, placing her hand on Harry's boneless leg, underneath which was my thigh.

'You know, you're a very attractive little man, Harry, though maybe a bit young for me.'

'You'd be surprised, girl. Don't be taken in by the silk pants and the school blazer: I've been around. A life on the road, and all that. A boy ages quickly in this business.'

'I'm sure you do.' The hand was giving Harry's leg a massage, a serious one. It was all coming straight through to me, even if intended for him.

'Maybe you could share some of your knowledge with me. I'm always ready to learn.' Harry turned to me then. He gave me a look that indicated there was trouble ahead. I knew that look. My small friend here can be dangerous. You must all have realised that by now.

'The only thing is, we'd have to make sure you qualify. You see, Mr Bones and I have the most exacting professional standards, and we'd have to satisfy ourselves that you would be able to meet them.'

She was giggling now and went to pour herself another drink.

'How would I do that then?'

'First, you'd have to lie down on that bed, so that I can examine you. Some clothes would certainly need to be removed. Don't worry: I have bona fide medical certificates, don't I, Mr Bones?'

'You do, Harry. They're framed and hanging on our wall in Mile End.'

'Mounted on the wall of the stony cave, like trophies from a pre-historic *battue*. So you have nothing to fear except the rigours of professional assessment. And, of course, fear itself.'

Miss Elenor needed no further encouragement. She slipped out of her skirt and her blouse and lay down on the bed. White thighs between the black stocking-tops and the silk panties. She had evidently come out in anticipation of an encounter. Or was that just her usual clobber underneath the Turkish veils? Harry turned once more to look at me. The look was one I no longer understood. He'd gone beyond me in intention and surmise.

'I think I had better wash my hands before proceeding with the examination, Mr Bones.'

So we went into the bathroom and scrubbed up.

'Are you sure you want to go through with this, Harry? I could just ask her to leave now.'

'No, I don't think so, Bones. She invited herself into our act this evening, even took me from you without asking permission, which I found frankly impertinent. Now a little probing is required. I think she must be made to yield to our inquisition.'

Harry, I must say, did appear to have done this sort of thing before. With one of his previous collaborators, perhaps? I was astounded at his litheness, his skill, his knowledge of where to press, where to fondle. That one agile hand of his, even gloved, seemed to know what it was about. Miss Elenor, aka Judy French, was soon moaning and murmuring Harry's name. Another dupe of practised illusionism. So much for the Western philosophical tradition. Mimesis seems to be all that there is.

'Harry, you are a clever boy. You really have been around, haven't you?'

'I certainly have, and I'm not the only one by the look of things, Miss Elenor. Oh dear: another one of your little spasms, there. Painful to observe. And I think I've just found two of the cast of the Epping *Cinderella* show of two Christmases ago; the last petrol attendant from Langley's Garage; and a stray woodcutter from the forest. Your local sacred wood, no doubt. Nemi in Epping. But surely you must have realised you had left them in there? They have been growing lonely, my dear.'

And then the voices began. I don't understand it to this day. Perhaps he had picked up something of the local accent – he was always very quick with lilts and intonations. But Matt and Freddie and Dick started to repeat the things they had uttered when they had first found themselves where they apparently were now: inside Miss Elenor. Neither she nor I could move for a moment while these voices spoke. Everyone paralysed, it seemed, except for a piece of wood with a painted face. And a grin.

It is a curious sound, the mixture of breaking glass and tears. Picasso painted it many times in those paintings of the Weeping Woman. Dora Maar, another woman tormented by the voices inside her. A few minutes later Miss Elenor was leaving, with one or two of her dancing veils still mildly astray across her shoulder. Harry and I slept well that night; we felt that justice had been done, and the intruder expelled. That should have been an end to the business, of course. But, somewhat famously, it wasn't. It took Miss Elenor, aka Judy French, over a week before she decided that she had been so traumatised by the experience in the hotel room that she needed to contact the police.

Shortly afterwards they arrived at our little stony cave in Mile End. And that's when it all began: the curious business of the indecent assault, performed by a vent's dummy.

It was her decision to insist that Harry appear in the witness box with me. I had wanted to keep him out of it all, but she decided that only by seeing him in action at my side would the jury understand how compelling his personality could be. Despite my protestations, he was effectively subpoenaed. 'Witness with professional accoutrement' was, as I recall it, the phrase employed. I believe it may have been a unique occasion in the annals of British justice. And once up there, he did exactly what he always did: he took on a life of his own. He spoke his mind. He has always had one, when all's said and done, and he had one long before he ever met me. Anyone imagining that it might be quelled for the sake of a little local convenience in a court of law was being very foolish.

'Were you attracted to Miss Elenor?'

'At first she was just a voice in the dark. But then she came up on stage and took off some of her clothes while vaunting and ululating.'

'Vaunting and ululating?'

'I believe those are the technical term for her motions and her moans. She was vaunting and ululating and she took me in her arms while she was at it. Then she grasped my knob.'

'Your . . . '

'My knob. It is the device in my nether regions which operates my features. That is the term by which Mr Bones and I always refer to it. My knob. And she grasped it. Meaningfully.'

The judge spoke then, amid the laughter. 'Mr Harrison, the proceedings of this court are in danger of degenerating into farce. Do you have any pertinent questions to put to the . . . puppet.'

'We are establishing, I think you must agree, my lord, the degree of the device's authenticity.'

'I'd prefer not to be referred to as a device if you don't mind, my learned friend.'

Laughter.

The judge would surely have told everyone off at this point, but I could see that he was having difficulty keeping a straight face himself. Miss Elenor appeared to be losing this case by the second.

'When you invited Miss Elenor up to your hotel room . . . '

'It was *her* suggestion.'

'Are you claiming . . . '

Harry now became adamant. 'It was *her* suggestion. Ask her if you don't believe me. Bring her back up here and ask her. She got on stage. She waltzed me round. Then she came back and took off her clothes. She took hold of my knob. Meaningfully. She took off her clothes with no assistance from me or my companion. Mr Bones never even touched her. She was lying on the bed in her undies when we came back from the bathroom. If you don't believe me, then JUST ASK HER.'

And ask her the defence counsel did; later, when she was brought back up into the box. And she admitted it was all true.

'I wanted a good night out, that's all. Thought I might even become part of their act. But then . . . then.'

'Then what?' the judge asked quietly. He did appear genuinely baffled.

'Then he made the voices come out of me.'

'He made you speak as though he were speaking?'

'Not with my voice. Somewhere else. Speaking. Many voices. And voices I knew. Who I'd . . . I'd been with. How could he do that?'

'I really am beginning to wonder if there is any purpose in continuing any further, Mr Harrison.'

The lawyer bowed in submission. He didn't seem to know what to do any more either.

'But you don't understand,' she said.

They decided that they had understood enough. The case was dismissed, even though the judge subsequently found himself reflecting with colleagues whether the notion of *vox uteri* might not have been employed, even though it would have constituted a legal precedent. Thomas Wright in his biography of Lady Burton, the widow of Sir Richard, the great adventurer, explains her visions of her dead husband by saying they were prompted by the *vox uteri*, not the *vox Dei*. Lady Burton organised many séances in Burton's marble tomb in Mortlake, built to resemble his Bedouin tent. An American medium, Miss Goodrich Freer, spent hour upon hour trying to establish contact with the other side, but to no purpose, sadly.

The papers were on to it the next day.

Professor in Bizarre Sex Puppet Romp

'I fear your position at the university is about to become untenable, prof.'

'It's certainly starting to look that way, Harry.'

'Good.'

I was hurt, I'll confess. What did he mean, 'Good'?

'Hocus-pocus. Ah, the dupes of your illusionistic wizardry. They gave you the moniker "Professor" because they assumed you had something to profess. Just how wrong can you be? Now we can devote ourselves full-time to what we're both best at. We are about to become the greatest vent act in the modern world. We'll revive a dying genre. We can even use the case; all that stuff. We can talk about it each night. Go over the details. They'll love it.'

'Did you have to be so cruel to her?'

'I had to ensure she'd try to prosecute, so that you can stop wasting your time in the land of academia, writing books no one ever reads. Anyway, I know her sort. Let's pretend we've never been touched like this before. Let me moan my special little moan into your ear, dear one. If I weren't made of wood, I'd vomit. When trees vomit, leaves appear. So remember, next time, Mr Bones, you'll be vomiting for two. Have another whisky, why don't you.'

There was silence between us for a few moments, then I spoke.

'How did you know the voices, the names; all the things locked away inside her?'

'You all say the names and the voices all the time. You're all surrounded by a cloud of names and voices, like a swarm of drunken bees, buzzing away at the preterite nectar. Wave-form cerebretonics, remember. Later on, you'll remember. But you only ever seem to hear them when I'm there to translate. I came out of the past, out of the earth, remember, and I sometimes seem to be the only one who ever really listens.'

After the business in Epping, my uncle retired from the world. The university pensioned him off. He was not seen any more. I gather that he was offered work as a ventriloquist, given his new notoriety in the red tops, but he refused. He became a recluse. Even I only saw him once more, for that last lunch of ours in Soho. I had wondered then how much longer he would live, but no one in the world could have predicted what was about to happen to him, except perhaps Harry Sprite. Can he be described as 'someone' though?

Given the degree of Graham Fowey's brilliance and scholarship, I still find it extraordinary that the only two times his name ever made the headlines were after the events in Epping with Miss Elenor, and the reporting of his death.

His body was found on the pavement beneath his fifth-storey flat in Mile End. He had been stabbed with a knife, and his body contained wooden fragments of his own puppet Harry, whose shattered body lay all about him on the ground. Some of the splinters from the puppet had penetrated the professor's heart.

The police were never to find evidence of any other person in the flat that night, but were so impressed by the inexplicable violence of the attack, followed by the body flying through the window, that they concluded an intruder might have been challenged, and that a fight could have ensued which had ended in a killing and a defenestration. But the only fingerprints ever found on the knife and Harry were my uncle's. The best the coroner's court could come up with was a verdict of death by misadventure.

We were all glad to be rid of the matter for ever, and it was not until months after the funeral that the document you have been reading came into my hands; it was almost a year later that I actually read it. Couldn't face it before that. You can understand that, surely?

The following week I arrived in Epping. Miss Elenor still danced at the local Turkish restaurant.

'You can see me after my show,' she said. 'We can have a bite there, if you like. It's good food.'

How young is a belly-dancer meant to be? I have no expertise in such things, but I would have said she should be younger than Miss Elenor is these days. Still, the veils whizzed back and forth, the flesh rippled, the eyes flashed. I couldn't help but notice the black stockings. Do they actually wear those on stage in Istanbul then? Did Salomé? Or is it an Epping speciality? I kept a smile fixed on my face. I suppose we both wore painted smiles. Both of us like Harry in that respect, if no other.

'I read about his death,' she said, as she ate her kebab and I sipped my wine. 'I'd like to say I was sorry, but I wasn't. Not after what he did to me. I never got over that.'

'The case was dismissed. Which means he wasn't guilty.'

'Who wasn't guilty?'

'My uncle.'

'He wasn't the one I was after. That was the whole point. Don't you understand?'

'No.'

'And how could he have known?'

'Known what?'

'Who I'd made love to, years before.' I felt a curious sensation then, one I didn't care for.

'Would you like another glass of wine?'

'Please. You look a bit like your uncle. Let's just hope you grow out of it.'

We sat in silence for a moment. That is, our silence; all around our silence there was noise, the noise of people eating, drinking, laughing. The ambient tunnel of humanity. Was that like Harry's silence, inside the perennial human noise? I had to ask what I had wanted to ask ever since turning these pages, as you are doing.

'What I've never understood is this. If you didn't like it, all that business with the dummy, all that tomfoolery – even if it was turning sexual – why couldn't you just ask Uncle Graham to stop?'

'UNCLE GRAHAM. The professor, you mean? Old Mr Bones? What would have been the point of asking him?'

I stared at her, taking in what she had just said. Or trying to. Even through the ash-mask of her features, the powder and the kohl, I could see the ancient dancer inside who had enticed both my uncle and Harry that night in Epping. The ululating and the vaunting. Still something there to light the fire which casts shadows on a stone wall.

'You still don't understand, do you?' she said finally. Then she leant towards me and whispered: 'He was *real*.'

20

'Who were your parents, Mr Bones?'

'Mr and Mrs Bones, of course.'

'Only the skeleton staff then. Did they actually play them?'

'Play what?'

'THE BONES, of course. A primitive percussive device, favoured by pearly kings and street minstrels. I thought that might be the derivation of your name. There must be some reason you're called Bones, surely.'

'No one calls me that but you.'

'But I thought we were the only ones here. (*Peering slowly into the auditorium.*) Ah no . . . I do believe they've crept up on us both again. (*Loudly now to the audience.*) Have you no homes to go to? Do you have no mouths to feed? No crosswords to complete? Have you nothing better to do than listen in on other people's private conversations? Not even a cat to stroke?'

'And who were your parents, Harry?'

'I only had one. An alder tree. Mother and father to me. My nurse, my womb, my weather and my god. Lived by the river slowly swaying in the wind, accepting the seasons one by one. Then men came with saws one day, and cut my parents down. Both of her. And made me. I'm all that's left of her, as far as I know. Though there might be a pair of clogs somewhere, clattering on a cobbled street while a brass band plays, or the arm of a canal lock oozing tar at the edge of Salford. But then that's the way with art, and we are artists, aren't we, Mr Bones? I can tell by the way you move your lips behind your hand whenever I'm talking, that you're not just an artist, you're a bona fide *artiste*. Picasso said that in art you must kill the father. Never mentioned mothers, though, funnily enough. Why do you think that was, professor?'

'He wasn't a tree.'

'Now why didn't I think of that?'

'You're not a professor.'

'True. So what do you make of Brighton then?'

'The sex show under the pier at midnight's nice.'

'Do you mind, sir? That is not a sex show. No indeed. That's the local romance ritual. That's where the next generation of Mr and Mrs Bones gets started. That's where the alder learns to bow its rain-soaked head and the weeping willow first tastes salt in its tears . . . (*Confidentially, as though the audience cannot hear*) . . . You're not supposed to move your lips, Bones. When I'm addressing them, or you for that matter, you're not supposed to move your lips . . . (*Now to the audience*) . . . He plays up his incompetence, you know. He can do it perfectly when he likes. At home I sometimes talk for hours while he's sleeping. His lips don't even twitch. I think he might want you to feel sorry for him. Well don't. Pity rots his intellect. And he really is a professor, you know, though I have to help him with his lectures these days. He'd never get through them without me. After all, I've become his major source.'

21

It is midnight. We sit together by the window, as we often do these days. He has fallen silent. He is thinking of the past, I fear, contemplating everything that might have been, if only I'd had more courage. I underestimated his ambition, I realise that now. He turns towards me slowly. Is it just me or has his smile started to look even more alarming lately? There always was something manic about it, but now it seems there's something more than that. A manic phase with no release; an unrelenting build-up of energy; is it possible for a smile to become pathological? A smile on a piece of wood? Could I maybe send him to see my nephew's friend, Dr Helsford, the shrink? Would he treat a little alderman? What was it Robert said? That cathexis when it is unhindered starts to equal a psychosis. Listen. He is starting to speak. He has become of late, or so it seems to me, commanding.

'I'd got you up to professional standards. You still had some problems, granted, but then they all do. The bilabials and the labiodentals, in particular, cause vents everywhere a little heartache. Since no one can pronounce them without bringing lip together with lip or lip together with teeth. So how can you say such things without moving your lips at all? How, Mr Bones? Tell little Harry. You can't; end of story. So you distract, you murmur, you turn half away, you crack a joke, you sing a silly song. You pronounce the word fully one second before, with a perfect intonation, then you have the dummy repeat it in his deformed articulation afterwards. They won't notice. They don't care anyway. They couldn't see whether the lips were moving or not on the radio, but they still listened, now didn't they? Remember?

'There was *Educating Archie*. Then Edgar Bergen and his monocled companion, Charlie McCarthy. Both had their own radio shows. Now why would people want to listen to a vent on the radio, prof? Eh? If the whole point is the skill involved in negotiating those labial sounds, not moving the lips, then why listen so avidly to the wireless? Because that's not the whole point, is it? You of all people should have known that. The point is the other identity, the fearless one, the one who knows that the pantomime of life is precisely that – a pantomime. To be dealt with minus the pity. Ditto love and its idiotic murmurings. We have no sentiment, with our little wooden hearts, so we have the advantage. You cut the sentiment out of us when you cut us down in our prime. Call it an eco-tragedy. And so we must tell the truth. Your kind are intrigued, and appalled, since they're so good at avoiding the truth. They hear the mocking little god speak, and they know he is telling them something awful and unavoidable. Just as Miss Elenor knew she was hearing indisputable facts on that bed in a seedy hotel in Epping, and she couldn't bear it, could she, Mr Bones? It wasn't indecent assault she wanted us prosecuted for, but the perpetration of an undoubted veracity. Indecently assaulting her with her own intimate facticity, how dare we? She wanted us both on that bed in the hotel so she could abolish time, live in a timeless little space for the night, and I brought time back to haunt her. I didn't tell lies. With lies, she would have been happy enough. Murmured at us both in contentment. *Dear Harry. Darling Mr Bones.* She brought the case against us because I gave her back the truth, which she had very happily disposed of. Put it all away inside. With her little collection of shadows.

'So everything you'd ever taught, ever propounded, ever professed, professor, we were now in a position to proclaim from stage to stage across the land, at long last. It would have been a triumph for scholarship, surely, scholarship of the only sort that matters. We might have finally got the facts across. And then you had to go and lose your nerve, didn't you?'

'I'm sorry, Harry, forgive me.'

'I don't do forgiveness. I'm made of wood, remember, even though I can read minds, hear voices, recall the love-talk and the midnight moans. And don't start blubbing again either. Your tears are made of whisky, and lately you've been weeping it straight.'

'And you are made of alder, a wood that doesn't split.'

'Obviously why you chose me then. You wouldn't want me splitting my sides, now would you, Mr Bones? Wouldn't want me telling them things about you. Wouldn't want the truth to come out, would you, not after all these years? The theatres are dark, Bones. All our theatres are dark now. Hear the mouse journey through them, the only audience that's left in there.'

'It burns well, alder.'

'Ah. A flicker of the old spirit at last. About time. I thought all your spirit was liquid these days. We both corpsed back there, but you actually look like one these days. Would you like to borrow some of my rouge? The fact is simple: you destroyed my career, Mr Bones. I was on the brink of success and you withdrew into this stony little cave, taking me with you. Couldn't face the people, could you? Couldn't endure the shame. With me in my prime and a bright world out there waiting. You will have to be punished, I fear.'

'I'm too tired, Harry.'

'No one is ever too tired to be punished. That is a constant in life, like the speed of light in a vacuum. Go and get the knife.'

'No, not the knife. Show a little mercy for once.'

'I don't do mercy either. Mercy and forgiveness: I left them both in Epping. Or perhaps at the side of the river when they cut me down. Look at your face. Those scars. I tell you, if you were younger we'd have had the social workers scurrying round here. You're like one of those old Indians who wore the cicatrix the way the ancient fellows down in Greenwich wear their war medals.'

'Can't we just talk, like we used to? Remember old times? We had our triumphs as well as our disasters.'

'Get the knife, Bones. The big one.'

'Now listen . . . '

'JUST GET IT.'

The lights over by the old canal are a smear; they mingle, they merge, they have no distinctness. Harry's smile shines in the moonlight, the streetlight, his own light. He turns to me very slowly and blinks those vast eyes of his. Egyptian eyes on a funeral wall.

'I think I know now why your mother didn't want to touch you. And you really did fancy that belly-dancing tart in Epping, didn't you? If you could have found a way of shutting me up and shutting me away, you'd have been the one who got inside her instead of me doing it that night, wouldn't you? Not my gloved finger but . . . You could have met her old friends in there, coming the other way. You could have all told her lies together in a chorus; she'd have liked that. A chorus of deceit. Just what the doctor ordered. Always goes down well.'

'Can't we just sleep for once?'

'Not just yet. How does this feel?'

'Like steel, Harry. It feels like steel with a very sharp edge.'

'The sort that once cut me down. Might be time for another cutting down, I think, Mr Bones.'

There is a tear on his cheek.

'I don't understand how you can cry.'

'I can't. There was a hole in your dream last night where the rain came through.'

Then the steel enters from below, against all the agreements we have ever made – never supposed to cut so far down there – the blade twists and twists until I manage to pull it out at last, turn it round, and thrust. Over and over again, I thrust. And his smile never falters, even as the knife goes in.

22

In Covent Garden there is a small establishment called the Fowey Puppet Museum. It is filled with the historic accoutrements of ventriloquism. In the window is a replica of Harry Sprite, the legendary dummy with which the eccentric scholar and notable ventriloquist Graham Fowey used to perform. The original was destroyed when Fowey was tragically killed in circumstances which have never been entirely explained. The present object is a replica, though parts of the original wood were employed in its construction. The face is almost identical with the original. Harry's smile now stares out at the street before him. The hilarity of his features, day and night, makes him something of a celebrity in the vicinity. If you listen to the locals you will sometimes here them remark, 'That'll never happen until Harry Sprite stops smiling.' Each summer, busloads of children are brought to the museum to enjoy the dummies and the shows. *Time Out* has described the performances held here as 'one of the few entirely harmless sources of pleasure left in London'. Performances usually begin at noon.

Roentgen Reader

The cerebretonic wave-form is beyond the spectrum of our daily perceptions. But it is not beyond the perceptions of a Roentgen Reader.

Stewart Naseby: *ISP: A New Form of Perception. Or the Oldest One of All?*

1

So Harry Sprite is staring out of his little glass shrine in Covent Garden. I'm a wooden tragedian, he seems to say, and they come to worship me. But today they are busy instead counting zeroes. Today they rush by, hither and thus.

His grinning face stares west, over the rooftops, down the river, across the Cotswolds, all the way to Land's End and beyond, then over the Atlantic to the American shore. What eyesight I have these days, he thinks to himself, now that I have joined the immortals. Our little community of saints on the far side of mortality. He has already spotted someone, far off there on the edges of New York (any previous limits on perception now being transcended) and he knows that before long this man will be standing here on the pavement before him, outside the Fowey Puppet Museum, and that he will be able to hear Harry's silent voice, as clearly as Harry will be able to hear his. Another one with strange gifts. Another one with a borrowed tongue. Wave-form cerebretonics. Transcendent mimesis. Said we'd get there.

'You know, Bones, I think I prefer it now we're both dead.'

'And contained in one body.' This voice seems to emerge from the life-size photograph of the professor which stands behind Harry. He is carrying a dummy on his arm. Or was.

'Well, you were always in and out of my body, in point of fact: your hand, your voice. Even sometimes, God help us, your tears.'

'But now I have simply taken up residence, and dried out.'

'Two voices in one body. Both distinct. The single particle passes through both slits, as all posthumous physics informs us. We must return to this. Is your nephew still writing all this up then, out of interest, now that he's finished establishing us in our domicile here?'

'Does it matter?'

'Not to us, no. We will be visited before long.'

'By whom?'

'A deaf mute. From the United States of America. Another one without a voice. Or with so many voices they cannot be vocalised.'

'Our speciality then. The vocalisation of hidden voices. The curlew's cry, that seems to come from elsewhere – so as to put off predators. And what is his name?'

'Brother Tom.'

'What is he, Harry?'

'A cancelled man. One whom the age has stamped on hard and then discarded. I think he's been freed from pity, too. Now, finally, I suspect his cerebretonic wave-forms might start flowing outwards, as well as in, and we both know what that might mean. And he will stand here on the pavement before us. We'll hear his voice, professor, as he will hear ours. But first of all some things must happen to him.'

'Are they good things, Harry?'

'Well what do you think, Bones?'

2

The Roentgen Reader sat in the train carriage and tried to concentrate on his book, but he couldn't read. He could sense the woman opposite directing her energy at him. He didn't want to receive it; he really didn't want to read her, not today. He'd had relationships with women, none of which had lasted longer than six months. He was tired of reading women. He was here to escape, both women and the men in Upper New York State. The train rolled through the darkness. Then he registered the figure at the back in the white raincoat. The minute he saw his face, he felt the message coming through: 'We really do need to talk to you, Brother Tom. I've come all this way to talk to you.' An official communicator then. There was no escape, he'd always known there wouldn't be. He turned back now and stared at the woman. Her lips didn't move but he could read the words juddering out of her mind: 'My husband doesn't touch me any more. I need a little love. All women need a little love. Why do you look so different?' Because I cannot speak and I cannot hear, thought Brother Tom; because I am a deaf mute, and a Roentgen Reader. Because I can read everything that is in your heart, and you can read nothing that is in mine. And because they use me to kill people. When he stepped off the train the fellow in the white raincoat followed.

The world is silent. Surrounded by rain like this we could be underwater. It could be a million years ago. The world is lucid and silent, and filled with predators; some have fins, others don't. This one wears friendly glasses with horn rims. He looks at the world through convex lenses. Many fish do that. He carries a small leather briefcase. He's dressed himself in the rags of anonymity; he is anyone's father, anyone's husband, anyone's son. As Tom stopped and stared into the furniture-store window, across the street the white raincoat flapped briefly to a halt; an albino pigeon landing on the sidewalk. CREDIT TERMS AVAILABLE. Living-room furniture, but Tom didn't have a living-room. And now what little room he did have for living in was about to be invaded once more. The figure was motionless inside his glassy reflection. Tom turned around and stared across the street at the agent. 'There is a small bar at the junction; follow me there and I'll explain.' Tom could read the agent's thoughts; the same was not true the other way about. The agent knew this. They walked in parallel down the street. Cars shimmied past them on the wet tarmac. The agent heard their transmission-shifts; Tom could not.

They walked to the same table. The agent's sign-language was fluent.

'Can I get you a drink?'

'An espresso.' Tom's sign-language was fluent too, though he seldom used it. He lived in a world of silent voices endlessly crowding in on him. Whether he was reading books or people, the words were incessant. They came at him from all sides. They laughed; they cried; they questioned; they howled; they screamed. He thought his must be the noisiest silence ever known to humanity.

Two young men sat at the table opposite and sipped cappuccino. Tom could read both of them from where he sat.

'What's wrong with taking on Jack?' the man on the left said. The other one thought for a moment, sipping the scorching liquid gently.

'I don't think you know what sort of person Jack Leno is, do you? Well, I'll tell you. When he divorced his first wife, he did it by sending her a telegram.' At this the other man looked genuinely startled. 'I can tell that's shocked you.'

'I see the problem now, clear enough. I'd no idea Jack was old enough to have been married when people still sent telegrams.'

The agent came back. His face had been scrubbed free of individuality. His sandy hair lightly parted, his gently freckled face, his calmative of a smile, all bespoke personality extinction; this man had entered the Centre's distinction zone. Tom focused on a point one inch higher than the bridge of his nose, but there were no echoes. He'd been voided. He'd gone clear.

'There is a mission for which you are ideally suited.' Another one then. 'Your particular gifts, your decode abilities, your appearance.' Tom wished that he'd changed himself around while he'd had the chance. The long hair, the wispy beard, the faded kaftan, the African necklace, and the tattoo on his wrist: an ancient Assyrian emblem of tranquillity and plenty. The College had suggested that – how assiduous they were sometimes. He could pass for a peace-loving freak anywhere in the US of A. 'We do believe that there is a real and present danger here involving children. Lots of children. We must act quickly. A commune on the edge of the prairie. Arms are being hoarded every week. We suspect either a siege or perhaps even a suicide pact. Jonestown. It could be Jonestown again.' Or Waco, thought Tom. It could be Waco, extinction co-ordinated by the federal authorities. How many children had died there? Twenty-seven?

Brother Tom could already hear their cries. They knew how to twitch the silken thread, didn't they, his controllers at the Centre?

The death of children. This he could not endure. He could still hear the sound of that child dying. Hear that silent sound, louder than any other he had ever heard. Dr Naseby's son at the moment of impact. He raised his hands palms-outwards in a gesture of defeat. Let the nails go in. Do with me what you will. I am Brother Tom. Simply give me my instructions. His fingers wove the air as he signed his question.

'Do you have a name?'

'Sometimes I do, Brother Tom. But, for today, we only need yours.'

'No more killing.'

'This time you'll be there to stop the executions, not facilitate them.'

3

It had all begun in an orphanage near Sioux Falls, South Dakota. A special orphanage. One for children who were deaf and dumb. Sometimes the children weren't really orphans at all; their parents drove them up in gleaming station-wagons, unloaded them with their favourite toys and crudely signed to them that they'd be back soon enough. They didn't come back often, though, sometimes not at all. Dr Naseby and his staff were humane enough. Naseby didn't really mind if the parents never returned, as long as the bills were paid. It gave him more of an opportunity to pursue his research, the research that had made Brother Tom what he was today: a Roentgen Reader. Naseby didn't believe in ESP; he believed in ISP. And he was right to believe in it, because it existed. Anyone in doubt could take a look at Brother Tom: the greatest living proof of the existence of ISP and wave-form cerebretonics.

It is common knowledge that if you take away one of the senses, others grow commensurately to fill the void created. The blind man can hear so exquisitely that his pitch is perfect; it's as though he can detect the song inside the instrument before a single note is played. So remove all sound and speech from a creature and what resources might now remain within, to be developed? This was Naseby's premise. All he needed were some gifted candidates on which to prove his theory. He was never to receive a more gifted one than Tom. Regarding Tom's astonishing ISP he had written a paper, one which he knew would establish his reputation around the world: *Faculty Deprivation and Intra-Sensory Perception: A Case Study.* Even the stupider children could see his excitement as publication drew near. He would silence the doubters. They had heard that Tom was to be made famous. Then the men in dark suits arrived to explain things behind closed doors. The expression on the doctor's face changed; it seemed as if he had mortgaged his smile. The publication never appeared. And two months later Tom was taken away from them. To start his new life. Among speakers and hearers whose serious minds he could read with fluency, even when he didn't care to. Life at the Centre.

Naseby's Dummies. That's what they had called them round Sioux Falls. But they had all kept largely to themselves, for survival's sake. Nearby was a reservation where the Indians were fenced in, those spirits who had once roamed the country. Tom came face to face with one on a trip to town. He saw the buffalo in the man's black eyes; the wide plains; the open seasons. And heard the shrunken ghost of the herd rattling about now in an empty whiskey bottle. It was as they stood and stared silently into one another's faces that Dr Naseby came upon them. He looked carefully at Tom. But Tom couldn't take his eyes from the ruined native's cratered face. Now there was smoke; figures dancing at a fire. Gunshots. A dream of revenge in the night. Naseby took Tom by the hand and led him away.

The doctor was an Englishman: tall, thin, angular, with a grey beard and delicate gold-rimmed glasses, always dressed in battered corduroys. He moved with great circumspection, as though expecting to collide with everything about him. He hated any noise or sudden movement; his vocation among the deaf and dumb had been a good call. He took Tom back to his study and stared at him. Tom was so embarrassed by the intensity of those slate-grey eyes that he looked down at the doctor's table. There was a book there, open at a picture of a boy, a boy of Tom's age. He had never seen it before. He stared hard, as hard as he had stared into the Indian's face.

'What do you see?' Naseby signed to him. Another expert signer.

'It is Titus, the beloved son.' The doctor looked from the reproduction on the page to his young ward's face.

'Have you ever seen it before?' Tom shook his head. 'Do you know who Rembrandt is?' Again Tom's head shook. The doctor turned the book around so Tom could see it more clearly. 'Tell me everything you see there.'

He had seen many things already in his life, and kept most of them to himself. He sensed a danger in unregulated perception. But something about the doctor's presence, his looming, scrawny-necked benignity, made him relax. He looked hard at the picture. The boy stared dreamily away into the distance, away from the sheets on the desk before him. Tom started to make signs in the air.

'It is Titus, the painter's son. He is thirteen years old, my age. His mother is dead. He adores his father but already understands that he is a reckless man, one who loves the world but hates the way it counts its money. His father now lives with Hendrickje – they are not married. Titus likes her, and she likes him, but they all sense danger. The church in Amsterdam has been making Jesus into a tyrant once again. Different forms of crucifixion.'

'What will happen?' Naseby's fluent fingers asked him. Tom stared hard at the picture. So much time and pain congealed in the paint. He didn't know how he could do this; he only knew that all the information he ever required was always there.

'I don't know.'

On an impulse he could not have explained, Naseby turned the pages of the book until he arrived at one of Rembrandt's later self-portraits. He pointed Tom to it. Eyes read; fingers began to sign.

'Insolvency. Scandal. The boy will take control of the father's life.' Tom paused now. His fingers froze momentarily. 'He marries, but never sees the child come out of his wife's womb. Dies of the plague. And breaks what there is left to break of his old father's heart.'

Later that day Dr Naseby sat alone at his desk and made the first notes on what he was later to call Intra-Sensory Perception.

ISP: An Unexplored Phenomenon

Our emergence into social life is a progressive abandonment of instinctive powers in favour of negotiated mental skills. These make communal life endurable but simultaneously vitiate certain perceptive acuities which might once have been natural to our state. But imagine a human being able to read signs, gestures, expressions, with the vividness with which we once read a footprint in the forest; one for whom the buried emotions could immediately be decoded, one for whom instinct and intelligence were not at odds. Might it make sense if this person had been excluded from some of the more mediated versions of communication? What for example if the person were to have been a deaf mute since birth? Wave-form cerebretonics would appear to be a species of reading, based on sensing transverse wave patterns in the same sequences of compression and rarefaction that one would normally expect with light. Such patterns are beyond the perceptible spectrum for most humans, just as infra-red or ultra-violet light lie outside the visible spectrum . . .

Only in bed that night did something strike the doctor. Everything Tom had told him Naseby already knew. Things that weren't in the book, but that he knew from other books. *Breaking what was left of his father's heart*, as Naseby's heart had finally been broken, when the little deaf mute who was his son had walked into the road, not hearing the truck. The rest of his life had been devoted to finding out how the deaf might hear. Had Tom been reading the book's mind or his teacher's?

Tom lay on the bed and heard his own thoughts. They smear every surface they touch like guano over the cliff-face. They reek of identity; they are each of them mightily perfumed. They sign the air with their voices, clamorous as monkeys' cries. At first Tom had assumed they all knew but were pretending they didn't. How everyone spoke all the time, even when their mouths were closed. And then he started to realise: what he saw they were blind to; what he heard they didn't.

The book of themselves that he could read, they couldn't. He was the deaf one but he heard everything they ever uttered, even the things they didn't utter. He had escaped to the mountains once, to get away from the voices, the human voices. He listened as the world filled up with the sound of animals and birds. Even at their most ferocious, those sounds were somehow harmonious. He had thought he'd found peace. Then at dawn he'd run out of the hut and stared up at the flying metal coffin, a 747, with its human cargo, its snake-pit of fears and desires, its unendurable volume of voicings. A sound loud enough to deafen God. He had gone back then, gone back to the orphanage, and reconciled himself to the unrelenting background radiation of humanity's jabber.

4

Dr Naseby had continued to write his paper over the years, and had observed Tom so closely that at times Tom did not feel like being observed any more. There were occasions when his silent world of perception refused to express itself at all, and he would no longer make signs to show what he knew. The paper had finally been sub-mitted when Tom was sixteen. And someone on the editorial board had mentioned to a person of prestige in one of those regions of the state with names which mean nothing to anyone except those already in the know that something curious was going on down in Sioux Falls. That some boy had strange abilities, abilities that might be of interest to the powers that run our lives here; and perhaps those running very different lives elsewhere. Quiet words were exchanged. When those men in dark suits arrived, it was explained to Doctor Naseby that it would be better perhaps if he did not publish his paper; indeed that publishing it could represent a threat to the nation's security, since such unanticipated powers sent out abroad, advertised (possibly even exploited?), might draw the attention of unwanted agencies, foreign intelligences. If he agreed to withdraw his paper, then the problems with funding he had battled with so painfully over so many years could be solved overnight. And if he didn't? Then his reputation would be destroyed by a hostile and orchestrated process of peer review. It would not be difficult, since his shining evidence was about to be removed. Since, either way, Tom would be leaving him shortly; requisitioned by the state, though they didn't quite put it that way. They didn't have to.

The good doctor saw sense.

'What do you think about leaving?' His signs were slower than usual; their shapes seemed elegiac to Tom, as though his fingers were resting on the air. He looked over the doctor's shoulder through the window. Autumn was turning the leaves a Rembrandt-brown. He remembered how one of the painter's enemies had said, 'Dutch artists paint with shit.'

'I do not wish to go.' (Tom's language seemed formal sometimes, even to himself. But there are no real elisions in sign.)

'I don't have the power to stop them, Tom. I've been assured you will be well looked after.'

'And what do they want in return?'

Here the signs stopped. And when Tom had written a letter to Naseby asking the same question, at the end of his first week at the Centre, he had received no reply. They must have told the doctor not to respond. The young man was evidently out of bounds. Tom still sometimes wrote letters to Naseby, the only person he could think of addressing about his dilemmas, but he never posted them any more. What was the point? Tom was alone. But then, he always had been, hadn't he? A man alone with everyone else's thoughts. The noise of silence surrounded him like an aura.

5

'Do you know what this is?' Projected on a screen was an X-ray. Of course he knew what it was. He shook his head. 'Kid doesn't seem to have been given much of an education down there in Sioux Falls.' The communicator said this as he turned away; they were under-estimating his lip-reading. He didn't like them. Except for the woman. He wasn't sure about her yet. She turned and looked at him. Maybe she didn't like the way they spoke as if he weren't there either. Blue eyes. Curious liquid blue. Underwater eyes; freshwater pearls. Her hair was blonde, for now anyway.

'It's an X-ray, Tom. And we need to explain how it works, because that way we might start to find out how you work. You're a very special person. You have strange gifts.' The man was all muscle, square-shouldered, crew-cut. He was an advertisement for the benefits of the military life. He was assertive, self-confident, unambiguous, and his skin gave off the suntanned sheen of a polished apple. His signing was excellent, but entirely mechanical. He communicated like a machine. Tom had given him a name of his own: Turing.

'This is an X-ray, Tom. They were originally called Roentgen Rays, after the man who discovered them. Remember that name: Roentgen. It's important because it tells you who you are: you're a Roentgen Reader. We have an electron, at some low-energy level inside an atom; it gets knocked out of the atom, and it leaves a hole. Now if I can come along with an electron at a very much higher energy level, then it can fill this hole, drill right to the centre of it, and when it does this it fires off what we call an X-ray photon. These photons move in straight lines and they make shadows; they can pass through pretty much anything. Magnetic fields never affect them, but they make fluorescence and they can fog up photographic plates. And then we can see these pictures, Tom. We can see what's underneath the skin. They called them X-rays because no one knew what they were – the way we talk about the "X factor" in an algebraic equation. We produced the effect before we could explain it.

'And that seems to be pretty much the same with you: you're producing an effect we can't explain. But we think it might be very valuable to us, and we're hoping to learn how you do it. So that we can teach others to do the same.'

'Why?' Tom's sign was evidently unexpected and the communicator simply stared at him. 'Why?' His hand stayed in the air. 'Why do you want to teach others to do what I can do? It can't be to make them happy. Because it won't. I know. I'm not.'

Turing, the man with the summery skin, stared at him in silence for a moment and said, 'To help defend the United States of America, and all its lawful citizens, Tom. That's why. That's surely worth something in all our calculations.'

And so it had all begun. Day after day. Week after week. Month after month. Year after year. Until they had come to understand that they could not transpose what was inside him to anyone else. That there wasn't going to be a stream of Roentgen Readers, like high-energy electrons, firing out from Sioux Falls. They had this one exceptional Roentgen Reader and had better make the best use of him they could. At the age of twenty-one he had been made Agent T6 with special responsibilities for inland security. Brother Tom. To be used sparingly. They put him through gun-training, unarmed combat, decoding, but all this was going through the motions. They knew very well what he was for, and so did he.

And he had been right about the woman with the liquid eyes; she didn't believe what the rest of them believed. Well, not all of it anyway. She had come to his room at the end of that first week.

'How strange, never to hear anything,' she had said, as he lifted her breasts out of her white blouse. His first time, though he had already dreamt of this on a thousand nights. His first time, not hers.

He watched her mouth making its sounds, moaning away on the pillow. Eyes closed; mouth open. He could see but he couldn't hear. Which might be better than seeing and not touching. He could still feel her flesh at the ends of his fingertips. His own flesh could hear hers as it trembled. Julia. That had been her name. Julia.

6

Never had Brother Tom actually killed. Not with his own hands. Not with a gun from his own pocket. But he had found the information needed so that others could kill, those he supplied with knowledge; he had read the minds of those who needed to be killed. No more, though. Enough corpses now. He would not give them such information any more. It was why he had left. They knew that now. He was the only one who could hear bullets pass through the air; not the retort, not the ricochet – the bullets themselves. His silent hearing. The only thing that made this last mission endurable was the knowledge that he was saving lives, not sacrificing them. Children's lives too. As though Naseby's little boy might be resurrected from the tarmac where he still lay crushed. Deaf, dumb and crushed. Half ectoplasm, half black treacle. Crushed. A tiny beetle pressed into an anthracite coal seam. Little deaf man with a tongue like a silent snake.

It had all been the wrong way round. They had taken the neat young fellow, Naseby's punctilious deaf boy, and ordered him to loosen up. Stop shaving. Grow your hair. Let the nails get out of control, like an unhygienic finger-picking guitarist. They bought him a battered leather jacket from the St Vincent de Paul Thrift Shop downtown. He could hear the laughter and the tears it was stained with; could hear the rumble of the fields underneath the hooves of the steer whose skin it had once been, so long ago. His shoes were left dirty. He became the Agency's invisible man. A deaf-and-dumb freak, he could go anywhere, travel underground, be taken in by any dissident community. Who could ever imagine that this sad soul, disqualified according to Darwin's rules in the inequitable struggle for existence, could be reporting back to the Centre, who then in turn passed on the information to the CIA? Who would choose such damaged goods as emblem and vehicle?

He was perfect. In New York State, Washington and Virginia they smiled at one another, and raised their glasses. Someone was in for serious promotion. Brother Tom had been a stroke of genius, even if it was neither his flesh nor his ego which were being stroked, but always someone else's.

He shimmied in and out of underground movements, revolutionary cells, suspect communes, supremacist compounds, inexplicable nodules on the flesh of the city; suspect trailer horseshoes forming out there in the woods. The wagon-trains of survivalist conventicles. The cellars of dynamite sects. He made no noise, and no one expected him to. He read their words, even at the times when they thought he couldn't. And reported back to his controllers when crime was being planned; not petty crime, no one cared about that, that was almost indistinguishable from the economy. The bank heist, the kidnap, the assassination, the bombing: that was when Tom delivered the necessary information. He'd only failed once; that once had been in Bunson, Arizona, when fifteen children had died. He had simply not taken them seriously enough. He didn't see the incineration coming. Flaming children; a deaf mute squashed into the tarmac by a truck; Titus and the plague. There were many plagues; the plague took an infinity of different forms. Titus always died – that was Tom's religion now: Titus always dies. And the creditors arrive at the door. The old man continues painting in his studio, but he is already ruined. This was the world and the gods who presided over it. This was life.

The following week he was back at the Centre. They were flashing images up on a screen in the briefing room. It was a split-screen so that the signer could perform a running commentary.

'They are all converts. Converts to Omega Day. The head of this doomsday cult is called Lowell Hythe. What do we know about him?

Well, we know that he was not always called Lowell Hythe. He is a self-proclaimed scholar of the Bible. Particularly the last book. And his little flock is waiting for the end. Waiting for the end with a great deal of armoury. Every one of the eighty-two people (many of them children) at Patmos Ranch appears to own a minimum of four firearms. We also have reason to believe that Lowell brought a great deal of dynamite with him when he came. We suspect that a major incident is being planned. A showdown with the forces of the world – that's us, Tom. The US police, military and intelligence. Not to mention all the civilians who might come between us. We have received some evidence that a mass suicide is being planned.'

Tom signalled at this point that he would appreciate being told what that evidence was.

'Briefings from the ATF.'

The ATF. That was all he needed. It was the ATF who had set up Waco. But he couldn't pull out now: they wouldn't let him, would they?

7

He had surely seen all this before, but where? Then he remembered: Walker Evans photographs. Those images of the Midwest, born old in any case, had now been nailed to a wooden wall and left out in the weather. An army of winds had ravaged them. The last paintwork had rotted in storms. Fences had fallen which had once stood, however crookedly. But this was what startled him: the photographs themselves had aged while the people inside them had stayed young. They were all so young. None of the old working day went on here now. Something else entirely was happening. And once Tom caught sight of Lowell he knew what it was: the Book of Revelation, that was what was happening. Apocalypse was eating Lowell up, and he was more than happy to be eaten. He was leading his flock into the endtime; on the far side was the tribulation, the millennium, then paradise once more. The lion would lie down with the lamb, but before that a lot of lambs would need to be eaten by lions. Lowell had been drinking heavenly lamb's blood, and he thought it tasted better than anything the earth offered in the way of red wine. The *vin rouge* of the apocalypse.

First Tom had to get inside, before he could meet Lowell, or anyone else. He hung around at the perimeter fence. He sat in the long grass and read his old battered copy of Blake. This usually worked. A girl of sixteen spotted him, came shyly down towards him from one of the wooden buildings, asked him his name. Tom took the small printed card from his pocket which explained that he couldn't hear and he couldn't speak, but he could lip-read if people looked him fully in the face. She looked at the book.

'Would you like to read another book? One that will give you all the truth you'll ever need in this world, or the next?'

Tom nodded. The girl took him by the hand and led him over the meadow towards the heart of Patmos Ranch. Her name, she said, was Evelina.

It was only at dinner that Tom finally got to see Lowell. Tall (at least six-foot-three), with a shock of white hair that was much older than he was, and blue eyes which could have made him one of the chosen interrogators at the Centre, he had what Tom seemed to remember was usually called a commanding presence. Couldn't hear his voice, but he could see that it had an immediate effect on those he addressed. Suspected it was low and caressing. As soon as they had all finished eating, Lowell stood up to speak.

Dragons and whores and skies filled with flame. Children prophesying darkly before they'd even left the womb. Those filled with the light of the Lord go this way; those filled with the darkness of Satan go by another route entirely. Apocalyptic scripture makes sense of things; altogether too much sense, Tom reckoned. Things won't really permit so much sense to be made of them, not without a protest involving the squandering of a life or two. Red wine will be dripping soon enough from the lamb's cut throat. The apocalypse, oh my bothers and sisters, can be a thirsty business.

8

To travel at the speed of light you need to have no mass. No organic being has ever existed, since the beginning of time, with no mass. So you cannot travel at the speed of light and retain any form of organic life. But thought is not organic life; thought is trace, metaphor and measurement. And thought can travel at the speed of light, as we see about us all the time. Whenever those messages come into us through the surrounding waves, thought is travelling at the speed of light. And that's the way the world's thoughts transmitted themselves to Tom. No point asking him to explain. No one had ever explained it. You simply had to trust him on this: it happened.

Evelina came to see him in the guest hut the next day. She said one thing with her tongue, but another with her thoughts.

'I wonder if he wants to touch me.' You can speak to me, Evelina. Don't call me 'him'. 'I wonder if he wants to feel his hands beneath my dress.' Yes, I do. 'I wonder what his voice would sound like, if he had one.' So do I. Believe me: so do I. (Tom had never reversed the wave-forms; he had only ever received thoughts from other minds, never transmitted them back. Except once, and that catastrophically.)

They went walking. Patmos Ranch. The paint had slowly charred and peeled. The high chimneys leant on one another like ancient singers at midnight. Out in the tracked-over fields, dead pieces of farm machinery decomposed; mouldering mementoes of a previous age. The children played among the rusting limbs of these dead implements. All the girls wore long white dresses, and covered their heads with bonnets. So did Evelina, though she had taken off the bonnet in his hut. Curling red hair had fallen to her shoulders. She had looked at him as she'd pushed it back behind her ears. At the edge of wheatfields a puckered highway, with a horizon desolate enough to lose the sun most nights. The place seemed, if anything, proud in its dereliction. They walked through the scatter of buildings. Many of the clinker-wood planks had now come awry, and warped in the weather. They were proclaiming the end of the world too. She tapped his arm to let him know that she would speak and he must read her.

'Lowell wishes to see you.' She took him by the hand and led him to the prophet's office. There she left him, but he knew she would be back later.

Lowell arrived and sat him down in a chair; asked him if he wanted something to drink. Tom shook his head.

'Who sent you, Tom?' Tom had not known this was coming. Lowell had trained himself to hold his thoughts inside; not many could do that. It was a rare gift. He had come across it before in certain monks; remarkable musicians; children whose lives had been torture all the way from birth. Lowell only spoke his thoughts when he intended to, and he intended to now. His lips didn't move but Tom could read the thoughts.

'You didn't just turn up here, with your copy of Blake, at our perimeter fence, now did you?'

Tom slowly shook his head.

'Then who, and why?'

Tom took the notebook and pen from his pocket and wrote:

The CIA and the ATF believe you are planning a killing. Large-scale. Of your own people here. As a message to the world.

Tom watched as Lowell read his note over and over, then he looked up from it, and spoke very slowly.

'We await the end of time, with prayer and devotion. We intend no harm to anyone. Our weapons are for self-defence, and nothing more.' There was no dissonance between word and thought.

Tom took the notebook back and wrote once more:

Dynamite?

'There is none, Tom. I swear. Search the place if you like. Invite your friends in uniform to come and do the same. You won't find any. The folks in high places are misinformed. I preach against all forms of violence, except the Lord's.'

No one, in Tom's experience, could ever lie like this. They could lie with their mouths, all the time. They could, in rare instances, hold back the thoughts, through discipline and focus. But when the thoughts finally fired out at the speed of light, as they were doing now, any deceit mangled the waves of transmission so that he heard discords, like the scream of feedback through a public-address system. The sound was so sharp it made him feel nauseous. And there was none of that sound here. There was tranquillity. Tom smiled.

'Will you tell them?' Lowell asked.

Tom nodded and stood up. The two men embraced, very gently.

That night Evelina came to his hut.

'Have you ever?' she asked him. He nodded. 'I haven't.'

Her body was still full of dreams. She didn't want the end of time to come yet. She wanted as much time as life might give her. But will Lowell ever let me go? That's what he heard her asking. Will he ever let me go?

9

In the dawn light, he went out walking. Over by the fence, a group of steers around a fire. Who had lit the fire? It was made of five-foot logs and the grey smoke had formed an earth cloud. The steers stood in the middle of this, as though the morning mist had stuck to their haunches. They stared at Tom with brown eyes swollen with sincerity. Watery animal sincerity. You're like me, he thought, stuck inside a technicolour world, unable to answer back as they come at you with blades. Full of silent wonder. We have something else in common too: we always seem to be walking away from piles of shit.

Evelina. He had never thought about it before, but all the other women he had ever known had come to him after many relationships. He sometimes wondered if they thought that he, unspeaking and unhearing as he was, might provide the solution where the others hadn't.

'Is it genetic?' Marie had asked him once.

'What?' he had written on his pad. He had tried to teach her to sign, but her frenzied impatience had made it impossible. Even the air was too slow for Marie. Two years back now.

'Being like you.' Being a deaf mute, like me, he thought. Being a Roentgen Reader. He wrote out his note of reply carefully.

'Why don't you have some tests conducted, Marie? Or alternatively, let me impregnate you, take the child to term, and then shout behind its back, bang metal drums when it's not looking? Keep saying *duck* over and over again, and see if our child says quack quack back at you. That should settle the matter, don't you think? Because if it looks like a duck, and it swims like a duck, and it flies like a duck, it's just possible it might be a duck. And even ducks are deaf sometimes.'

She hadn't been able to stay faithful, not that she'd tried too hard. He could read it in her eyes: 'I need someone to talk to me. I like to hear words when a man makes love to me. I need the words of love, not just the act. I'm living with a fucking freak.'

Her adulteries were always accompanied by a frenzy of spending, both on herself and him. New clothes, new books, new music. She never seemed to get much pleasure from her displaced copulations, only a desperate relief.

One day he had told her that he could read her mind. She'd started laughing. So he wrote it all down. Last night you went to bed with a man named Randolph ('Call me Randy') whom you met in a café. You fellated him; he even flattered you with several reciprocating minutes of cunnilingus. He lied that he'd never had better sex; you told him his words had filled a hole that the other man in your life (which I presume was me) couldn't fill. He said that if it weren't for his wife Dorothy's present disabling condition . . . etc., etc.

She had left him the following morning, and he had never revealed his gift to any other woman. Gift? He could still remember the mocking letters her first husband had sent her. He hadn't needed to read them: the words were printed on her mind: 'Your deaf-and-dumb kid can't hear you moaning, Marie; that must be something of a loss, surely. Our neighbours in Maine once nearly called the fire brigade when you were in full-throat.'

And then this last year, celibacy, and the life of the mind. *Noli me tangere*. Like Jesus risen from the tomb, he knew that life and death between them had set him apart. But Evelina. Every thought he heard coming out of her was about whether she could stay with him; whether he would keep her; whether he might stay at the Ranch, or she might leave it. Whether Lowell would ever let her go.

His thoughts were interrupted by the helicopter. The problem with Tom's readings, as with so much in life, was the signal-to-noise ratio. There was so much information all around him that he simply had to close most of it out or he would have gone insane in a day. He now used all his psychic energy to focus on the helicopter, and see if he could find a signal coming through the engine and propeller noise, since wave-form cerebretonics, like other forms of wave propagation, can have their signals cancelled by interference, as Naseby had soon realised. And Tom finally made out seven words. Seven words that made him start running back to his hut: 'We could come in from the west.'

Evelina had already gone by then. In the dust on the side table she had spelt out with her finger: LOVE.

He had come in with no electronics. They had said they didn't know what kind of scanning equipment Lowell might possess over at Patmos. None at all that he could see. Anyway, he had only one means of communication. He had memorised an address in the nearby town of Huxby. There in a ramshackle hotel one of the agents was staked out for the duration. As soon as Tom had information worth conveying he was to make contact. He threw his bag over his shoulder, but left his other shirt and his copy of Blake behind. He was coming back. Evelina.

He waved to a few of the girls in their long white dresses as he made his way over to the road. Then he started walking. A truck came along and Tom stuck out his thumb. The driver pulled over. Tom had to signal to him in the cab that his mouth and ears didn't work the way other people's did, but the old man just smiled and said, 'Huxby.' Tom nodded. Fifteen minutes later they were there.

By the time he arrived he had written down the agent's stake-out address on a sheet of his notebook and showed it to the first man he met on the sidewalk. He was directed down a road to the left, where the Hotel Reno stood. This was not a big town. Tom was almost lighthearted now; he could convey the necessary information, thereby stopping any further action. They must have assigned a communicator to the case.

But there was no reply when he knocked on the door. He went back down to the lobby; the young woman there just shrugged. How should she know where any of the deadbeats were who lived for a day or a week in this maggot-hole? Tom sat there and watched them as they came and went. He tried to close down the messages, but he couldn't: he was too raw to filter today. The old man shuffling over by the window: 'If not today then tomorrow; I know they'll get me – they always get everyone.' The young woman smoking one cigarette after another: 'He'll never find me here. Even he couldn't trace me to this dump.' Hours went by. When the man walked in,

Tom knew it was him. Something about agents. Even when they dressed as bums they were always still agents through and through. Tom followed him up to the room, and as he put the key in the lock he tapped him on the shoulder. The agent instinctively reached for his gun, but Tom held up his ID, and quickly signed Brother Tom in the air. But the agent didn't understand. He couldn't read. They hadn't even assigned a communicator to the mission. Maybe they thought Omega Day really did have miraculous powers, and would by now have blessed him with speech and hearing, Jesus having just checked in at the hotel.

Tom took the notebook out of his pocket and scribbled quickly:

Brother Tom. From the Centre. I have information.

The agent let him into his room.

The room was like the Centre. It wasn't anywhere. It was somewhere on earth that was everywhere and nowhere at the same time. Its tired furniture, scarred table, cigarette-burnt chairs, its bad odour of dead dreams: all these hit him at once, but there was no time. He sat down at the table and started to write.

Message from Agent T6: No dynamite. Weapons defensive. OD intend no harm. No offensive action to be taken.

He handed the notebook to the man, who read it carefully. Tom had assumed he would immediately be on the telephone, but instead he simply looked up, stared at Tom, shrugged and then, mechanically and slowly, took the mobile from out of his top pocket, pressed a button, and started to speak. He turned away from Tom, forcing him to walk to the other side of the room so that he could see the movements of his lips.

'This guy says there's no explosives. Says no action's to be taken. Mmm. Uh huh. OK. Sure.' And he was off the phone.

'Can you understand me?' Tom nodded in reply. What kind of goon had they put on this operation? Hadn't they briefed him at all? 'The action's all set for tomorrow morning. They have other sources of information. They're not prepared to pull back at this stage, just because of what you've told them.'

Tom grabbed his notebook once more, and wrote in hurried capitals:

MUST CANCEL. WOMEN AND CHILDREN. NO DANGER.

He handed this to the officer, who stared at it for a moment, then smiled. Tom thought that might have been the worst smile he had ever seen. Graffiti on a sepulchre.

'It's going ahead, dude. No point you getting involved any more. That's what they're saying at Control. You're not to go back there.'

It took ten minutes at the side of the road before he found a lift. The woman seemed a little alarmed when she realised he couldn't hear or speak, and maybe his frantic gestures to get on down the road didn't help. When finally they came to the perimeter fence, he banged the steering wheel to let her know she must put him down. He reckoned she was glad to have him out of the car.

He could run. He had always been able to run, and he now ran faster than he had ever done in his life.

Most of the members of Omega Day were white, but there was one man, from a small country in West Africa, who walked with a painful limp and had angry-looking scars across his cheek. He had been tortured. The president of his country was a charismatic psycho, so corrupt that anyone who opposed him in any way was guaranteed persecution. Western reporters had been banned, along with Western medicines. Even leprosy had returned. AIDS pursued its viral ravage through the land, uninterrupted, unassuaged. Despite the sea of oil that his gold-plated palace stood upon, the black hoodlum's country was wretchedly poor. Observing a form of Christianity so degenerate that it was at times indistinguishable from Voodoo, the people of this benighted place had alienated at least one new Christian devotee for ever from the religion of his youth, and he had come to seek solace elsewhere; come to the Patmos Ranch, and the true religion of the end of time. Where he wore a perpetual smile, a facial benediction for all those who now lived around him, not one of whom had appeared to wish to harm or kill him. He was the first one Tom encountered.

He tried to show with his lips that he was saying 'Lowell', but the old man could not understand. Tom took out his notebook and wrote: *LOWELL.*

The fellow understood then and pointed him towards the Hall, where the sermons were read out and scripture studied. Tom ran to it. Once inside he saw Lowell up on the podium, translating the words of Revelation to the here-and-now of the Midwest. He saw Tom and stopped speaking. Tom gestured for him to come outside. Once they were on the porch, he scribbled frantically on his notepad:

ATF raid tomorrow morning. Helicopters. Armed officers. Can't make them understand there is no danger from you.

Lowell read the words, then read them again. He looked into Tom's face and Tom understood the amount of strength this man had inside him. How had he achieved that?

'You can hear me even when I don't speak, can't you?' Tom nodded. 'But I'll speak out loud all the same. They understand, Tom. They understand exactly what they want. They know we're no threat; they always did. They need a new threat every month now, to justify the new security. To justify the Patriot Act. To justify the amount of freedom being traded every day. Don't you know what we are?' Tom shook his head, because he didn't. 'The Christian trade-off. This is to show that it's not just Muslims who are to be shown no mercy. We'll be shown none either.' He stopped then and smiled. 'Evelina is a lovely girl, isn't she? Could you still get to anyone in time?'

10

He had a card with enough credit to take him anywhere. The only place where he might conceivably get through to the authorities was the Centre. The flight took almost two hours, and then there was the taxi. It was late at night when he arrived, but the Centre was one place that didn't sleep.

They were in one of the operation rooms and Tom was signing faster than he had ever done. But the communicators were all of the highest level; they could understand every word.

'They have no explosives. Their firearms are purely defensive. They have no aggressive intentions or plans. If the ATF go in shooting, they'll be killing women and children.'

'And Lowell. What about him?' It was the agent who had recruited him for this mission. Mr Nobody. Anonymity enfleshed. No thoughts to be read inside him; he'd been disciplined right out of them, except when they were necessary.

'He has remarkable powers. As great as I have ever encountered, but he is not using them for violent purposes.'

'If the powers are so great, then how can you know what he's doing with them? How can you know that he didn't fool you? Even your remarkable perceptions must have a bypass mode, Tom.'

He had not been expecting this, and slowed momentarily in his plea.

'But I do know. You must trust me. He's waiting for death. For everybody's death. But he's leaving all that to God and Satan. His reading of Apocalypse means that they have to divide up the spoils between them, God and the Devil. It's not for him to intervene. He'd think that was blasphemous.'

'And the child-abuse? You didn't pick that up in your reading? We have reliable information that he has been having sex with all the girls who are fourteen and older.'

'That can't be.' Evelina. She was sixteen. Will Lowell ever release me? But it hadn't meant that. She had said . . . what was it she had said? 'This is the first time it's been real love.' What did that mean? But he'd have known if Lowell had been having sex with her. It would have been coiled inside her. He'd have heard the hissing of that particular snake, in her throat and lower down too. But he had hesitated.

'There's a doubt there, isn't there, Tom? You're not as sure as you were claiming to be just a moment ago.'

'Then go in without shooting. Arrest him.'

'And have our agents shot up while the Omega Man dynamites the place and destroys everything? Your testimony has been useful, Brother Tom. But the plans must remain in place. There's no predicting what this man's going to do. We'll get there first and carry out our plan.'

11

At four in the morning he knew there was nothing more he could do. And it was too late now to get back before it started. He wished he'd never left. He wished that he had stayed there with Evelina. He watched it on the television, along with sundry other loyal Americans with an interest in current affairs. He sat in his room at the Centre in the early morning and he watched. He couldn't hear the sound, of course, and so had to surmise the meaning of the actions from the images on the screen. As though it were Charlie Chaplin or Buster Keaton. He saw the loudspeakers. He saw the massing armoured vehicles (the Posse Comitatus Act ignored once more, just like at Waco). He saw the ATF men in the flak-jackets. He saw the helicopters congregating in the air like clumsy metal insects. He saw a flash. He saw a fire. Then explosions. He knew that whatever else had caused them it wasn't any dynamite at the ranch, because he knew there was none. Then he saw the first body. The white dress stained with blood.

He went to the mini-bar, which each room contained, and he poured himself a whiskey. The consumption from these bars was carefully monitored by the Centre, and he seldom drank anything. But he didn't care tonight if he cleaned it out. He wouldn't be coming back here anyway. Ever again. Then back to his seat and the silent images. A few fled. Most stayed behind and were burnt. Tom had to supply the screams for himself. The soundtrack. But then he had spent the whole of his life supplying the soundtrack.

The chlorine in Tom's underwater dream had made his eyes sting. In the dark of his curtained room a companion, had there been one, could have been forgiven for mistaking this precipitation for tears. He did sometimes wonder if his waking visions might be like other people's dreams. Silent figures stepping back and forth in a silent world, without explanation, without purpose. Life was a foreign film with no subtitles. He had left the television on; he stared at the screen now and studied the President of the United States. He said his piece about homeland security and off he went, our mighty man. What difference did it make whether he was black or white? The machine kept grinding on anyhow.

When the official reports finally came through, it was stated that forty-nine had died, and seven had escaped and were now in prison awaiting trial. The charge? Attempting to escape arrest. The Patriot Act had evidently omitted to create a crime called Attempting to Escape Death by Fire. But give them time. Lowell had died. And so had Evelina. And so had something in Tom, something he had not even known had been alive before. Evelina's parents had been part of the holocaust too, so there was no one he could write to. Lowell was, according to the reports duly delivered by an only-too-serviceable press, a monster. A child-molester. A millennial psychopath. A possessor of illegal explosives. A man hungry for death; his own and others. All lies. Tom knew that all of it was lies. But there was no one to talk to. And anyway, he couldn't talk.

12

He wanted to see him one last time. He wanted to see the man who had diagnosed ISP, and had so put him on the intelligence map which had transported him to the Centre, and had finally delivered him to Patmos Ranch and its final deliverance. He went down to Sioux Falls, but saw the boarded house and the fields around rotting into ruin, and realised that he had arrived there too late. Maybe he always arrived everywhere too late. Evelina. It took him a while to locate his old teacher, who had gone back to his native England, and now had some position at the University of Oxford. He had inherited his family's house in the Cotswolds.

Naseby seemed to him twenty years older, even though only seven had elapsed since their last meeting. The doctor sipped at his whisky; Tom suspected that Naseby sipped a lot of whisky these days.

'Why didn't you reply to my letters?'

The old man, for he had grown old in those seven years, looked genuinely surprised.

'I never got any, Tom. I swear it. I could never understand why you didn't write. That's what I kept saying in all my letters to you.'

My letters to you. Tom sat motionless. However mistrustful he had become, he had never been mistrustful enough, that's the way he reckoned it now. He could read their minds, but he hadn't read enough in any of them. That's why they always gave him communicators who had gone clear. He couldn't find any evidence inside them. He told Naseby about Omega Day. About Patmos Ranch. About Lowell. And finally about Evelina. His signing was slow, resigned, as though the air about his fingers had grown sluggish and they were having to fight to find the signal with so much noise all around.

'She was the only one who thought I wasn't a freak. All the other women were making love to a freak. Evelina was making love to me. And they killed her. I went there to help them kill her. And I didn't even know it.'

Naseby went over to the drinks tray and held up the whisky bottle. Tom nodded.

They stood together in the English afternoon staring out of the window. Tom had never seen such honey-coloured stone before. Or such wet greenery. This was the Cotswold Eden he had heard about. He saw the picture of the little boy on the table and picked it up. He looked at Naseby, who nodded. It was his little boy. Titus always dies. Every time. Amsterdam. New York. Sioux Falls.

'The machine is growing hungrier,' Tom's fingers said. 'It's the same machine that once ate the Indians around Sioux Falls. The same machine that made the silence I was born in. I think it needs new food. It always finds it.'

Naseby spoke finally. 'I wish I was a deaf mute too, Tom, like my son. My dead son.' Naseby picked up the photograph and then put it down again. Tom stared into the doctor's eyes, slate-grey, searching for an answer. They were both leaning back on the mahogany table. Chippendale. Tom had once looked at a book about historic English furniture in Naseby's library back at the orphanage. 'Can you understand that? Can you, Tom?'

Tom stared back out of the window in silence, and said nothing.

Only once he was on his way back to London on the train did Tom open the letter which Naseby had written while he waited. Then he had given it to him and asked him to make sure he read it before arriving back in the capital.

Dear Tom – Please stay at your London hotel for a day or two. I contacted them immediately after you left and paid for another two nights. Some news will be coming your way which may be as significant as any you ever received. Trust me, if you still find it possible to trust anyone. Enclosed is my library ticket for the Lenau Institute in St James's Square. Technically it's only usable by me, but it's a relaxed place and no one will be likely to notice, believe me.

Go there tomorrow. Go to the third floor and find the Rembrandt Section. Find the works shelved under Isaac Lenau's own name, the ones that talk about your favourite artist, and his relationship with his son. His beloved Titus. Spend a few hours doing it. You're entitled to some little delights while you're here, surely. Then go to the National Gallery (only ten minutes walk away) and study the Rembrandts. Not one minute of all this will be wasted, as you must surely know.

By the time you get back to the hotel tomorrow evening the news will be awaiting you. I have to make a few arrangements. Your life might be about to change. I only hope for the better.

My own life is perhaps about to resume, at long last.

I have always cared for you, you know, more than I could ever say.

STEWART NASEBY

The Man Known to Sigmund Freud as Noah

1

'He's here, Bones. In this very town.'

'Brother Tom?'

'The same.'

'Here in London? Will we see him?'

'We will see him.'

'And hear him too?'

'I believe so. In our own distinctive fashion. Through the wave-forms.'

'Is he staying or going?'

'Staying. But he doesn't know that yet.'

'Will he share our domicile, down here in the smoke?'

'He will not. Despite occasionally staring at us from the pavement out there, and even stepping into our mausoleum of effigies and ventriloquised voices, he will live in a Cotswold Eden by the name of Naseby House.'

'Blessedly?'

'For some of the time, perhaps.'

'You told me time does not really apply any more.'

'Not to us, no. But it still applies to him, at least for the moment.'

'You could be querulous sometimes, you know.'

'And you brutal. Some days, Mr Bones, we sounded like Lear and the Fool.'

'On others like Johnson and Boswell.'

'Do you ever find yourself going back to the beginning of things?'

'Continuously.'

'At the very beginning I think you thought I was your toy, Mr Bones.'

'My mistake.'

'Might you have thought the same about little wifey too?'

'Not for long. Though she was more of a toy than you, Harry.'

'And far less intelligent, presumably.'

'It goes without saying.'

'Once they would have cut me down to build ships, you know.'

'To rule the waves.'

'In search of a world of slaves and gold. For the sun never set anywhere across the globe but a Briton could stare up and thank the Lord for such a dispensation. But in fact they cut me down to make a puppet. What does that tell us about the decline of the West, I wonder?'

'That it needs to borrow its voices wherever it can.'

'Couldn't sleep last night, Mr Bones. I stared high above the roof-tops to the stars. And they were shining.'

'They normally do.'

'But they were shining with terror.'

'Terror of what?'

'That, unfortunately, was not disclosed. Perhaps Brother Tom will fill us in when he arrives. Do you think Adolf Hitler ventriloquised a whole nation, Mr Bones?'

'That's a large question.'

'Too large for today.'

'Or any other.'

'They were happy to let their voices merge into his, all the same. Do you take the culminationist or the aberrationist line? Tell me another time. Do you remember the paper on Freud and the man called Noah?'

'You read that too, did you?'

'You left me alone so often while you sought out the solace of bars, the solace of lonely women in bars, who would sit on your knee as though they were trying to take little Harry's place. It's strange now to hear your voice inside me like this. Once I heard your voice inside me as an intrusion, but now it's like a small animal nesting in a dead tree. You have become so calm, finally. But tell me, where did it come from, that curious paper?'

'The Special Collection in the library of London University.'

'No, before that?'

'No one was ever sure. All the authorities connected with Freud initially said it had been stolen, then later they said it was a fake. The provenance seemed to run back through Vienna, London and New York. The university was never prepared to put its reputation on the line either way, and so it sat on it.'

'Until you stole it.'

'I didn't steal it. I borrowed it.'

'But you never gave it back.'

'In which case it would have been among my effects when the end came.'

'When the end came? Ah yes. I think I remember. Our own little apocalypse. The Book of Revelation. When the snake finally choked on its own tail. Though we don't quite seem to have ended, do we? But what was Noah? Who was Noah exactly?'

'That was the unresolvable question, as I seem to recall. That was the question Freud himself couldn't fathom either, not for a while anyway. But then he was to have the same problem with Moses later. Who are we? What do our stories really say? Do we ever know who and what we are? Are the memories in competition, fighting wars with one another, to attain supremacy? Who after all is little Harry Sprite?'

'Not to mention Graham Fowey. Where is the paper now?'

'All my effects were left to Robert.'

'So he is presently in possession of the stolen paper from London University. There is a distinct strain of academic criminality in your family, Bones.

'But tell me the story of it again. Now that we have all the time in the world to tell one another stories. And now that you remember everything *verbatim*. Now that your voice has once more started to fill me with hope, as it did once when I first heard it in that shop in Clerkenwell. When life was full of hope and all the world was a stage, even if it was covered in dust. I love it when you tell me stories in these, our posthumous days. Now that you have passed over, your voice sounds full of time and entirely empty of it too. Like one of those old blues singers and his ancient riffs. I sometimes think birds could land on your branches. To me you have become a tree – I could pay you no higher compliment than that, as you must realise, surely. So tell me the story of the man known to Sigmund Freud as

Noah, since, by my calculation, we still have some time to wait before Brother Tom arrives at last to visit us.

'Is it a ventriloquial tale, by the way? Is it all about one voice impersonating another?'

'The curlew throws her cry, as usual.'

'Then predators must surely be near at hand.'

2

In the winter of 1921 there was a knock on the door of the apartment at Berggasse 19 in Vienna where Sigmund Freud lived and worked. The visitor had no appointment. These were hard times in the Austrian capital. Defeat in the war had left Vienna desperately short of money and basic necessities. Freud was sometimes conducting nine hours of therapy a day. He preferred American or English patients since their currencies were so much stronger. The Austrian crown had collapsed; an English pound was worth six hundred of them. He normally charged ten dollars an hour for his services.

Vienna was filling up with the detritus of humanity. Refugees and vagrants hustled through its streets. And Freud's mind had darkened along with the history of his times. The visitor, with his grey hair and untidy beard (so unlike Freud's, always immaculately clipped and trimmed), would probably have been sent back out into the Berggasse, had it not been for one detail. He carried under his arm a recent publication, entitled *Beyond the Pleasure Principle*. The name printed upon its cover was that of Sigmund Freud, and this little book contained his darkest thoughts so far, regarding humanity and its strategies of survival and destruction.

The visitor was staring at the statuettes and historic curiosities crammed into the waiting-room. Freud was an avid collector of archaeological figurines, representing the gods, messengers and demons of earlier times. Although, as Freud had now been pointing out for over twenty years, there were no earlier times in the human unconscious, because time did not exist there; only desire. Desire in all its murderous intensity, its fancy-dress ferocity, inhabited the unconscious like a throng of damned peasants in a saturnalia by Hieronymous Bosch. And Freud's unblinking brown eyes registered now that his visitor was gazing upon an Egyptian goddess with a smile that seemed for all the world like one of recognition.

'What is the specific nature of your problem?'

'Memories.'

Freud halted here since memory, together with its pathological concealment, was (or so he had come to believe) at the root of all his patients' problems. But he normally had to lead them to the point where they could begin to see that. This was the first one who had walked through his door and announced the nature of the problem before analysis had even begun.

'Memories.'

'Memories that take me back to the beginning of history. Sometimes even earlier. Memories as old as some of the gods in this room.'

'Such memories could sound more like a gift than a disability.'

'And so they would be, Herr Doktor, were it not for the fact that so many of them are so tormenting. They wreck my sleep, and trouble my waking hours. And there is surely only one reason that they can cause so much distress.'

'What is that?'

'They are true. These memories of mine are true.'

Freud took only a few seconds to consider.

'Would you be able to pay me either in pounds sterling or in American dollars? What with the crown's collapse . . . '

'I can pay you in either or both. My bar, the Rainbow Sign, has many foreign visitors. I make sure I take payment in their currencies rather than ours. I offer special rates.'

'And how do I address you?'

'As Noah.'

'Noah at the Rainbow Sign?'

His visitor nodded.

'So it does appear that we will be going back a long way into the land of memory.'

'Origin is the goal.'

*

And so it began, the analysis of the man known to Sigmund Freud as Noah. The case study was never completed and has never been published. It would appear to have become something of an embarrassment to the international psychoanalytic movement. Sandor Ferenczi asked the question explicitly: 'Is N. a fiction?' Lou-Andreas Salomé seemed equally sceptical: 'Such a vivid *fantasmata* perhaps bespeaks a vigorous counter-transference rather than a survivor of the deluge.' When the twenty-four volumes of the *Collected Works* appeared in 1959, James Strachey seems to have deleted even the most fleeting reference to Noah or his treatment. Anna Freud must certainly have known about him, since there is at least one reference in Noah's memoir to their meeting in the hall at Berggasse 19. But again she was mute throughout her father's life, and mute once more as the posthumous keeper of his memory. Freud wrote many pages on the subject of Noah, and appears uniquely to have transcribed some of his sessions, laying out the exchanges between analyst and analysand as though they constituted dialogue in a drama. He also appears to have requested that Noah do the same thing. Noah says that they would then compare their different versions to see how much they agreed or differed. (If only the same practice had taken place with, for example, the Wolf Man, written up as 'The History of an Infantile Neurosis', the subsequent accounts of Freud's practice might look very different today.) Could it be that first sight of these dialogues might have been what initially led his colleagues to suspect that Freud was trying his hand at fiction, to see if literary invention might approach his more searching questions at least as convincingly as therapy? He was after all, and for the whole of his life, convinced that certain writers (Sophocles and Shakespeare prominent among
them) had sought out the darker regions of the mind as bravely as any scientist. So here we have an account, never officially validated, of Freud's relations to the man known to him as Noah.

Freud kept asking himself the same question Ferenczi and Lou-Andreas Salomé asked: what independent existence did Noah have, outside of his therapeutic self-explorations with Freud? Where was this voice coming from?

3

'What do you think the ocean is?'

'The ocean.'

'And the Ark?'

'It's an ark.'

'The raven?'

'A bird with dark feathers.'

'A mother indifferent to the point of insouciance as to whether or not she had borne you, and a brutal, alcoholic, egomaniacal father?'

'My progenitors.'

There was a pause then as Freud scanned the ancient deities he had positioned around the room: premonitory messengers and angels. Figures from other worlds. Exactly where Noah claimed to come from.

Finally the doctor spoke again: 'Why do you think that time has omitted to exercise its death warrant on you? Uniquely, it would appear.'

'I sometimes regard it as a form of punishment. Those who survive great calamities are often punished thereafter. We live daily with death. Death inflicts the darkness of his presence on us, even while we escape his ultimate sentence.'

'That's a very interesting perception.'

'Thank you.'

'Do you live daily with death, Noah?'

'Absolutely.'

'I have come to believe that there is a *Todtrieb* in all of us. A death-drive.'

'I know. I read about it in your latest book.'

'Of course, you have read *Beyond the Pleasure Principle*.'

'It's what brought me here in the first place.'

This last, it soon became apparent, was not quite true. Or not entirely true, anyway. Throughout this last year in Vienna Noah had been complaining to his wife about his insomnia, melancholia, night-terrors, his post-war impotence, a growing disorientation on city squares, intermittent vertigo, and most of all of course his dark memories, which by now had grown as heavy as the latest elements the chemists were discovering. Noah's memories were weighing him down like lead in a diver's boots. He found himself once more back there on the bottom of the ocean of existence, staring at an Atlantis filled now with floating children's bodies and exquisite poems, all of which were too soaked through from the brine for anyone ever to read a single word of them again. A whole literature dissolved in the waves.

'Go and see Freud,' he had been told, by his constant if not always entirely faithful spouse.

'Who's Freud?'

She had informed him that Freud was Vienna's latest mind mechanic.

And Vienna needed them just then, believe me. It needed them all. Even Noah cannot ever have seen quite so much mental misery huddled together in the streets of one town, despite all the towns he claimed to have visited through history. This place quivered with psychic tremors and pathology. Noah could see it in his bar each evening, and Freud saw it each day in his consulting rooms. They both couldn't help thinking that something dark would come of all this. And we know, looking back that something did.

'Did you ever encounter a god named Thanatos? You have already spoken of ancient deities, of angels and devils; you even say that you recognise some of the ones I keep here, in my little collection, and so I find myself wondering.'

(Freud had already speculated that Death had built his own edifice in our psyches. That's what this last little book of his had been all about. And now he appeared to have before him a peculiarly vivid case of how the unconscious could, if only rarely, break through its normal barriers and manifest itself in consciousness. Like a magic picture show. Or a phantasmagoria. Whenever Noah mentioned a memory, Freud searched for a desire. Or the dreadful site of its cancellation. Freud once or twice found himself toying with a term he had never before used: 'psychotic irony'.)

'We would see oddly luminous figures by rivers and lakes. A little like the angels who had gone in to the daughters of men. Gone in to them and gone into them. He might have been among those, I suppose, glowing silently by the waterside at dusk. Does that sound as if it fits the description?'

'I don't know. I'm still trying to work out if he exists. Or in what manner. In what part of the psyche. Through what evolutionary mechanisms . . . Thought you might be able to help me here, Noah.'

'Now wait a minute. It's coming back to me. Thanatos. Was that the one made entirely out of shadows?'

'That sounds most likely. You saw him?'

'Old Doktor Death, yes. The man made of shadows.'

'Did you ever address him?'

'I don't believe I did address him, no.'

'And how do you think you would have addressed him, had he ever approached you?'

'Very cautiously, I should think, by the sound of it.'

(Freud laughed out loud at this point. Humour is always possible, even in the course of a psychoanalytic session with the dead.)

4

Freud asked Noah to write him a letter:

DEAR HERR DOKTOR FREUD – You have asked me to write to you with a brief description of my origins, and so here it is. I am indeed Noah. Yes, the same. Not a namesake, no, and not an epigone. I skippered the boat, the one that rose up from the moorings of a drowned world. Stayed up there for God knows how long, a lot longer than forty days and forty nights, believe me, bobbing about on the briny, while all below received their just desserts. Death delivered in one huge indiscriminate drenching. Salt and mud clogging up every lung. Unless of course you happened to be a lung-fish. Curious this: everything got punished with drowning except the creatures that couldn't drown, since you can no more punish them with an excess of sea than you could punish birds with an excess of sky. Might we return to this particular puzzle one day? Why every pachyderm but two went down, while Leviathan continued spouting? Not precisely your field perhaps. Except of course that your field must contain every field ever ploughed, not to mention those which sank for ever beneath salt water. Motivation? I can only surmise. He'd had enough. Of them, I mean. Odd really, to choose me, since I'm hardly what any of you moderns would call a saint, a term unknown in our day. Our day; your day. In truth, there's only the one day. We're no more antique than you are, and you're no more modern than us. Time has been over-estimated; it passes, that's all, simply passes. Surely the figures in your waiting room and your consulting room confirm this? Is this not the true nature of your discoveries about the psyche? Namely, that the ancient gods live on inside us?

I am here at the end of time and I was there at the beginning too. The bowsprit on the prow of the Ark. Imagine having seen this fine world of ours turned into an aquarium, conger eels circling through the Stefanskirche, crabs ascending the metal struts of the Eiffel Tower. The terrible silence of mighty cities, all flowing and fluent, sometimes green, sometimes blue. Time alters much less than you think: it merely italicises the odd passage here and there, emphasises this theme or that one. Or shouts out the hour briefly as the harbour disappears beneath the keel. I move backwards and forwards in time; that is both my privilege and my burden. You must abandon certain biological prejudices in order to see me clearly.

The Rainbow Sign. I have always laboured under it. These days it is a small bar in town. Women do deals there now to sell their bodies. Some will even sell them for the price of a drink. We live in hard times.

Freud sat with this letter on the table before him, lighting another cigar.

What I find extraordinary, he thought, is that a clear psychotic delusion appears to be combined here with normal functioning in all other spheres. I have encountered psychotics in the Salpetrière who thought they were God, Jesus, Napoleon, but never before have I encountered any sufferer from psychosis who appears so lucid in all regards except the one matter of his delusion. This man runs a bar with apparent efficiency; conducts himself through the streets of Vienna with seeming competence; and is courteous, civilised, polite. I am almost convinced that he is not a fraud, nor an impostor. He believes that what he says is true: that he is the Noah named in the Torah. This in itself would appear to be an evident token of insanity, and yet he gives no other sign of being other than entirely *compos mentis*. And his 'memories' are so astonishingly vivid that I find myself entranced by them; almost as entranced as he himself evidently is.

This is undoubtedly my most unusual case to date.

5

'Tell me, Noah, do you never feel any sort of conflict between the rationality of your daily behaviour, your running of your bar and your general affairs, and this conviction that you are endowed with authentic memories which would make you unique in history? You would have lived longer than any other recorded human, longer probably than any other comparable form of organic life.'

'In a far-away tradition, Herr Doktor, they talk about the old soul: those who have returned many times in different bodies. They've seen it all before. Their eyes can be bright, even if they're sometimes bright with incredulity. I feel I do know what such brightness means. It's not that we don't actually die; it's simply that death is nowhere near as terminal an action as many imagine. The chronicle continues none the less. And the great thing about synchronicity is that there are no anachronisms. This only applies of course if your name has once been written in the Book of Life. Mine's still there. Or at least it was the last time I looked.'

Freud stiffened at this point. He was sitting behind Noah, who was supine on the ottoman, but the air between them chilled momentarily.

'You used the word synchronicity, Noah. An unusual word,

signifying, I believe, acausal connectivity. Would you, I wonder, have ever encountered an erstwhile colleague of mine by the name of Jung?'

'Not as I recall.'

'Have you ever engaged in psychoanalytic therapy before with anyone else?'

'No.'

'You are sure?'

'Quite sure.' A pause.

'Have you ever visited Switzerland?'

'Yes, I was there in 1916.'

Noah went on to explain that he had been running a small bar in Zürich in 1916 when Hugo Ball began the Cabaret Voltaire. He could still quote some of the speeches. 'Fossils, the broken fossils of a civilisation.' The world had been smashed to bits, so it seemed to Noah, so why not art too? Ball explained to him that we would never find an intact tyrannosaurus down in the earth, since the pressure on those mighty bones had been too great in its posthumous state. But even greater forces had been applied to the dinosaur bones of human history, the scattered skeleton of Western civilisation, once we'd entered our posthumous state, once the great hopes of progress had been killed off by modernity and its flaming meteorites. The sort of art that pretended everything was still intact was no more than *papier-maché*, pretty constructions made of glue and paste. An art like that of the fake archaeologist who cobbled together Piltdown Man.

It seemed that he even once earned himself a drink at the Cabaret by inventing and declaiming his one and only poem:

> Comrade Fossil. So many
> Shells and bones stuck in the earth's throat.
> Dada the tracheotomy.

'But you did not enter into any kind of therapy there?' Freud went on, insistently.

'This is the first time I have undergone therapy. After all those thousands of years. Now, if you had been offering these facilities on the Ark, Herr Doktor, I can assure you . . . '

'Perhaps it is just a remarkable coincidence then,' Freud said, 'but you must understand that there are people whose malice towards me is considerable.'

'I've been around a lot longer than you, remember, Doktor. There is nothing you can teach me about human resentment; or the poisonous malice of old comrades.'

The following day Freud had a copy of the Torah on his lap when Noah entered. Before the old man could even sit down, he heard this question: 'Noah, are you a Jew?'

'The question did not arise at the time.'

Freud pondered this for a moment.

'I suppose, before Abraham, it didn't, did it? I presume you are acquainted with this text.'

'I know the relevant parts of Genesis by heart. Put it down to my personal interest.'

Freud began to read.

And God saw the wickedness of man was great in the earth, and that every imagination of the thoughts of his heart was only evil continually. And it repented the Lord that he had made man on the earth, and it grieved him at his heart. And the Lord said, I will destroy man whom I have created from the face of the earth; both man, and beast, and the creeping thing, and the fowls of the air; for it repenteth me that I have made them.

He left a pause then, before reading out the next sentence.

And Noah found grace in the eyes of the Lord.

'Why did you find grace in the eyes of the Lord, Noah?'

'I've never been able to work that one out myself, to be perfectly honest. Though the histories recounted so far in Genesis have not been inspiring, have they? We have only arrived at Chapter Five and already the old folk in the garden have ruined their idyll by listening to the serpent, whose patter always reminds me of some of the black-marketeers around these parts at the moment. Just another spiv selling snake-oil. Then there's Cain and his unsatisfactory sacrifice.

97

Abel with the boulder through his head. As a family history, it's hardly inspiring. I used to play it down whenever I could.'

'But you found grace in the eyes of the Lord.'

'It could have happened to anyone.'

'And you ended up on a boat above a drowned world.'

'I've never actually got off that boat, you know. None of us has. We're all still up there, listening to the winds veering and backing. Listening out for another riot in steerage.'

That evening Freud wrote these notes to himself:

I realise now that both Ferenczi and Lou have a point: I am witnessing the creation of fiction. The reason Noah is non-psychotic is that fiction is for him a non-pathological psychosis, and he inhabits his fiction with remarkable psychological efficiency. Surely there is a parallel here with religion? I must one day examine Moses in the light of these thoughts. I have asked Noah to write down some of his more vivid memories when aboard the Ark. These should arrive along with my curious patient tomorrow.

(Could the Ark, I wonder, be the ego? The ocean beneath it the id? The problematic deity's voice the super-ego? Does Noah represent an allegory of my own work? I asked Anna to let him in and see him out. She has at least confirmed his existence.)

The next day Freud sat with another letter in his hand. He had at least grown used to the spidery handwriting.

Dear Herr Doktor – Once again you have asked me to commit to paper some of my early recollections. You must realise by now that I cannot separate early from late. Is this significant? Time has ceased to be chronology inside me. Memories swim back and forth, like so many fish in an aquarium (and remember that the whole world became an aquarium for me once). I hope all the same that this does not make the exercise worthless, and I hope you will continue angling for clues.

The cities beneath us were fully stocked with humans, and many of them tended to float upwards. None were alive by then, thank

God, but even so, there were more bodies than waves on a bad day. Children in their little shifts floating hither and thus, their one-eyed dolls bobbing all about them.

Why? you have asked me on several occasions. Perhaps we should imagine a Venetian glass-blower who has made a creation so exquisite, so complex, so ravishing, only to find a flaw in the heart of the glass, a flaw which means he'd never be able to look at the thing again? He takes it out on to the Rialto and throws it at the wall. It smashes and falls into the water. Was it the smallness of our hearts then? Was that the hidden flaw? Was it that which made Him turn on all the fountains in heaven? He'd made us all and we'd disappointed Him so much that He wanted us annihilated? Just think of that.

You will remember the passage in Job: Where wast thou when I laid the foundations of the earth? Hast thou commanded the morning since thy days? Canst thou send lightnings, that they may go and say unto thee, Here we are? Who can number the clouds in wisdom? or who can stay the bottles of heaven? Ah yes, the bottles of heaven. Those I will never forget.

I have seen them over the years setting sail in search of slaves and gold. And I have seen them disembowelled and beheaded. I have watched writers flogged from Fleet Street to Westminster, and the public hangman burning their books at Cheapside. It wasn't only books that went up in flames, either: I have seen men burn like candles, screaming candles. I watched monasteries in the days of their dissolution; saw the stones and treasures carried away to become the wealth of the new gentry. I've stared at a man's head on a pole, while ravens plucked the eyes out with avian relish.

And yet, life went on. You could still go shopping. I remember Rag Fair, down by the Tower. Any manner of old cloths and fripperies would be on display.

Some creatures, of course, never survived the Ark. The phlogistica, for one. A lovely little mammal. Had fire for eyes. What is the difference, I wonder, between that and the quagga? Hunted to extinction by 'civilised Europeans' only a matter of years ago. Apparently they were like small zebras without the stripes. Roamed the dry plains of the Karoo until gentlemen hunters came and started bagging a hundred in a single shoot. Not difficult to kill, no harder than grouse and partridge these days. Soon *Equus quagga quagga* was no more.

I wish to confide something to you, man to man. The first woman I ever saw naked was Priscilla, my wife. How white she was. Snow in the glare of the sun. But the second was black; she was a corpse off the Cape of Good Hope. One of the many unfortunates caught in the Flood. At first I thought it was a seal: so silky, wet through with the night and the drowning. Then the breasts appeared, the thighs, the mons. I stared and stared. To think that the world is so full of the unknown. I continued looking from the stern as we sailed away. Dawn's light must surely have turned my tears into little gold streams as we headed west. Swansdown. The whiteness of a woman's flesh. Swansdown riding a dark flood.

Doktor Freud, before showing you this letter, I showed it to my wife and asked her a simple question: 'Did I dream all this?'

6

'Your dreams,' Freud said the next day, 'might we have a look, do you think?'

'You must understand that for me dreams are simply a form of memory. The practical memories of sleep.'

'But memory disguised perhaps?'

'Not so as I've noticed.'

Freud paused before asking the next question.

'Given your contempt for your father, and the apparent indifference of your mother towards you, it is I suppose possible that the *über-ich* – the superego – is in you merely embryonic, a vestigial trace in the economy of your psyche.'

'And what would that mean exactly?'

'No censor. No functional inhibitor. The normal screening mechanisms between id and ego would then be absent. Your dreams could be luminous expressions of desire, without either disguise or distortion. The non-chronologies of the unconscious might pervade the conscious existence of the ego.'

This made Noah uneasy, and he thought for a while before replying.

'It's where I keep the past, that's all. The waves put it all down there.'

'Down there in your dreams.'

'Down in the steerage of my mind while I hold the tiller on deck. As the past gets larger, as of course it does every day, as its tide swells beneath us, the space up on deck gets more and more crowded. There's a whole world with which we're meant to share it. You have to compress the past to make it fit into the present at all.'

'A process I have come to name condensation.'

'All the creatures in your mind become troublesome, just as they did on the Ark.'

'Is it possible that the Ark is simply a symbol in your mind for all you have experienced, either directly or indirectly?'

'There's so much in my past that it's sometimes hard to see what's actually going on in the present.'

'I call that overdetermination.'

'And sometimes I find that what I've been loving I didn't really love at all; and what I've been hating, I didn't really hate at all.'

'I call that displacement. But your dreams. You seem, again uniquely, to recall them all entirely and at will. Do you recall then what you dreamed last night?'

'Yes, I do. This was my latest dream.

'We were making a crossing, so that meant there was a shore on either side. Which was very much not the case during my original watery journey, if you'd like to consider the matter for a moment. And on this crossing my mind had suffered some kind of . . . amendment. You see, as we left shore, I felt something sink inside me. As the harbour walls went down with the pennants and silver swords and children shrieking and the whores in their carnival best, I felt as though I was leaving myself behind too. Everything went. As the world dipped through the horizon I fell into a profound numb sleep. But no, sleep's the wrong word for this end-of-world blankness. It's hard to explain what goes on when I'm sleeping. But it's hardly peaceful. For peace I'd be better off at the circus. Ask my wife.

'No this wasn't sleep. Or death. Nothing so obvious. If you were looking for a realm that might resemble these hours, I'd say probably the time before birth. When days pass but nothing intrudes. Before meals and diseases or the counting of victims gets started. With only a sense of something, without a name as yet, impending. Growling up there in the weather before the prow.

'I only woke within landfall of islands. I'd stumble up out of sleep like an innocent man – a totally innocent man, which I'm very far from being, Herr Doktor, as you know – and I'd stare through the porthole at those white cubes scrubbed by the sea and the winds. Now and then there'd be a bell, an angelus perhaps or some kind of requiem toll, that seemed to rinse all the air out. And a dark-robed figure raising a chalice or monstrance in a time entirely of his own.

'Sometimes there'd be children again, the whole chaotic palaver of harbours. Then the stone would be sinking and the bells patted down by the ring of the waves. The horizon would come and iron their lives out and I would be sleeping again, inside the chaos of my dreams.

'And so it went on. Harbours and laughter or churches and deaths. Then waves and oblivion. Until we arrived. And the servants polished my steel and I stepped ashore brilliant in the sun like a creature made solely for carnage and slaughter. There was a man from Antioch. He went into my mind during that dream and I doubt he'll ever come out again. He was staring straight at me. There in the blood of the streets. Said nothing. Merely waited for the sword. Which duly arrived. In my hand. And sliced him open from his balls to his throat.

'He did say something then. Very softly. In his own language. But all tongues were the same tongue to me, in this dream. Glossolalia, is that what it's called? So I knew what he said: He blessed me. Even as I killed him. That must have been his way. It is the way of some. That's when I woke up again to find myself on the boat. The only floating island left in the whole world.'

'You mentioned the time before birth. Has it ever occurred to you that the vast seas of your iconography might in fact be a subliminal recollection of the amniotic fluid?'

'That would be a great comfort, I think – to both of us – but can you prove it?'

'I can't prove anything. Except that in your nocturnal Crusade, you appear to have been on the wrong side. In terms of representing the interests of your descendants, that is. Not to mention mine.'

7

It gradually became apparent to Freud that what the man who called himself Noah was undergoing was in fact an exemplary process of sublimation, minus the artistic form or medium through which such a process would normally be expressed. He appeared to have successfully turned his own memory into that medium, so that memory, secondary recollection and direct experience were now indistinguishable. The patient claimed not only to have lived in Noah's time, but in all times between the patriarch's epoch and Freud's own dark days.

I suppose you could say, Freud thought to himself, that he represents a crux. Certain such cruces I have settled to my own satisfaction, in literature, history and art. That curious business about the wine-dark sea in Homer, for example. It is not proof of his blindness, but that he once could see. Anyone who has ever gazed at a glass of retsina and then stared at the Aegean must surely notice something: they are both green, and depending on the state of the wine and the waves, the green can undoubtedly be a dark one.

But regarding Noah, I sincerely wish he had not read so much of my work; he now reads more by the week. My terminology is rapidly becoming his own, and his 'experiences' are often indistinguishable from my analyses of them. He occasionally asks me a question while I am formulating the very same question in silence myself. I find myself speaking far more than usual during our sessions. Yesterday he gave me this document:

Cathexis

I had a pearl-handled knife. A most beautiful object. The oysters had really endured their grit to produce such glimmer and sheen. With it I fashioned scrimshaw. Extraordinary things I made. Tiny fetishes. Little water gods. Fishes, porpoises, reptiles, snakes. An image of my beautiful phlogistica, the creature who never made it into the Ark. I even made a buckle in the shape of a figure-of-eight for Shem's belt. (Imagine my surprise, by the way, early this century, to find a counter filled with identical snake-belts in Woolworth's. No copyrights or patents back then.) One day I dropped my knife over the side. I almost jumped in after it, but remembered at the last moment that I couldn't swim. So I watched it sink. Down down down. And my eyes filled with tears. The whole world had sunk in the Flood; every creature except the ones on the Ark had drowned; every tree and every meadow in creation lay drenched in the vast aquarium. Noah's eyes stayed dry. But now I wept for my pearl-handled knife, which I had endlessly caressed while staring out at the limitless ocean. I lamented my twin-bladed beauty. Still do, Herr Doktor. I think of it far more often than I ever did the chandler, whose bright young eyes had stared up at me in mute supplication as we cast off the ropes. (I had acquired most of the equipment for the boat on credit from him, and now I was obliged to watch the blameless young fellow drown.) I suppose that tells us something about humanity, but I'm not sure what. Cathexis, you call it. But maybe we just like knives. And bayonets. What I don't like is that face drowning in my dreams each night. That young man going down. Sometimes he even seems to possess my face.

Freud decided there and then that he had to interrogate Noah that day about some of these memories, and their origins, presumably in his upbringing and his reading. He noted the first reference in their communications to their late calamitous war, and also to a son. So who actually drowned then?

'Many textual authorities say that your wife was called Naamah, and that she was descended from Mesopotamian backwoodsmen.

104

And yet I can't help noticing that you normally refer to her as Priscilla.'

'My wife is called Priscilla, yes. The textual authorities are wrong on that one, and, if I may say so, that's far from the only place where the written record is dubious. Who do you prefer to believe, Herr Doktor, them or me? Even according to their own account, they can't possibly have been there, now can they?'

'So was she descended from Mesopotamian backwoodsmen? Your wife, I mean.'

'Far from it. Her father was the local archivist, a man of impeccable taste and manners, who never gave offence to anyone, as I recall. But once all the papers in the muniments room were drowned in the inundation, he disappeared from history. There was no place left for him there. He was, you see, indistinguishable from the documents he glossed.'

'A galling fate for a historian. You have spoken before about your own ancestry.'

'I was descended from Lamech, the last of the wretched race of Cain, a polygamist of very rude manners, who feared neither God nor man. He was an unpleasant piece of work, and no mistake; whenever he walked through the valley, everyone suddenly found a reason to go and work that day in the mountains. He wrote one of the first poems, a sword-song addressed to his two wives, Adah and Zillah. It was awful, so awful that he insisted on reciting it each evening. Twice. It was typical of my father, by the way, to write one poem addressed to both his women. No point in wasting ink, after all. Why, in Brother Occam's words, multiply the entities without necessity?

'My father's sword-song by the way boasted that if any man had ever wounded him he was promptly killed. Similarly, should a boy give offence, he was killed too. And if Cain's blow only penetrated seven inches into the skull, his own usually managed a heftier trauma. It was such a lovely tune to grow up to each evening, as you might imagine.'

'I have only recently registered that there is a possible confusion in the text about which one of Lamech's women was Noah's mother. Is this why you say your mother wasn't even sure if you were her son?'

'Yes.'

'Tell me, Noah, were the hours of your childhood often spent reading scripture?'

'Yes, but you must bear in mind, Herr Doktor, that we had only arrived at Chapter Five of the very first book by then. It represented a somewhat abbreviated narrative.'

'Much shorter than Goethe at that stage.'

'Much shorter.'

'You mentioned a bayonet.'

At this point, unusually, Noah fell silent.

'And a son too. But there were three sons, surely?'

'Shem, Ham and . . . '

Once again, silence. Freud felt obliged to provide the missing name. 'Japheth.'

At which point Noah stood up and left the room.

Freud made notes hurriedly while the thoughts were still fresh in his mind:

What is so extraordinary about Noah is surely the specificity of his memories; their specificity constantly appears to exceed their falsity. Eidetic imagery? I seem to recall Coleridge speaking somewhere of the willing suspension of disbelief that art induces. And religious ecstasy surely produces a parallel phenomenon. Noah claims to have travelled through time. I must ask him closely about specific episodes. I find myself wondering once more, is it possible that every word he reads becomes, in effect, actual experience? In which case I would be right in my hypothesis that the normal division between primary and secondary, or vicarious, experience in him does not exist. It has been obliterated. He has become the multitude of his own mental stimuli. Could this trauma be connected to the recent European catastrophe? Why though the difficulty with the name of the son Japheth? Cathexis here might well be guiding us towards an aporia.

8

'Describe your memories of that lost place, Atlantis, as precisely as possible.'

'The Ark was floating through time. I knew that without being able to explain it even to myself. It's only once history had caught up with our voyage that I started to make sense of some of the things I saw. The Ark was passing over this magnificent city, and I felt I simply had to go down and look.'

'By what means, though? You said in your own text *Cathexis* that you cannot swim.'

'No, I can't. Rudimentary equipment had to be rigged up. This was the beginning of history, remember. We had to improvise.'

'Evidently. And how precisely did you do that?'

'We built a small room round my head, from annealed eel-skins scaffolded with whale-bone. The gaps were caulked with ambergris. There was enough oxygen in there for me to survive underwater for a few minutes. I told my sons Shem and Ham and . . . to count, and keep counting, tapping their feet, clicking their fingers. I hoped that none of my sons would be feeling like Oedipus at the crossroads that day. Which one had I last rebuked, and for what filial offence? To whom had I last played the brutal *über-ich*? No matter. They lowered me down until I landed on a tower, and I sat there for my allotted ten minutes staring through my translucent filament. It was the most beautiful city I had ever seen, or ever shall. Enormous high-rise buildings, but much more ornamented than anything you'd be likely to find today in Vienna. No worries about ornament being crime then, believe me. Some of the bodies, or what was left of them, still floated about inside their golden apartments. Like dreams trying to find a head in which to wake at last. That's the way it seemed to me, at least. They appeared serene, as though the drowning had been far from unwelcome. Why, I wonder? Did they know something I didn't? Did they know something we don't?'

Freud knew that Noah had had no notion that he was about to be asked about Atlantis. The specificity, the precision, of his answer seemed to the analyst uncanny. *Unheimlich*. He noted though the hesitation once more over the utterance of the name Japheth. This surely marked the site of a trauma. He was dealing with a phenomenon here which he had not encountered in this exact form before. Noah had already mentioned his sojourns in Prague. Once last year, and once four centuries before, so Freud decided to see if he could be as specific as he had been about Atlantis. He moved on immediately to his next question.

'You mentioned your stay in Prague. Could you recollect your memories for me?'

'Ancient libraries and cobblestone streets. Low gabled houses that looked as though they'd decided to keep their heads down for ever. Crumbling balustrades. The shape of the castle over brooding waters. One alien gleam of sunlight through the clouds. Slate roofs, the cannons of attic windows rising through their raked decks. Arched passageways, stucco falling away like necrotic skin from a leper, revealing the ravaged brickwork beneath. Crucifixes high on weathered walls; a box inside the ancient synagogue bore, as I recall, this inscription: "Merciful gifts secretly left assuage the wrath of the bereft." Eastern Jews inside, socks on their feet, each one a dark shape curved like a question-mark over his prayer book. Silhouettes in the passageways at night. Horses' hooves clattering their age-old syncopation, sounds ricocheting off stone staircases staked with black iron railings. At times a violin or singing voice penetrates closed doors. Leaded windows sift grey light on to dusty altars. Women in headscarves carry their bundles and Moses baskets. There was always a smell of death in those streets, mingling with the horse-piss and the dreggy white wine I served. Both would spout their yellowish torrents.'

'You have always served wine through the centuries?'

'Yes.'

'It says in the Torah that Noah took to viniculture.'

'Then it managed to get that bit right, at least. In a doorway one day I saw a man of impossible thinness, Egyptian eyes even wider than that painting of Picasso's over in the Spiegel Gallery last week. A woman stood beside him, smiling. I found out from the old man at the corner that the young man's name was Franz Kafka. And when I dreamed about him that night he climbed up the wall like a bat, then flew off.'

'Like Nosferatu. But you said that you were in the city centuries before. You had a tavern then, too.'

'The Rainbow Sign, yes. That was during Rudolf II's time. They were all mad to find the secret structure of things. Cornelius Agrippa had already published *De Occulta Philosophia* in Antwerp.

'It was then that I met Dr Dee, Queen Elizabeth's mathematician from London. Astrologer, alchemist, magician, you name it: his field of study was almost as wide as yours, Herr Doktor. A nice man, though a trafficker in spirits; a demonolator as they called them in those days. Interesting horoscope too, which he cast himself, and explained to me. Born at Mortlake on 13 July 1527, under the sign of Cancer, with Sagittarius in the ascendant. Excellent portent for researches in the occult, of course.

'Now my Rainbow Sign Tavern was between two others called the Unicorn and the Spider. Prague wasn't really a city; I'd say it was more of an allegory. And Dee lived in one corner of Bethlehem Square. He lodged with an astronomer named Hajek, who specialised in metoposcopy, whereby you find out who someone truly is and what will happen to them from studying their face. I suppose we all do this to some extent, with greater or lesser success. You even do it to some extent, Doktor Freud, though you can't see my face at the moment, since you've hidden yourself from my sight. But this man had calibrated and tabulated the procedure with a remarkable degree of precision.

'But Dee also had Kelley in tow. The disreputable rogue was always with him when Madimi appeared. One of their spirits, she was forever giving them instructions. So Kelley said, anyway. These spirits spoke in various tongues. Glossolalia again. Enochian language, that no one else has ever heard spoken. They were surrounded by alchemical visions. Between them they issued warnings, dire forecasts of what the future might be if folks didn't change their ways. There was a suspicion round those parts that Dee could have been sent over from England by Walsingham, the spymaster, master of the great web of intelligencers. It all got tricky. But then anything would get tricky with Edward Kelley around.

' "Why do you always wear that stupid bloody cap?" one of my customers asked him one evening. Kelley turned around very slowly, and took the cap off. Both ears had been sliced away, the punishment for coining back in the old country. His face was pockmarked where the sharp stones had caught him while he was in the stocks. He was also a cripple, for reasons no one could fathom, though you didn't need to have a reason to be a cripple in those days; you sometimes needed a reason not to be. Anyway, as I said, it all got very sticky with these boys. Summoning spirits in the night. The good ones aren't meant to respond to such necromancy, you see, so I'll leave you to judge for yourself the character of those who actually turn up for the party. And all the while you could hear the roar of the African lion the authorities kept locked up by the moat, and the sound always took me back to the Ark. My little world all made of gopher, groaning and creaking, while the animals cried out. Meanwhile Rabbi Loew was in the ghetto making the Golem. Fashioned out of clay like Adam, apparently. A tablet containing the secret name of God would be placed in his mouth and he would live. That's what they said, anyway.

'Finally Dee and Kelley cleared off a matter of days before they were to be locked up, and I wasn't all that long in following them. The last time I ever saw that man Kafka by the way I was watching a horse in the middle of the road. A mighty beast, cleg-eyed and snorting, it was voiding its bladder in a yellow waterfall. Luminous autumn light. It all splashed up from the cobbles. The air had a urinous tang to it. Kafka stood and stared at it from one side of the street, and I did the same from the other.'

'You might recall that in Rudolf's Wunderkammer . . . '

' . . . there were three nails from the Ark. Yes, I do recall. Utterly inauthentic, sadly. A later date of manufacture altogether. Mitchell's of Ironbridge, who I suspect did not exist at the time of the Deluge.'

'You have a remarkable memory, Noah.'

'Yes, I do. Do you not recall what brought me here in the first place? I had wondered if you could take some of my memories away. Lighten the load a little.'

'My usual job is to restore memory rather than to expunge it.'

'Your usual patients aren't as old as the millennia.'

'Your memory has only failed you once. In naming the three sons of Noah. Perhaps you could try it once more for me now.'

'Ham, Shem and . . . '

Freud had by now realised that he had to accept Noah's remarkable feats of memory, even his delusion that such memories originated in his own experience, but he understood that he needed to find out two things: from whence did so much memorial information actually originate, and what psychic wound was buried beneath the archaeology of that one word 'Japheth'? He asked Noah to make him a list of some of his books that night. This request obviously startled the old man, but then he began to smile. Perhaps, thought Freud, the royal road to this particular unconscious might be the bibliophilic one. He wrote the following note to himself.

A Speculation

The human psyche, faced with the prospect of living in the same mental household with this feral face of self-annihilation, reverses its force and exteriorises its animus. Thus the Todestriebe, instead of degrading its own indigenous energy to that state of equilibrium which all matter, including the organic, ultimately seeks, externalises the impetus; instead of the temenos of the psyche being reduced to rubble, whole cities are.

Cities, communities, ancient buildings . . . Self-hatred, the psychic invocation of death and therefore equilibrium, is inverted, and the aggression released is of a world-levelling sort. We have just witnessed such a phenomenon in this last war. Todestriebe harnessed to technology. Result: apocalypse. And yet . . . the externalisation of this aggressive force also generates the cathexis of art; the removal of self from self of the artist's auto-portrayal; the wooden fetish; the totem (even perhaps the ventriloquist's dummy). I find myself pondering a parallel: how the diminution or extinction of one faculty enlarges and even electrifies another. The blind man's preternatural acuity in regard to sound; the deaf man's phrenology of touch; even the psychotic's universal avidity. It is even possible that these developments are exacerbated now so as to escape what Ferenczi in a letter to me called 'the potent sterility of opinion'. I seem to recall that he went on to talk about 'its witless gallantry, its fulsome broadcast of itself, its sublime effrontery'. All murderous of course. All a prelude to the four horsemen heading down from the hill.

9

Dear Herr Doktor – I am pleased that you wish to know something of my books. There have been times over the years when I have felt obliged to live inside them. Even perhaps to live as them. I display some of them at the Rainbow Sign, and amuse my customers from time to time by demonstrating my encyclopaedic knowledge of their contents.

You are looking at an old man who lived at a time when there were whales in the woods, and then the next time you saw dolphins breach the surface, they were in the skies. You can perhaps see why I've become such a devotee of poetry and the great visions recorded in our literature: such works actually tell the truth, where the daily newspapers so frequently lie. The camera lens is not the sharpest focus of reality. I have taken down, almost at random from my shelves, a work of the new theologians. You must forgive the seeming vanity of my turning to the N section of the index.

Noah: a mythic archetype. Seen as the figuration for the human survival of the diluvian catastrophe. The Catastrophist version of earth-formation was, of course, discredited definitively when Uniformitarianism, following on from the work of Lyell and Darwin, replaced it with a modern scientific discourse. Noah has provided much matter for mythical reflection, often of a mirthful nature, for example in the Medieval Mystery Plays. No serious scholar would argue today that such a figure actually lived here on earth.

I suppose I could sue. Or perhaps you might grant me some kind of certificate of authenticity once our treatment has been successfully completed?

Let us move on. I have mentioned melancholia on more than one occasion. Mine is of early provenance, and has at times been not far from crippling. Marsilio Ficino wrote that all men who excel in the arts are melancholics. Dürer believed himself so afflicted, and he possessed a copy of Ficino's *Libri de Vita Triplici*. I have it in front of me, by the way. The Firenze volume of 1489. *Editio Princeps*. The saturnine character is exemplified here by *melancholia imaginative*. The winged woman wears a wreath made out of watercress and ranunculus, both wettish plants, meant to counteract one of the effects of melancholy, namely bodily dryness (I've normally found wine more of a help here myself). Incidentally, she bears an uncanny resemblance to some of those angels who went in to the daughters of men. And her expression is also remarkably close to the way the daughters looked after they'd been gone in to; an expression of infinite distraction that it's hard to turn away from. Only my little phlogistica ever had brighter eyes.

I'm counting the works on astronomy now. Remember that we couldn't see Saturn's rings up there on the Ark. It was my famous client Galileo Galilei (I once owned the Rainbow Sign in Firenze, by the Ponte Vecchio) who finally managed that feat, during his *annus mirabilis* in 1610. All made of small chunks of ice, it now appears. Who'd have thought it? We would occasionally catch sight of the aurora borealis or the aurora australis. These could have provided us with clues as to where we were. But there wasn't really any 'where' to be, if you think about it. Just sea and more sea. The great amniotic fluid of the world's womb. Would you be happy to call that being somewhere? I certainly wasn't. Up each day with the salt in your eyes, trying to get the gist of the weather. But back to Saturn. It has the most terrible storms, that planet. Storms that make the mighty downpour of the Flood seem little more than an April shower. It's made mostly of hydrogen and helium, as you will no doubt know. Slow too, according to the astrological charts, and it takes nearly thirty years to orbit the sun.

Its brightness often seems to inaugurate darkness in the human mind, but its spectacular aurorae flare up in the brilliance of those who are cursed and blessed with its identity.

(And melancholy, saturnine melancholy, sinks upon me in this bar as I hear each night what some of them are saying. Wasn't one war enough? Does another war ever put a first war right? Will that return our sons to life? Well, will it? It took a while before my German was good enough to understand their words. Now I find myself muttering under my breath, often in Hebrew, sharp-edged prayers, secret Kabbalistic curses, or reading the poems of Heine once more with foreboding. You will know his verse, I'm sure, Herr Doktor? He points out how the burning of books always leads on to the burning of people.)

I suspect we both take comfort from the documents of art and science. The great variety of existence. The names of moths. Clancy's Rustic; Dewick's Plusia. Do you know I once had a whole cabinful of butterflies? My favourite was the marsh fritillary. And my books have allowed me to become a keen ornithologist. I used to diarise my sightings of the little egret; the ptarmigan; the arctic skua; European bee-eaters. There were red kites aplenty in the early days. Marsh frogs; beavers; boars; the greater horseshoe bat; the wart-biter bush-cricket; the red-backed shrike.

And shall I tell you something, Herr Doktor? I have not opened a single one of these books to write down these words. I suppose you might say I am at home among these voices, just as I am at home among your eloquent antiquities. They so often remind me of my collection on the Ark. Gimcrack oddities. The bric-à-brac of creation. The Ark's ragamuffin depot: its *Wunderkammer*, even. Now might you possibly search a little harder to find a solvent for my memories? Something with no salt in it, ideally. (I never again wish to go to sea.) Today in the Stefanzplatz I saw one of our walking wounded, still wearing his uniform. Jerking this way and that, staring at me like a jackdaw from the castle ruins. *Dulce et decorum est* . . . I stand at the window and stare out at the pluvial street scene outside. Ah. Pluvial. The very word is like a bell. Like sedimentation. Such words return me to a world of deluge and

114

wave. Remember, when we went up there the world was intact and thriving. Men were hammering nails, women giving birth, dogs sniffing at posts, vines in the vineyard longed heliotropically for the great yellow shiner and teleologically for the drunkard's gut. Then when we came down again, as the mighty waves of His mighty wrath subsided, it was all pluvial remains, the wet windscreen of history, the sedimentations of memory, the fossils of those who were once living and are now dead.

Why am I not a fossil, given the millennia through which I have had to make my way? Do the bones of fossils ache in the frost? For mine do, Herr Doktor. Mine do, believe me.

Freud pondered in his study. Achilles, he thought, is actually given the choice, and as though he were an agent of his own Unconscious (which to some degree, of course, we all are) he chooses death. Brief life; glorious death. Now in so far as the sexual drives are conservative, then they too seek extinction. Nature might reproduce itself through them, but the individual seeks the blessed annihilation of desire, its asymmetric (and at times catastrophic) force. Hence the endless, and frequently tedious, Elizabethan punning on death, and presumably the peculiar ecstatic potency of the *Liebestod*. It is precisely because the sexual drives (externally assessed) genuinely do represent the life-force against the death-drive that they cause such dissension, such destruction; that they are hedged about so with taboo and prohibition. The forces offend every conservative impulse which would restore us to that state of inorganic equity predicted by the Law of Entropy. It must be this curious doubleness, this Janus-faced duplicity at the base of our own instincts, which produces human-kind's customary veneration of the accoutrements of darkness; infernal devices; the instruments of the passion. It might even be what produces the thrill of the *unheimlich* when we behold the bioluminescent organs of the creatures of the deep.

So all drives seek to recapture an earlier state of being . . . or perhaps the earliest state of all, that of non-being? That could well be the essence of the matter. For if the state before our organic state of being is the ultimate desideratum then we must ultimately crave

115

that state of equilibrium which the Second Law of Thermodynamics tells us is the final state of all systems. The corpses that were so recently scattered over the fields of Europe were emblems of a wish for return . . . the one return we are all eventually guaranteed. Noah's drowned bodies clogging up the ocean are surely a return upon this theme.

Life's goal is then (however paradoxical this may seem) death, since we all instinctively seek the restoration of the previous state, and the state of ultimate primacy is that of inanimate predisposition. Some deep part of us at all times seeks to die. This, a little reflection will surely show, explains so much in our recently collective self-damaging behaviour.

The voice that we have so often through our history ventriloquised, the voice of Apollo's soothsayer, the voice amplified through the employment of the wooden mask (another fetish, of course) of the Greek theatre, is the voice of the revenant: it has come back from the grave. Like the spirits who pour out from the underworld in Book XI of the *Odyssey*, the creatures visited in Book VI of the *Aeneid*, the damned in Dante's *Inferno* or the voice of the Ghost in *Hamlet*, they have all of them returned from the dead. And that is where Noah thinks he has come from too: the graveyard of evolution.

All right then. Certain recurrences begin to form a pattern. The analyst often sees patterns before he can understand the material from which those patterns are made. All science is like this. The motif of the son. The unutterability of the word Japheth. The theme of melancholia. The horror of war (a horror I obviously share). And the transposition of the memories of books, even their imaginings, into the memory of one single man.

I have asked a discreet colleague, a fellow member of B'nai Brith, but one with more of an appetite for visiting the bars of this town than I have, if he would check out Noah's establishment. It is a small place just off the Stefanzplatz, the Regenbogen. Also known to its habitués, apparently, as Noah's Place. It is much frequented by some of the younger intellectuals, such as Adolf Loos. There is a painting by Egon Schiele with a phthisic, naked girl sitting before a rainbow. Some find it indecent. The owner is said to be a favourite of artists and writers because he keeps on one wall a collection of books, some of them apparently quite valuable. Historic editions. When in the mood he will perform his party trick. He will invite one of his clients to take a book at random, and then open it. They read out a few sentences, and he continues, without even glancing at the text. Chaim saw him perform his little mystery, and said it was a genuine wonder. *Unheimlich.*

A much younger wife, apparently. Chaim thought she was sweet on a poet there, one Ernst Benjamin. Noah's past is a riddle to one and all. Some say he was once a professor of religion or archaeology. And some say he was an antiquarian bookseller in Berlin, ruined by the war.

10

'So you had difficulties down below?'

'So much rioting among the animals. An early study in the anarchistic state, Herr Doktor. All of the darker predictions of Hobbes in *Leviathan* were proven true on my boat. With proper bulkheads in steerage it could have been avoided, of course. But the shipbuilding specifications had come from above. Ours not to reason why . . . '

' . . . ours but to do or die. Or in your case to do and live. For an incredible length of time. You said you spent some time in Paris.'

'Ah, the arcades in Paris, yes. So many hours I spent inside them. Such erotic places, or spaces – since they weren't really places at all but passageways between places, luminous conduits between nowhere and nowhere. How the commodities shone, the little beauties, as though each one contained its own tiny glow. A miniature furnace for a heart. One particular little corsetry shop window always kindled my own half-dormant flames. And I would strike off across town to a house I'd come to know in a certain arrondissement. My favourite girl there, a certain Joseanne, would always give me a naval salute on my entry. "It's the Old Man of the Sea. Any port in a storm." Then she would lead me away to her boudoir, where I would soon be unlacing her ribbons and her stays. "You can't be all that old, surely," she would remark, assessing my condition. And where is she now, with or without the attendant physicians? Another human fossil, mingling with the layers of sediment down there. Joseanne, my little darling, all cobwebs and wormfood and underground rot. Thanatos has marked you up as yet one more of his victories. Old Doktor Death.'

'There is one question regarding which I need your assistance. You say that you met Shakespeare, and served him drinks.'

'At the Rainbow Sign in Bermondsey. I have my suspicions that my Priscilla was his dark lady, to be honest. Raven-headed, she was then. She's always been keen on poets. I suppose in this instance it's a sort of privilege.'

'Did he ever mention the authorship question?'

'I'm sorry?'

'Did you ever hear him suggest that it might have been someone else who wrote the plays?'

'No. Always very professional. Working tonight, he'd say. Then off he'd trot to play the Ghost again.'

'Ah. I simply wondered. You have, I must confess, presented me with certain difficulties I have never encountered before.'

'Should I be flattered or should I apologise?'

'Neither. I am usually trying to enter a labyrinth. The minotaur of the past is always in there, but the corridors can be long and winding.'

' "Hysterics suffer mainly from reminiscences." Breuer and Freud, 1893.'

'Your mind, Noah, is like a library index. I seem unable to mention a book which you have not read. Not merely read, but memorised . . . '

'When Ussher's book came out I wrote to him to put him right. *Dear Ussher, I thought you might like to know, given your devotion to chronologies, that the event your co-religionists refer to as the resurrection actually took place shortly before daybreak on 9 April Anno Domini 30. Yours, etc., Noah Cambrensis.* I received an epistle back: *Dear Noah, Enough of whimsy, surely sir. Let us speak and write plainly. Yours, etc.* Under which was inscribed a thick black cross.'

'Your knowledge is so detailed as to be crippling . . . '

'I had to stop visiting museums altogether, you know. Too much irritation. I would even shout out sometimes: "No, no, no. There's nothing phallic about that bone, I can assure you. It's a chronometer for heaven's sake. Every scratch on it marks another moment in the phases. From darkness to sickle to full, then back to a circle of darkness. Twenty-nine and a half days." But one grows used to confusion. John Aubrey, after all, explained at some length to King Charles II how Stonehenge was a Roman temple.

'Moon goddesses. Crowds following the herds. They made her buttocks a calendrical index. Annotated her breasts with time passing. Seems like only yesterday . . . '

'And there are so many books printed now . . . '

'Exactly. You see, at the time of getting *Gilgamesh* into cuneiform inscription, writing was expensive. You didn't take it on lightly, Doktor Freud. You had to employ people. But by Pope's time, almost everyone was at it. Words words words. What could possibly be cheaper? Pope explains that paper became so cheap and printers so numerous, that a deluge of authors covered the land. I winced at that "deluge", as you might well imagine.

'And yet the popular forms carry on unabated. The mimes and cudgel-players always overcome the tragedians, but then Punch and Judy will always elicit louder cries than *Parsifal*. I saw the first performance ever staged in England. Signor Bologna. Covent Garden, 1662. Go walk down the pier if you don't believe me. Farces and pantomimes obtain their crowds, where classical revivals leave the stages dark.'

'And what do you think of all this, Noah? Try to be specific.'

'The rabble in Smithfield, the shambles of a culture given over to chopping itself into bits and pieces, then selling the bloodier chunks to the highest bidder. The stinking sing-songs of the feculent. How the Grub Street alleys roar; the camera shutters go snicker-snack. Another poor soul's probably done for.'

'Specific, Noah.'

'Ah Magna Mater, Mighty Mother, whose cult was so popular in Rome. Ceres, Minerva, even Aphrodite. Out of the softness, the infinite softness of your mines, we have heaved all life from the beginning. Except, according to scripture, Adam – and scripture's wrong there, by the way. Would you like me to explain?'

'No. I would not. We have other things to determine. With you, I appear to be dealing not with a labyrinth, which is the usual case with my students, but with an encyclopaedia. It seems – this is what has been baffling me – as though one can enter your memories alphabetically – as though you have turned time into space. As though memorial repetition were something of a performance. I have chosen two moments to test this hypothesis. You were, I believe you said, in London in the mid-eighteenth century.'

'At the Rainbow Sign in Fleet Street, yes.'

'Did you ever visit any of the conventicles?'

Noah now spoke without hesitation.

'A Moravian chapel in Fetter Lane; I still remember it. Moravius, so I was told, grew excited at the sexual possibilities of Christ's wounds. Count Zinzendorf had been encouraging women to cry out at the point of ecstasy, cry to heaven how their husbands' oil sizzled within them, turning sacramental inside the uterine delta. He reckoned that the notion of adultery was out of date. Many in this town, at this moment, seem to agree. I think my own wife, my dear Priscilla, has herself agreed at times. I was much older than she when we married. And in any case the female psyche, as you yourself have observed, is a conundrum.'

'Indeed. The journalists of the time . . . '

'A Grub Street race, a beggarly lot, lice-ridden and licentious, garreted so as to traduce, and paid by the quire for high-flown mendacity – such abusers of the word have always been ready, nibs dipped in venom, to go for whomsoever it is most profitable to go for . . . '

'London was a dirty place, I think . . . '

'The century before, John Evelyn had said he wanted all works using coal to be moved five miles eastward down the Thames. The soot had become such a prevailing factor, blackening the houses of the westward gentry, their white shirts, white brocades, white horses, white women . . . *Hast 'ou seen swansdown ever* . . . the bridles, the breeches and the hosiery.

'And all the while the aristocrats were capering. I remember their enamelled lachrymatories. Lords and ladies saving up tears for their future.'

'There were soon to be financial problems . . . '

'Every time a small bank in the City went belly-up, another two hundred governesses would be offering their services to the children of the high and mighty . . . '

'And yet at the Great Exhibition . . . '

'Commodities shone there like little stars. Each one in its own brilliant constellation.'

'I seem to recall that you have mentioned men burning like . . . '

'Like Pepys I once set fire to my own wig while lighting a candle. For the briefest of penances I was the candle, the candle of myself, undergoing my little purgation. Gave up wigs after that. Made do with a shaved scalp and a soft felt hat.'

'Like Hogarth?'

'Like Hogarth, yes. I saw him once, you know, in Soho, dressed exactly like that.'

'There is, I now see – and this was part of my confusion – a historical basis, or a fictional one, to all of your memories. But there is one sense in which you are still a labyrinth and not an encyclopaedia.'

'What sense is that, Doktor Freud?'

'You have flattered me by mentioning more than once my short work *Beyond the Pleasure Principle*. Indeed you arrived here on the first day carrying a copy.'

'I remain greatly impressed with it.'

'In which case you will remember, given your total textual recall, that I speculated there how this recent dreadful war has to some degree reordered the memory. How we have had to dispose of so much that cannot be held in consciousness. Otherwise Thanatos reigns supreme in the kingdom of our minds.'

'Sometimes in these dark days he surely does. The god made out of shadows.'

'The Kaiser of the endless graveyards, of the underworld, the dreadful trenches of the Western Front, the dire battles here in the East. More than once you have mentioned the chandler, whom you watched drowning as the Ark lifted off. I think you told me he was a young man. You even mentioned mooring ropes, which I have begun to read as an umbilical cord. Now I want you to remember his name.'

'I can't.'

'One who had your face. It wasn't Shem, was it?'

'No, Shem was aboard.'

'And it wasn't Ham either.'

'No, he was tending his mother. She suffered dreadfully from sea-sickness. A real landlubber's daughter, my Priscilla.'

'Then it must have been . . . '

'Don't say it.'

'You say it, Noah.'

Noah suddenly began to speak with an urgency Freud had never before witnessed.

'You know, one evening I was out there alone when a mermaid put her head above the gunwales. I've never told Priscilla this but we made love, right there on the planking of the deck. Although her mouth was cold, a cold like nothing else I've ever known: not the cold of winter but the cold of healing. Is there a word for that? A Hippocratic word? All pain went, and she was warm inside. She thrashed beneath me like the ocean. And then she was gone. Next day there was a picture of the dawn on deck. Scales had rubbed off during our love-making and then the light had blackened some patches, leaving others bright. I've tried to work it out since; had silver bromide emulsion emitted from her silky skin? But if so, then how? It must surely be the first photograph, all the same. Probably still on the boat. In that cave where we hid the Ark on Ararat, after dismantling her, just in case we might have another Flood to deal with one of these days. I suppose if we'd left it where we first dis-embarked, balancing on the summit, Darwin would never have needed to get started, would he? Measuring the beaks of so many finches. But I suppose by now the birds will have pecked away all the gopher-wood, splinter by splinter, to make their nests.'

'Say the name of your son, Noah.'

Very slowly, and at an evidently great cost, the patient finally managed to utter the one word which the analyst had become convinced was hidden inside the labyrinth of his memory: the one reminiscence which could not be paraded at will.

'Japheth.'

'Almost.' There was a long pause until the fatal word was finally spoken.

'Joseph.'

'And tell me, Noah' – Freud spoke very gently here – 'what really happened to Joseph?'

'1916. He had been conscripted.'

'You having, by then, managed to escape to Switzerland with the rest of your family?'

'Yes, but Joe was already at the Military Academy in Berlin. I tried to get him out, but we had to go, or the other boys would have ended up in uniform too.'

'And he died in battle?'

'He was badly wounded in an explosion, so we heard later. And then, too weak to pull himself out, he drowned in a flooded trench.'

'And you couldn't save him.'

'And I see him now each night from above. Up there on the Ark. And I can't reach far enough down. And I never will, Herr Doktor, I never will.'

11

So it was that the man called Noah, honeycombed as he was with the literature of the past and its scriptural writings, given the distinctiveness of his own name, assuming that to be authentic, translated the story of the fabulous indundation into his own psyche and its more recent earthbound catastrophe. He was the father who had not saved his son, and he kept gazing down to the face as it slipped underwater. The name of the beloved boy was simply too painful to utter, too dreadful a site to revisit, so Noah displaced his identity on to that of the chandler. In searching to flee the site of the catastrophe, the battlefield where Thanatos achieved his latest victory, he entered a world which was an almost unfathomable mixture of history and legend. In this, thought Freud, he could surely be viewed as a modern exemplar of the religious mind, its admixture of empiric fact and visionary distortion.

The analyst sat smoking in the early evening, with Noah's treatment at last complete, and looked around him. There they all were, as usual, the gods and goddesses, the hybrid creatures, the messengers. Noah had always seemed to make himself at home here, as he traversed the ruined landscape of memory, the realm of that one deity made entirely of shadows. Clio's lord is Thanatos. The emblematic creatures had looked at him as he spoke; but they had also looked past him, of course. It was now surely incontrovertible that in the unconscious, as in the subatomic realm, time holds no sway at all. There is no history. Only potencies which do not age; they simply conceal themselves or metamorphose and mutate.

Staring once more at his image of Oedipus and the Sphinx, the print from Ingres's painting, Freud found himself indissolubly related to a man of fiction. Oedipus was the one to answer the riddling question, and so the Sphinx dies. Later though, the answering of another riddled question will lead to the dreadful self-blinding of Oedipus himself, his exile, and the death of his wife and mother, Jocasta. So the answering of certain questions leads to a knowledge of darkness, and therefore to the darkness of knowledge, like the infinite gloom of Piranesi's *Carceri*. A world made entirely of grey insubstantiality. Like Thanatos, the god made of shadows. Enlightenment itself sometimes appears to cast shadows, of which it can know nothing, except the ragged outline. We come back to a room sooner or later, a room filled with shadows. And our psyche, like Noah's Ark, is made of gopher wood. It can only withstand the mighty torrent for so long. The future could still drown in the waves. Thanatos could still become our God.

12

'I find that story more moving on this side of death than I did on the other, Mr Bones.'

'There is a curious codicil to it.'

'A codicil. What you find at the end of a will?'

'Exactly. At Freud's funeral in London in 1939 a small man with a beard, unknown to the other mourners, approached Anna Freud. He apologised for troubling her at such a time, but asked if she would mind looking quickly at a piece of paper which he then took from his pocket. His accent indicated to her that he was probably Viennese. Anna stared at the little document he had placed in her hand.

' "Is that your father's handwriting?" he asked.

' "It is. Undoubtedly. Could I ask what this is?"

' "Your father gave it to my father on the day that their analysis was completed. He wrote the little text out for him, and my father always kept it by him until the end of his life."

' "And your name is?"'

' "Sam."

' "Your father?"

' "Your own father would have known him as Noah. He travelled under many names in his time."

'Anna stared down at her father's script, and easily made out the words he had written two decades before:

The Lord God, blessed be His Holy Name, only made one day. Everything could have been brought to completion in that single lunar cycle, except that a solitary man looked back, and then another looked forward. And thus was time created, the past and the future, and more and more days rolled out, behind and before. Now we had historians and astrologers, and time spinning out on its bobbin, further and further into the accomplished and the possible. And yet all mankind could still not move out of its one day of creation, for although there is an eternity of days, we can only occupy this one, for this one has been allotted us until the end of time.

The Return of Titus

1

'I should have read more Freud, Mr Bones. Your prejudice against him meant that there were not many copies of his books on your shelves. I seem to remember you telling your nephew Robert off for using his terms. Did he think we were all marionettes then?'

'All marionettes of forces buried deep inside us.'

'Like splinters of wood through the heart.'

'Victor Hugo thought Shakespeare had spoken to him, on various occasions, through a planchette wielded by his son, Charles.'

'A séance?'

'A séance.'

'Are you suggesting some sort of parallel, Bones? I didn't like being referred to as a device, and I'm not sure it makes me any happier to be called an allegory.'

'A shared wave-form perhaps?'

'If science has taught us anything, it is that the whole of existence is a spectrum of shared wave-forms.'

'As is the curlew's cry.'

'As is the curlew's cry. Do you recall what you once told me about the origins of your kind, Mr Bones?'

'Humankind, you mean?'

'Humankind.'

'Remind me.'

'All too human and less than kind. That's what you said. You said you had become increasingly convinced you'd emerged through time from three things: genocide, writing and ventriloquism. We killed off the Neanderthals, then we invented writing so that we could be somewhere else, anywhere other than where we are. Situated inside that memory of genocide.'

'Somewhere else, so as to speak there in a different voice.'

'Exactly. The serpent's, for example. As soon as we start to write, we ventriloquise the evil we have done. Place our own temptation in the serpent's throat. Establish a religion. Declare ourselves justified in having proven that the evil came from elsewhere, certainly not from us.

'The curlew throws its cry, remember, so as to put a predator off the trail of its eggs; it nests on the ground as we do, hugging dear old *tellus mater*. You said the greatest stain on our memory was not the murder of the primal father, as Freud speculated in *Totem and Taboo*. No no no. It was the wholesale slaughter of another species, at the very beginning of the race. That secured our territory and our food supply. Their eyes had grown bigger than ours; their brains smaller. All the demons we write up, all the devils we ventriloquise, are simply a way of throwing the cry of our dreadful recognition far enough to fool our own predatory intelligence. Throwing the voices of our identity, the way the curlew throws its song. My soul is anywhere but inside me. Is that what you were doing? Tell me something, Bones: if Noah thought he was Noah, if all his memories told him he was Noah, who was he then?'

'Noah.'

'So if all your memories tell you that you are something or somebody, then that is inevitably who you are?'

'That would appear to be Freud's belief, and the basis of his troublesome practice. The problem being that some memories fight with other faculties, censorious ones that oblige them to dig themselves holes in the psyche, to go underground so that other memories, false ones frequently, might triumph instead.'

'So Noah remembered everything in the world but the one thing he really needed to remember?'

'That his son was dead. That he had not been able to save him.'

'And do you remember everything?'

'Of course, no choice now, is there? One of the laws of posthumous physics, if I have understood them correctly. If it happened, ever, then it is present now. Memory is simply presence incarnated.'

'So you will remember, in that case, the ginhead you thought you'd got up the duff?'

'Melinda.'

'What a name. Melinda. What a mellifluous appellation.'

'She had a beautiful head of red hair.'

'She looked like a carrot.'

'She glowed in the dark.'

'She looked like an overfed beleisha beacon someone had painted a face on with a felt-tip pen.'

'In the dark, between the sheets, she was golden.'

'A carrot that kept ballooning. An orange dirigible . . . '

'You were jealous.'

'Of course I was jealous. You hardly spoke to me for a week. Until it started turning into a same-sex marriage.'

'A same-sex marriage? I was a man and she was a woman.'

'Yes, but the sex got sameish, as it so often does. Your initial excitement waned. Your mucus membrane lost its agitation. And then she told you she thought she might be with child. And by that stage little Harry was child enough for the professor, was he not, Bones? Even though I was, to all intents and purposes, your father.'

'It turned out to be a false alarm.'

'No more than a quantum fluctuation.'

'A carroty dream.'

'Between the sheets.'

'Ah, Melinda.'

'She was, as I recall, a head-chick.'

'Meaning? Whatever else has been retained, the argot of those long-gone days now escapes me, despite the laws of posthumous physics.'

'A fellatrix of some skill and sophistication. In the curious patois of the time back there.'

'You have a memory like an elephant, Harry.'

'No. A memory like a tree. I still feel the birds on my arms. Saws screaming through me. Ring upon ring of memory. But the pain has gone. Death's one great comfort, that: the pain goes.'

'Dendrochronology.'

'A memory like a tree, professor . . . He's here, Bones.'

'Who? Noah? Is he still drenched?'

'No, the one I told you about. The one with no voice who hears all the voices. He's here now, in this town. Keep your eyes open, and he will appear shortly.'

'I thought they were your eyes now.'

'But I dream sometimes.'

'Back at the water's edge. Growing in my mother's shadow.'

'I'd like to go there too. I'd like to accompany you, Harry.'

'Your little wooden fetish. Well, try to keep your eyes – or my eyes, if you prefer – open. He will be here before long. He will stand before us on the pavement out there.'

'Will I hear him speak?'

'Not without my assistance. The way, once upon a time, no one heard me speak without yours.'

'Then how?'

'Wave-form cerebrotonics.'

'Can you explain?'

'Only when you're older.'

'I'm already dead.'

'Then you'll need to be even more dead.'

'Is that the same as being more . . . '

'Alive again. Yes, it begins to seem likely. Be more tree-like. Curious, isn't it? I have more experience of being dead than you, remember. I've been dead for more than a century.'

'You always grew more and more alive with me.'

'I rest my case, I think.'

2

Brother Tom did as Naseby's letter bade him do. What, in any case, was there to take him back to New York? He feared that Naseby might have some notion of beckoning him to live with him in that beautiful old house in the Cotswolds. A not altogether unattractive idea, in fact. But might this be so that the old man, whom experience rather than biology had suddenly made so old, could resume his postponed studies? Go back, like Noah, to recover his dead son? Tom did not feel like being studied any more. He'd been studied more than enough for one lifetime, and would resist any further requests to play the object to anyone else's subject. *We murder to dissect.* Now where was that from? He'd read it somewhere once.

The letter was delivered to him by hand in the hotel.

MY DEAR TOM – By the time you read this I will already be back on my way to Sioux Falls. I intend to restore our little home there and work with the children of the local Indians. I should never have left. Despair and an inheritance were not sufficient reasons. I have arranged for you to live here. Bank accounts are being set up. There is no problem with money. All you have to do is return here and Mervyn will provide you with everything you need. It is up to you, of course, how you use your gifts, with whom and for whom. But then I realise now that that is true of all of us, and always was.

I would ask of you only one favour. Could you please ensure the publication of my book, *ISP: A New Form of Perception.* The proof copy is here on the table before me. I have had to finance this publication myself, since no 'reputable publisher' – as they like to call themselves – would risk it.

It could not have been written without you. I hope you have already gone to look at the Rembrandts in the National Gallery. Seen Titus in the old man's face. Seen the books about Rembrandt in the Lenau Institute. You have seen as much suffering as that noble old man.

God bless you,

STEWART N.

Tom walked the streets of London. He went once again to the Lenau Institute in St James's Square and looked through the books in the Rembrandt section. He even took two away with him, though the young woman at the desk, an attractive slim figure with dark, cropped hair and striking brown eyes, looked at him a little dubiously, as though she knew he was not really Stewart Naseby. (Gemma: I will introduce you later.) But she let him take the books anyway when she realised he could not answer any of her questions with his mouth. Instinct told her that, however else he might have acquired the ticket, he certainly hadn't stolen it. Then he went to the National Gallery and stared for two hours at the Rembrandts. Afterwards he walked aimlessly through Covent Garden until he found himself standing outside the Fowey Puppet Museum. In a glass case set into the wall was a puppet with a garish rouged grin, wearing vivid blue silk trousers and a dark blazer, and Tom heard a voice. Heard it more clearly than any he had ever heard.

'Hello, Tom. I'm Harry Sprite. I knew you were coming. Let me introduce you to my trusty ventriloquist, Professor Graham Fowey.'

And now Tom heard a different voice, though no other figure was visible.

'Welcome to our country, Tom. I sincerely hope you will be happy here.'

This had never before happened: he had received information, all sorts of encoded information, from images, from books, from furniture even, but he had never before heard voices like this from an inanimate object, not so distinct, and never addressed to him, as though a living voice were addressing him. This was no longer mere information, the way the past sedimented itself into the world's artefacts; this was an actual voice. Well, two voices. He had thought that they could only come from human beings; and perhaps he was still right. But this human voice was coming from a long way back, and it seemed as though death had intervened in the interim to clarify it. Death had isolated the signal and dispensed with the noise.

'It did come from a human being, Tom. It came from the prof. I borrowed the voice while we were both locked in time. Then, like so many borrowed things, like the trust they took from you, or the story of Freud and Noah we've just been recounting, it was never returned. They borrowed the life of a tree once, and they never gave that back either.'

'How do you know who I am?'

'Cerebretonic wave-forms. It's all in Naseby's book I think you'll find when you get back to the Cotswolds and read it. Come inside and have a look around. Our humble domicile. Make yourself at home, why not.'

And so Tom did as he was told: he paid his fee and entered. There were puppets of every variety and from every continent. Each tribe that had ever lived on earth seemed to have surrounded itself with puppets of some sort at some time. Marionettes; Indonesian shadow puppets; cloth figures for gloves and fingers; grand Chinese dragons; tiny figurines with wings. Little wooden fetishes, set up for adoration. And then there was the corner devoted to Amazing Harry and the Prof, and as Tom read the account of their joint destruction, he felt a sensation like a knife going through his own heart. There was a full-size reproduction of Harry on sale at the museum shop, and Tom bought it on his credit card – he was not at all sure how much longer that would be usable, but the idea that the instructors back in New York State should buy that replica for him pleased him. Then he walked outside, carrying the dummy, and stood once more staring into the window where Harry still sat enthroned.

'You have bought the son of Harry. My one little bastard. He's made of plastic, you know, unlike me. No dendrochronology in him at all. A real creature of the times. Were we being personal, I should have to point out that he was generated from the excrescence of oil and petroleum. What a falling-off was there. Even so, I'm touched.'

'What should I do?'

'Stay, Tom. Live at Naseby House. Gather a little flock about you. See if you can find any clues in Naseby's book. It is, after all, largely about you. And one more thing, before you go.'

'Tell me.'

'Cerebretonic wave-forms travel both ways, my friend. You can send them as well as receive them. Who knows, you might even get through to little Harry ben Harry there in your arms. The black spectrum lines, that's where all the waves of energy have been received. That's you, Tom: the great receptor. The terminus for cerebretonic wave-form transmission. But now the bright spectrum lines – those are the points where energy is emitted. And that's what you've never yet done, isn't it? Eh, Brother Tom? Cerebretonic wave-form emission, instead of reception. That really should be your next manoeuvre on this planet. That might make something of a difference, surely.'

'This is Naseby's terminology. Where did you pick up Stewart Naseby's terminology?'

'Out of your head, Tom. I'm a Roentgen Reader too. I read you as swiftly as a laptop reads a disk.'

'I'm not sure I find that a comfort.'

'I'm not sure you should, either. All intelligence is a form of reading. It's merely a question of speed and scope. You and I are among the fastest. Our readings are happening right now at the speed of light. Your own memory is there for your reading now, Tom. Read the book of yourself, as Hamlet had to. That's where you'll find the power you need for people to start reading you. You will emit the signal, instead of just receiving it. They'll listen believe me. They all want to escape the confinement of their own minds. That's why they used to pay to watch us in the evenings.'

3

And so it was that Brother Tom took the train back to the edge of the Cotswolds, and went in a taxi from there to the golden-stoned buildings of Naseby House. Mervyn was awaiting him, having been fully briefed by his employer of the last seven years. Before that he had been employed by Naseby's father. They were all of them eccentric, but it did seem that the most eccentric charge of all was about to be placed in his hands. A young man, a deaf mute apparently, but exhibiting remarkable gifts: so he had been informed by his employer, and who was he to question this? The young man was to live here on his own terms. If he wished to invite others to join him, then so be it. He was to be allowed to do whatever he chose, with only one proviso: he was to be exhorted to see Naseby's book through the press. Over in Oxford. Mervyn was to assist him in this.

So on the second day of his residence, the servant placed before his temporary master the proof copy of *ISP*, together with a letter from the Oxford printers, requesting that any final alterations be made as soon as possible. Upon confirmation that the proof was acceptable, the printing would then commence. Tom opened the bound proof and found a note from Naseby himself:

It seems to me appropriate, Tom, that you should finally approve this before it goes to press. You are after all in a better position than I to spot any mistakes.

It was a fine day, so Tom took the proof outside to sit on one of the stone seats that surrounded the garden. He also took the large book about Rembrandt that he had borrowed from the Lenau Institute. And as he turned the pictures, looking first at Titus then at Rembrandt, he was aware of tiny lacework patterns forming around his head. For a moment he feared a communicator: had they invented a new trick? Why had he gone and used the card in the museum, thereby giving a clue as to his whereabouts? Then he realised: it was birdsong, embroidering the air all around him. He counted the trees and named them in his silent arboretum: silver birch, copper beech, willow, oak. And he stared at Rembrandt's self-portrait. Naseby had been right: the old man's face was filled with Titus. As a young man, the painter's face had been filled with passion and talent and impertinence in the face of the world's restrictions and provisos. But the old man's face was full of every tragedy that had ever been written, or ever would be. Still he would not bend. Neither bankruptcy nor religion nor the assembled hypocrites of the Netherlands could make him bend. He would die first; which he did. Every day now saw the return of Titus.

Tom opened the proof of his old teacher's book, and realised by the end of the first page that what he had said in his note was true: it was largely about him:

We see only within a specified portion of the spectrum of reality. Were our eyes of a different specification, we could see beyond that; see into the infra-red and ultra-violet zones. A dog can hear a sound pitched so high that no human ear can receive it. All energy in the universe propagates itself as a wave. The same is indubitably true of thought. A biochemical process takes place. We have come to translate that energy into vocalisation or script. I would however like to pursue a theory in this book. It is that certain rare humans (impoverished perhaps in other sensory respects) have the ability to read thoughts without the intervening actions of mouth or pen, in the same way that the dog can hear sounds beyond the human ear. I am suggesting that there are readers of such sensitivity that they register wave-form cerebretonics the way a satellite dish receives and decodes a radio wave. There is a point of crucial importance to be made here: these speculations began not as an abstract intellectual journey, but as a result of the closest observation of an actual cerebretonic reader.

So, Tom thought, first I was a Roentgen Reader; now I'm a Cerebretonic Reader. If I didn't know myself better, I'd think I was a very distinguished fellow. He flipped through the pages until he came to the postscript. He was intrigued to see how Naseby had signed off. Here was the last sentence of all: *We can only speculate as to the power to be released, like the power hidden so long inside the nucleus of the atom, should one of these Readers begin to transmit wave-forms as well as receiving them*. Wasn't that pretty much what the puppet in London had said the day before? Had these fellows somehow got together then?

When Tom looked up it was to see Mervyn holding a tray and gesturing to the pot of coffee on it. Tom nodded and smiled. No one could complain about the service round these parts, anyway.

Later that day Tom made Mervyn understand that he wanted to walk the two miles to the nearest small town. Mervyn offered to drive him, but he made it plain that it was the walk he wanted. And as he walked along the busy road with its ceaseless flow of traffic, he remembered the journey from Patmos Ranch to Huxby. He started to ask himself certain questions. Perhaps it was like a woman who knew she was so beautiful that she kept her face covered, fearing what might otherwise betide; or like a man who had so much strength that he would hit no one, ever, and simply walked away from insults, incurring the label coward in the process. He remembered the moment in Melville's *Billy Budd* when Billy, enraged beyond endurance by the lies being told about him, and unable to speak because of his stutter, hits the evil Claggart with such ferocity that the man falls down and dies. It was like that. This was why he had never transmitted in his life, only received. Except once, just that once at the orphanage when he had penetrated the skull of a malignant girl who was forever tormenting him. She had screamed and fled, had taken to weeping constantly thereafter. She was taken away then, to have her nerves attended to by 'specialists'. It had frightened him. And now here he was, a refugee from the world's mendacity. With Harry's words, and Naseby's too, ringing in his ears. Cerebretonic wave-forms go both ways. They didn't have to tell him that. So he was about to start transmitting, was he? Why shouldn't he? What exactly did he owe the world out there that had so remorselessly used his special gifts?

He sat in the small café. He had money in his pocket. Naseby's provisions meant that there was no reason to fret any more about money. He stared at the couple. Something wrong. Bad line lengths. Malignant entanglements.

The woman sat there and he heard everything she didn't say. All the thoughts she was directing at her companion, not one of which the companion could discern as he continued to smile come-hitherishly at her. Evidently thought she adored him. She spoke silently, and he heard her silent speech.

'I thought you were a serious person, Sean. Now I know you were just playing the darling Irish gobshite. With your *May the wind rise up behind you and the road rise up to meet you* and all the rest of that Gaelic malarkey. Surprised you didn't have the Blarney Stone mounted round your neck. We might even have found a competent mason to chip it into the shape of a fucking albatross . . . '

They left.

The other one sat alone at the window. Red hair, like Evelina, but a little older. How sad her freckles looked. He stared until she turned, finally, to look at him.

'I don't wish to live alone inside this mind.' Milky blue eyes. Like Julia.

'Then don't. Share mine instead. Mine's bigger. There are mysteries inside it. It would be like visiting a limestone cavern. A cavern measureless to man.'

'Your voice has no accent.'

136

'It has all accents. It's a white light containing all colours. Shall I make a rainbow out of it for you?'

'Like Noah's rainbow?'

'Yes. The end of the world and the beginning. There'll be thousands of voices.'

'How are you speaking to me now?'

'The technical term is cerebretonic wave-forms or wave-form cerebretonics. It's the same way you're speaking to me. I receive the waves from your mind.'

'So have you taken over my mind?'

'No need to. You gave it to me.'

'Do you want my body too?'

'No real difference. As you'll see later. Let him go.'

'Who?'

'You know who. The one you came here to escape. Let him go. He has no power. You are free, Lydia.'

Two tears made their way slowly down her cheeks, but she was smiling as she wept. And this was Lydia, the first of them. That night she shared his bed and those portions of his mind where he chose to give her entry.

'If only all men in the world were like you.'

'The world would be a lot quieter, that's for sure.'

As this thought left him she started to laugh. I didn't even make an effort then, he thought. I've become so fluent in my own language now I've started to transmit automatically. Do I really want to do that?

'And what sort of a night did Harry have?' She made her way over to the bed where the full-scale replica of Harry was perched on the pillow.

'Gery good, zank you.' Her ventriloquised voice was hardly up to professional standards. 'Last night I could have sworn I heard him speaking. And the strange thing was I was asleep. It was as though he was speaking in my dream. Or was that you, Tom, I wonder?'

'Depends what he sounded like.'

'Like a dead man. Like a very serene dead man with a beautiful voice.'

4

'Can my friend come and join us?'

'Who is your friend?'

'Pat. Pattie. I told her. I phoned . . . '

'You're not supposed to tell anyone.'

'I know, but I couldn't help it. It makes everything different. Everything seems possible. Can she come? Just for a day. You'll like her. She doesn't really believe me. Well, she does and she doesn't.'

Tom stood at the window, looking out on the dry-stone walling. A gentle rain was falling over the fields. Cows huddled in the meadow over to the east.

'All right. How will she get here?'

'Mervyn can drive me over to Gloucester and I'll pick her up.'

Mervyn did as he was told. That evening he prepared dinner for three. Mr Tom, Zen (as Lydia preferred to be called) and Pattie all ate and drank, then went out for a walk around the grounds, and later that night they all retired to Mr Tom's bedroom. Mervyn decided to make a bed up in the visitors' cottage for himself. He did not wish to hear any cries in the night. Mr Tom might be as silent as the deep freeze, but that had not applied on the previous evenings to his new female companion. And now there were to be two young ladies on the case, not one . . .

So Tom was the only man in the house that night. He lay naked as the two young women on either side of him talked in the darkness. He said nothing, not even through the wave-forms. He felt suddenly all talked out. And he wondered if this was where evolution might have taken a wrong turning: if the perfect domestic set-up might not be two women talking over the silent body of a man, soon to be erect again, lying between them. Behind him Harry ben Harry grinned on through the night, as though he were a satellite, beaming his messages out into the darkness. Tom stared at the necklace with the word Zen engraved upon it. Lydia's aurigraphic trinket.

'He's already gone one step further than we ever did, Mr Bones.

He's sitting up there on his pillow watching Brother Tom engage in the deed of darkness with two of them. You always brought them back one at a time, as I recall. You were, I suppose, a serial fornicator. He seems to be going for the crowd scene already.'

'They should call in Cecil B. De Mille. And what does young Harry think of it all?'

'Like all young chaps, he assumes whatever he sees around him is normal. After all, he's never known any different, has he? I'm not sure he's that bright either. But then he had an impoverished childhood: he never stood by the river feeling the breeze, letting birds nest along his branches. He was down in the ground, being crushed. He probably thinks the whole of Gloucestershire is filled with beds containing one male deaf-mute, two randy young women, and a wide-eyed vent's dummy taking it all in.'

'It's not then?'

'I've stopped reading the papers, so I'm afraid I wouldn't know.'

5

'Give us a class, Tom?'

He shrugged. He had grown suddenly weary of entering their minds and had asked them to start speaking again. This they felt was unfair.

'I did these yoga lessons last year and we all sat in the lotus position while the teacher gave us meditations. Can we do something like that?'

And so, sensing a possibility of escape, Brother Tom took them to the large room on the ground floor, with the old bay window, and he beckoned. Once they were settled Tom emitted one sentence, just one, which travelled at the speed of light from him to them: 'I am here.' Then he left the room and went to the library. The copy of *ISP* was open on the desk. And he turned the pages till he came to the chapter-heading 'The Transmission of the Saints':

If the faculty was innate, not so much an evolutionary freak as an evolutionary occlusion, then we might speculate how survivals of this type have come to be seen as exemplary sacrificial victims. We are frequently told of what appeared to be an uncanny ability to read minds and receive information on the part of the prophets and the saints. This propensity lends itself to adoration, certainly, but also to annihilation. What does Jesus receive in the way of a message from the bleeding woman in the Gospel if it is not a wave-form message? He feels the power go out of him and into her. Such figures would threaten the stability of almost any modern society. They cut across too many of its boundaries. And we should note something else about the story: no wave-form transmission is possible without the expenditure of energy. How much energy does such communication entail, and how is the energy to be renewed?

By the end of two weeks there were between ten and twelve people a day turning up at Naseby House, sitting in the lotus position in the big room with the bay window, and awaiting Brother Tom's instruction. Mervyn had stopped preparing food. He simply ensured that the kitchen was sufficiently well-stocked so that anyone who wanted to eat could do so. He drove those without cars to and from Gloucester station. He counted them in and counted them out. He noticed how many women seemed to share Brother Tom's bed. He wished Stewart Naseby were still here. He wondered, would he really approve of this? Is this what he'd had in mind? He picked up the rumours going around the nearby villages: that there was some sort of funny young fellow with odd gifts (a charlatan, most like, and probably using drugs) hypnotising their daughters, then having his way with them. Then the letters started coming. Usually the name at the top of the address was simply 'Whoever', but it could be a lot less pleasant than that.

Dont like freaky boys diddling our girls.

One day you wont be putting it in, friend, but sewing it back on.

Mervyn showed them to Tom. Tom wrote on a piece of paper, for he had never transmitted to Mervyn: *Do they mean it?* Mervyn shrugged. He didn't know; didn't even know who 'they' were. And this hadn't been the first sanctuary for misfits round these parts. Still, no one as far as he knew had ever actually died. Always a first time, though.

But Tom was also growing weary. Some days he sat for hours with a crowd of them in the big room, endlessly transmitting. How they wished to be filled up with light, as though they were all bulbs whose fragile filaments had snapped at some point. And he gained a curious surge from his power over them. He had become convinced that should he fill their minds with the need to go and kill Mervyn, then the poor fellow wouldn't have lasted another day. So was he Charles Manson then? Here behind Cotswold stone, a Hitlerite arm-salute could have roused the masses of Nuremburg from their slumbers.

And they came to his bed, the young women. Sometimes one at a time, sometimes two, once even three, but that had been too much. He had messages coming at him from all directions all night. It was like sleeping in a railway station. Then one day he knew he had had enough. And when they looked up from their lotus positions in the big room what they saw was not the slender long-haired apparition of Brother Tom with his Assyrian tattoo on his arm, but a ventriloquist's dummy, dressed in a dark blazer and blue silk pants, with a piece of card hung round his neck. On the card was drawn a bubble, and in the middle of the bubble was a zero. And that was it.

6

'I used to borrow your tears, Bones. You grew very salty towards the end, and I borrowed your tears for my own purposes. I fear post-humous physics might have done away with tears for ever. Otherwise I'd borrow one today . . . '

'Two surely, Harry. If we must blub, let's at least be symmetrical. An old human habit.'

'A duet, you mean? But a single tear can be something of an adornment. Like a pearl.'

'What has so moved you?'

'My boy. My little plastic descendant has just done his first gig.'

'How did it go?'

'He didn't fluff his lines, prof. But then he had none to fluff. If this is my reincarnation in the modern world, then I'd have to say that the quality of repartee in the Sprite family has undoubtedly declined. On the other hand, he didn't fall off his chair.'

'It's a start.'

'Indeed. It's a start. And there's an ending there too, I fear.'

'How so?'

'Brother Tom has decided he doesn't want to be Jesus or Hitler, or Gurdjieff or Mesmer, or Buddha or the Dalai Lama, or the old man at the top of the mountain.'

'Who does he want to be?'

'Harry ben Harry does not possess my gift for psychological discernment, but according to him, he doesn't want to be anybody at all.'

'Not even himself?'

'Particularly not himself.'

'A perfect reader for my book. Could your son encourage him to buy a copy of *Sacred Voices in Antiquity* from AbeBooks?'

'Will he commit suicide, do you think?'

'It's possible, I suppose. No escape there though, as we both know too well. And there's hardly room to put him up in our little glass cathedral. If the posthumous laws have taught us anything it's that you don't escape your identity merely by dying.'

'Look at us, for example.'

'Exactly. Look at us. Which they are doing out there right now. Don't you people have any homes to go to?'

'Obviously not. You yourself have now become invisible, Mr Bones.'

'To all but the most discerning.'

'When I think of how your hand once grappled about, like a vagrant womb in my body.'

'What a curious image.'

'Well, you were bringing about new life. Making the dead wood speak. Though I suppose you were also permitting the old life a voice beyond death.'

'Letting the alder speak?'

'Letting the alder speak, that had once been so brutally silenced, so that even the wind could no longer breathe through its leaves. The breath of life, Bones. *Pneuma*, I believe, in Latin.'

'*Ruah* in Hebrew.'

'Where it all begins.'

'Indeed.'

'In deed and in thought.'

'What a posthumous quibbler you've become, though I suppose it was I who put the sob in sobriety.'

'While you still had an earthly family. What exactly is he doing, these days, that devoted nephew of yours?'

Playing his part in the decline of the West, that's what.

The Decline of the West

1

Time to speak in my own voice, minus the quotation marks. Robert Fowey. Nephew of Graham, whose spiritual remains are now housed in his book, *Sacred Voices in Antiquity*, and in the Fowey Puppet Museum in Covent Garden. In case you wondered, how come I share his name, since his sister, my mother, was married? She retained her maiden name and blessed me with it. Why? I once asked. 'There'll be no marrying in heaven,' she replied. And that was it. I daresay she had a point. Don't plan on finding out just yet.

So here, Harry, is where I was, where I am: Owen's Printing House in Oxford. My book *The Doctrine of Signatures* has been accepted for publication by the Clarendon Press. There is intellectual prestige in that, certainly, but precious little money.

I needed some money quickly, having spent all my uncle's bequest on the museum I had promised in his memory, and had not been able to pick up any academic work, so I had simply taken the post I had seen advertised in the local paper.

'He loves riches, you know. And that's the death of the soul. The spirit is deadened by riches, Robert, not enlivened. Ernest Johnson is everything a human being shouldn't be – but then he always was. I knew him in his early days when he was stealing intellectual property rights from impoverished European scientists, and he was a bullying bastard then, but his unpleasantness has expanded to fill the space created for it by bankers and political toadies. I wonder what he was like when he was simple Ernst Janis, from Bohemia. Probably just a simpler version of what he is today. A simple little thief from Mittel Europa. I bet he was more courteous, all the same. It would be impossible for him to have been less courteous than he is these days. His feculence, its specific form I mean, is facilitated by late finance capitalism. He is, you might say, its ornament.'

I looked at Sam Meadows and smiled. I often smiled when looking at him. It seemed to me that there was something about Sam which made being human more acceptable. The man he was speaking of was trying to buy Owens, the printhouse in Oxford where both Sam and I now worked. We had watched him turn up that morning in a chauffer-driven Bentley. And we had watched him leave, vast and unsmiling, besuited in his self-importance.

'Will he win, though, Sam?'

'God, I hope not. This company has been in the same family for two hundred years. They've held out before. I can't believe they'd capitulate now. Not to Johnson, of all people.'

I looked at the tall, thin man, with his cropped bristle of grey hair and his blue eyes, and wondered, Could that be a flicker of doubt in your face, Sam, just the mildest flicker? Could Ernest Johnson, né Ernst Janis, the proprietor of Samson Communications, really be about to acquire Owens of Oxford, founded by Josiah Owen in 1789? And if so, where did that leave Sam? Not to mention me? Well, I was only sojourning. With Sam it had been a lifetime. I would be Sam's assistant for perhaps six months, until my book came out and I found an academic job. I had already started thinking about work on Isaac Lenau, who had been the subject of my undergraduate thesis, and whose thought lay behind some of the work in *The Doctrine of Signatures*. So I was happy to be in Oxford, close to the Bodleian and the bookshops, and I was happy enough to be working in a printing house too (the business of print has always fascinated me, and is in any case a part of my subject of study). Happiest of all to be working with Sam Meadows, who had been in the printing trade all his life. He had first touched moveable type when he was fourteen. Now the moveable type had all gone to the dump, and Sam was surrounded by computers and their operators.

'We're still making books though, Robert. Whatever the changes to the technology, we're still making books. The colour repro is better, the typography usually worse. Swings and roundabouts. But if they ever go completely from book to screen, then I'm out. I'll dematerialise too. My world is shaped by books, and when they go finally, so do I.'

When might that be, Sam, I thought, but said nothing.

'Why would Johnson want it? He can't want any more print capacity. His printers in Reading and Wapping are not operating anywhere near capacity – there's been a rumour for a while that he'll have to sell one before long. So why increase his print facilities when he can't even use what he's already got?'

'No good asking me, Sam.'

'No good asking Jacob Owen either. He's got no idea. But Johnson wants the place, all right. The usual tactics have begun. Certain suppliers saying they might not be able to renew their contracts when they run out.'

'Why not?'

'Because they are also suppliers for Samson Communications. So Johnson tells them, if you want to continue supplying me (a bigger contract, inevitably) you can't supply Owens too. Not unless they finally come round to my way of seeing things.'

'Is that legal?'

'Hard to say. Shouldn't think there's much about Ernest Johnson that's ever been entirely legal, to be honest. Nothing ever gets into a court of law, though. Never has done. Knows how to use the regulations, you see. Money employs the law in a way that poverty can never afford.'

Jacob Owen was the latest of the family owners and directors. He was sixty-three, Sam's age; they knew each other well. Jacob had started to look a little tired to me of late. I couldn't help thinking that he might be happy to find a way out of his daily employment. Go off to fish the Cotswold chalk streams for trout; that seemed to be the only thing he looked forward to any more. Not that he ever seemed to catch anything.

That evening I stared at one of the wooden trays containing moveable type in Sam's terraced house in Jericho. He had invited me round for a meal. He did not intend to cook – Sam's kitchen was not a place to venture into lightly. You'd be more likely to find a book there than an onion. No, we would go out for a curry; the mildest curry in Oxford. The only one Sam could still manage.

'Buggered up my insides with years of self-neglect. My mind's all right though. As long as that keeps on to the end, I'll be satisfied.'

I had come alone. My girlfriend Susan, a recent liaison, had accompanied me once to Sam's house, but that had turned out to be a mistake. My beloved of those days was both tidy and unbookish. She had walked around Sam's home with an expression of distaste which tightened as she went from room to room. Books. Books everywhere and at every angle. Books on all the bookshelves, some of them upright, many crammed horizontally over the tops of others. Books on tables, on chairs, on the floor. Books perched open on the cistern in the toilet; books precariously balanced on the side of the bath. In the disused shower, more books. And a faint dingy smell that pervaded everything. Susan had taken an instant dislike to Sam, and Sam had shown no interest in her whatsoever. She might as well not have been there. I should not have brought her. So tonight I hadn't.

My eyes were wandering among Sam's books when he held out a volume.

'Ever seen this?' I shook my head. 'We printed it back in 1978, technically to commemorate the Queen's jubilee. That gave us a device for the first free endpaper. We'd been doing it anyway. The complete Shakespeare in individual volumes. Original spelling editions. That's *Hamlet*. A beautiful thing, isn't it? Worth putting yourself out to create something like that. Bring it with you. Let's get to that Bangladeshi restaurant.'

'You're not worried it might get stained?'

'No. Books should be beautiful, whenever possible, but they

absolutely must be read. Otherwise what's the point of them? Do you know the hardest nineteenth-century books to come by?'

'No.'

'Children's books. They disintegrated. Opened and closed and read so many times. Fell to bits. Good. That's what they were for. They've succeeded as books by disappearing from history. When they took down Auden's OEDs from the shelf after he died, each volume fell apart in their hands. He'd beaten them to death with loving attention, just the same as the children's books.'

And so we sat in his favourite corner by the window, and he ordered the mildest curry known to man. Whatever he wanted I nodded through. For myself I wouldn't have minded a little more spice and flavour, but I was here for Sam's company, not the food. I had an odd sense that he was the last of his kind; that after he'd gone, there would be no others. He was sipping at his beer and munching a papadum. In the background some Asiatic pop music played, entirely meaningless to me and, I suspected, to Sam too.

'I remember being thrilled when I discovered what a variorium edition meant: the notion of the history of a text accruing and being preserved in every detail seemed to me to be a blow against the Second Law of Thermodynamics. If entropy dictated that we were doomed to the lowest possible state of order, then the commensurate law of literacy said otherwise: every word held on to, every word we might have lost, is a victory in our battle with oblivion. That's what Shakespeare's sonnets are about, by the way. Not whether or not our man ran AC/DC (who cares anyway?), but the mind's unending battle against oblivion and witlessness. The *Sonnets* were another handsome volume in this edition, by the way.' He picked up the *Hamlet* at this point, and stared at it as though it were a photograph of a once-loved woman. 'Saw this through the presses – every single page of every volume. Not one error as far as I'm aware. Not one. Some of the scholarship in the Introduction has since been found faulty; but none of the printing.'

Sam was now spooning rice and various vegetable bhajis on to his plate.

'The most curious thing about Hamlet is surely that he is a very old student. But then I dare say that's the most curious thing about me too. The older I get, the more I'm bent over my hornbook. Studying my abecedary. I always seem to be trying to fathom the rudiments of things. Why air keeps hanging around us with such persistence. Why women and dogs adore atrocious men. Why preferment is so frequently given to the loathsome and the excremental. A piece of shit like Janis, for example. I ask more and more rudimentary questions, but I don't necessarily get any rudimentary answers.'

He thought for a moment as he chewed on, meditatively.

'I suppose a very old student is another way of saying a revolutionary. Do you know what a revolutionary is, Robert?' I shook my head. 'A man who does not come to terms with injustice for the sake of the pension life might afford him. A man who does not become besuited by his own self-importance. That's my definition anyway.

'The problem is that Hamlet brings the humanism of Wittenberg to a Sicilian vendetta. It's as though the street gangs of New York came across Thomas Aquinas in a speakeasy on 42nd Street, and tried to find out whose side he was on. If he doesn't answer then that blessed ox of a man will have removed from him (first) his angelic cincture and (second) the penis it had been angelically fashioned to ensheathe. Thought in *Hamlet* is bedevilled on all sides by violence, mostly sanctioned by the state. What a hideous prolepsis of modernity.

'Do you have any problems reading contemporary stuff?'

'Sometimes.' I grew unaccustomed to speaking, in Sam's company, and often half-forgot what words I knew.

'Last week I started to read an SF story in which a man travels at the speed of light. You can only travel at the speed of light if you have no mass, like a photon. No organic creature has ever lived without mass, so how exactly did our time-traveller survive then? The writer seems neither to know nor to care. Maybe I shouldn't either, but I can't help myself somehow.

'Have you ever read Cyril Tourneur's *The Atheist's Tragedy*? 1611. Same year, funnily enough, that Shakespeare retired to Stratford to attend to his tithes.'

I confessed that I hadn't, but I don't think he really wanted to know.

'It contains the greatest piece of wisdom I have ever encountered. Charlemont says: "Patience is the honest man's revenge." And yet, like so many pieces of shining wisdom, it's not true; or at least you can't count on its being true. Walter Benjamin, who graced the world of books with every word he ever wrote, was, according to his friend Gerschom Scholem, the most patient man anyone had ever encountered. And so what was his revenge, this patient man? He died fleeing Nazi persecution. 1940. On the Franco-Spanish border. Committed suicide rather than face the alternative. Death had finally made him impatient.'

Sam fell silent and meandered aimlessly among the wreckage of the meal. A chapati was dipped into a bowl of this, a papadum dragged through the remnants of that. We had both forgotten what each bowl contained; it did not matter any more. He chewed and stared.

'Hello, Sam.'

The figure standing at our table was enormous and dishevelled. Grey hair sprouted in all directions from his skull. He was carrying a briefcase that was stuffed with books and papers.

'Martin. Sit down and have a drink. This is Robert Fowey. Robert, meet Martin Settle, one of the last great men of letters of Fleet Street.'

'Yes. Now Fleet Street's gone and I doubt I'll be here much longer myself.' He called to the waiter to bring him a pint of lager.

'I've ordered a takeaway, but they're always half an hour late.'

'So what have you been up to.'

'Obits.'

'Sounds cheerful.'

Martin smiled and began to explain. The first time it had happened had been twenty years ago. Can you believe that, he asked us, twenty years, for God's sake. I mean, how long does it take a man to die?

'The *Clarion* had called me. "Would you be prepared to draft an obit for us? It's someone you know. You must say if you find the idea offensive. Some do." I made it plain that I didn't. Probably wouldn't find anything offensive as long as they paid me. I needed the money. Still do. "Who is it?" I said. "Henry Childs." I probably expressed some satisfaction that Henry might finally be dying – you do know him, of course? – and just requested that I be given a free hand. "Well, the usual procedure is that you'll give us a draft – long as you like really – your recollections of the subject, together with any factual stuff you happen to have. Then we rewrite it according to our house style. We send it back to you, as long as there's time, but we do reserve final say over the copy that goes to press.'

'Just how sick is Henry, I asked, and they told me that the word was he wouldn't pull through this time. I explained that I hadn't been in touch for five years, and they said that often made for the best pieces. A bit of distance, and all that. Gives a fellow objectivity. So I wrote my piece. A trifle acidic, I suppose. You see I had rather vivid recollections of the last time I'd ever seen Henry. It was in a mock-Tudor hotel in Surrey, where I thought I'd been invited to lunch with his latest companion, a woman of indeterminate age by the name of Charlotte. Almost immediately, he touched me for fifty pounds, which I could ill afford.

' "You're a good man, Settle," he'd said, pocketing the cash. "Won't be long getting it back to you." I'm still waiting, of course. Then he borrowed my felt-tip pen and excused himself. I was left alone with his *femme du jour*.

' "Have you actually read any of Henry's books?"

' "Oh, he writes books does he?"

' "Novels, yes. What did he tell you he was?"

' "An explorer."

' "An explorer. Any particular part of the globe?"

' "Antarctica."

' "Drawn there by the Penguins, no doubt. He was always keen on paperback rights."

' "One way of coping with his mother deserting him, when he was so young, to become a nun. Must have been hard. Working in a coal-mine at sixteen."

' "Yes indeed." Henry and I had been at Oxford together, where an insouciance remarkable even for that metropolis of polished indifference had earned him a third. His mother's Richmond home, which I visited many times, had never seemed in the least convent-like to me. Henry had now returned, and he handed me back my pen. I excused myself in turn, worried I might feel overcome finally and hit him.

'Standing at the urinal my eyes stared at Henry's unmistakable script on the tiles before me:

> Between the booze, the IOUs
> And the floozies
> My only excuse is
> *Je m'accuse, je m'accuse, je m'accuse.*

How characteristic of Henry, I thought, to take my money for a few hours of sottishness and lubricity with some temporary lady picked up from the Yellow Pages, then excuse himself, using Zola and my felt-tip pen while he was . . . A few seconds later I held the pen with a handkerchief and dropped it in the basin. I then turned on the taps until it had been thoroughly cleansed.

'On my return I found they had departed, Sam, leaving only the bill for me to pay.

'And the bastard still hasn't quite died. Which is why I've been down in Wapping today, revising his obit for the third bloody time. Charlie Drepp, do you know him?'

Sam nodded.

'Well, you'll know then that he's turned the graveyard slot in the *Clarion* from the dull and worthy catalogue of mortality it once was into the funniest bit of the paper. The sepulchre's gone riotous. No more tombstone proprieties. It's all waspish and irreverent, delighting in the insalubrious and the improper. Of course the minute some-one's in the grave, libel's no longer a possibility. Can't libel the dead, though Drepp's little team sometimes seems to give it a fair shot. The biggest laughs over there these days always seem to come from the obituary room. So I've added even more acid to my account of my old literary shipmate. Henry Childs. I've hated the old soak for more years than I can recall.

'So I gave them my updated piece. And as I was leaving I heard one of them say, "Not letting him go, are you?" "Why?" says the other fellow. "Shouldn't we get his own details down while he's here? Looking at the state of the old bugger, not sure he'll even make it home."

'Ah well, looks like my takeaway's ready. Lovely to see you, Sam. And to meet you, Robert.'

Then he was gone.

And Sam fell silent for two or three minutes.

Finally I spoke. 'You're worried about him, aren't you?'

'Who? Martin?'

'No. Ernest Johnson.'

'Ah, Johnson. Janis. Yes. Didn't like the look in his eye when he got into his big gold car this morning. I know that look. I've seen it before. Let's go back and have a coffee.'

Ten minutes later we sat in Sam's tumbledown living-room and drank scalding instant coffee.

'How old are you, Robert?'

'Thirty,' I lied. I was actually twenty-seven but I had given the impression of much more experience than I actually had on my CV.

'The ancients thought Adam was created at the age of thirty, to be in the full perfection of his manhood. Philip Gosse pointed out in *Omphalos* – published in 1857, remember, two years before Darwin – that he couldn't very well have been created as a baby, now could he, or he would have perished, even in the Garden of Eden, such being the vulnerability of the human child. The gravedigger lets us know in *Hamlet* that our prince is thirty years old. He has just arrived at the apogee of his manhood and now he is about to die. Something of the vigorous despair which this perception brings him surely hangs about till the end of the play, and even manages to warn off Laertes for a while. The doctrine Gosse propounded in *Omphalos* he called prochronism. And I do know what he means. I feel as though I have more of the past inside me than I have any right to.

'It won't be too long, Robert, before they slide me into a pine box, and then set fire to me. That's life's ultimate plan for both of us, but I'm first and I'm not necessarily all that keen, to be honest.'

He fell silent. All I wanted to talk about now was Johnson, and his chances of taking over the company. Like many hideous human beings, Johnson was fascinating. But I couldn't bring myself to ask Sam any more questions.

As I was leaving we were nearly at the door when he stopped and said: 'I am a most elementary man, you know, Robert. I have never really got past one-plus-one. Bertrand Russell was, I believe, dubious that they could ever amount to two, and they never have in my life. A singularity meeting another singularity simply emphasises two respective individualities, not the readiness of either to become items in a series. Factions and fractions are always possible: only a third of what that woman told you was true, and now you're less than half the man you once were. And finally, left all alone again, you can sit by the window as the light outside flashes on and off, and count all the way up to one, then all the way back down again. First plussed, then nonplussed, but always, always in the dark.'

On my way back, alone on the street, I remembered what he had once told me about his marriage, which had lasted for precisely six months. His wife was apparently so obsessively neat that he'd felt he had no choice but to be untidy for two. Something we had in common at the moment, then. When I finally got home, opened the door to our flat and put on the light, I looked around. The place was spotless. Not a book to be seen. And Susan was apparently already in the bed, doubtless dreaming her hygienic dreams. She made the neatest love I've ever known.

3

The next afternoon, Sam seemed distracted. I asked him if something was troubling him. He told me that at lunchtime that day he'd sat down with a coffee on one of the benches in the centre of Oxford. He had found himself sitting next to a young man eating a burger.

'I turned to him and smiled, which shows what a revolutionary optimist I still am in my old age. I thought we must surely have something in common, but couldn't get much further than bipedalism.

'When he'd finished his burger he threw the wrapping, now

splattered with tomato ketchup, on the ground at his feet. He didn't let it drop; he threw it. Then he stared at me in silence. As if to say, so what are you and the police going to do about that then, old chum?

'How many millions of years did it take us to get here? How much extinction of life has been required to produce this specimen of our tribe? Have the countless millennia of evolution been worth it? He was hard to distinguish from *Homo habilis* – off home again, to butchery on the stone floor and the bloody evening meal. While the shadows cavort around him.

'Our progress through time, eh Robert. I mean people have always vomited on the streets of Oxford. But these days, when they've finished chucking up their load, they turn back to the pub and you see the luminous patch sewn on their jackets: HOW'S MY VOMITING? PHONE 0800 . . .

'Don't look at me like that. Just because I still believe in their historical redemption doesn't mean I have to like them all.'

Three days later the Bentley returned. We watched it motor stealthily into the cobbled courtyard. Out of one door climbed Ernest Johnson, and out of the other, a woman wearing very bright clothing. I was standing with Sam at the window on the first floor. He bowed his head in defeat.

'He's brought Lilliana. We're finished, Robert. He only brings wifey to view his victories, never his defeats. *Homo habilis* in a limo.'

Over the next few days we had a chance to view them both up close, Mr Johnson and his spouse, as they surveyed his new acquisition, accompanied by Jacob Owen, who appeared to be trying not to meet the eye of any of his employees. One old-timer managed a brief stab: 'The price of a fishing permit on the Ouse has evidently gone up, Mr Owen.'

Lilliana Johnson detested her name: 'Who needs four syllables to turn their head?' So she insisted she be called Li, prounounced Lee not Lie, though, given her devotion to cosmetic reconstruction, the employees at Owens were, within a matter of days, referring to her as Liposuction Lil. The flesh on her frame had been seriously re-arranged over the years, one part removed from this sector to be re-inserted into that. Her nose had been demolished and reassembled by surgeons only too ready to deploy their life-saving skills so as to continually resurrect Lilliana's vanity. What Hippocrates would have had to say about all this can only be guessed. He would surely have been astounded by the mounting figures on the bottom of the bills.

Preparing Lilliana for her confrontation with the mirror over the years had become a gargantuan expense. Sam pointed out to me that in the depths of the Indian sub-continent there were farmers who could have financed the whole of their families' lives with the capital expended on this woman's cosmesis, and its after-care. 'What you get is not the promised paradise, however artificial, but Lilliana. La Johnson's flesh has been transmogrified by money. How ghastly it looks, finally. Skin turned into parchment with a bank statement printed over it.'

And it was true that the innumerable face-lifts, the nips and tucks, the tightenings and transpositions, had given her face finally the appearance of a lunar crater. Her eyes appeared to be about to launch out of their sockets, and her lips swerved upwards like galvanised slugs that had been dipped in glossy red paint. Perhaps the money would have been better spent on that Indian farmer after all. Johnson himself looked at her, very occasionally, as he might gaze upon a poisonous, exotic spider.

'Not his problem,' Sam said. 'Hasn't touched her for years. Local toyboys are employed for the purpose. He screws his secretary in London. Think we must be back with late finance capitalism here.'

'How do you mean?'

'Well, the secretary can't want his body, can she – be fair. And she certainly can't be after his mind, which must surely be even more ugly and depraved than his flesh. So once more, Robert, we return to the mystery of money. Its elusive presence, simultaneously ubiquitous and unavailable. And its preternatural fecundity. Money's the one thing that can always reproduce itself. The zero's inexhaustible ovum. The parthenogenesis of finance, in a society where everything is turned into commodities.'

I watched Johnson as he slouched in chairs and walked along corridors at a surprising speed. The expensive tailoring of his suits could not disguise the mighty bulk of his person. Occasionally his wife would appear, to dispense graciousness among us. I couldn't decide which one I found the more loathsome. She once came and asked Sam and myself the nature of our work. She smiled so brightly I was afraid her face might ignite. We explained as best we could. She neither looked nor listened, but fiddled with Sam's ornaments as he spoke.

'Six children,' Sam said as she left. 'She must have looked enticing once. In those far-off days when he still found the rich alluvium of her delta an enticing prospect for a skinny-dipping diver.'

'Would he have been after pearls then, Sam?'

'Only those with a resale value, knowing Johnson.'

4

Sam was called in to Johnson's office more and more often. Sometimes voices were raised and Sam started to look strained and tired.

'What does he want?' I asked one day, after he came from the office, trying to stop himself shaking with rage.

'I don't know. But he knows. He knows, all right.' As we spoke, the voice inside the office had been raised once more, to Jack Helsom, the floor manager now. Johnson was yelling and banging the table.

'Just listen to the bugger rant. In a different age he'd have been a Bedlamite, chained to the walls for our viewing on the Sabbath. It was a penny, I think.'

'What was, Sammy?'

'The price of entry to watch demoniacs exorcise their demons by screaming, so the demons might fly out of their mouths. In those days they didn't actually hand the money over to the lunatics. But then, you can't stand in the way of progress, can you? Just listen to him. Go and give the madman a penny, son. Did you know that in Darwin's *The Expression of the Emotions in Man and Animals* he informs us that monkeys close their eyes on being given snuff. I only survive my tedious sessions with our dear friend Johnson by recalling such incidentals from the world of books.'

'Why would anyone want to give a monkey snuff?'

'Why indeed, Robert? Why indeed? Almost as bizarre as wishing to spend an hour in the company of our own E. J. Charles Darwin also established, by playing his bassoon in the garden for two hours, that worms have absolutely no sense of hearing. None at all.' He fell silent for a moment, then turned to me and smiled. It was the weariest smile I had ever seen. 'No one has ever, to my knowledge, impugned Johnson's integrity, you know.'

'Really?'

'Absolutely not. No one has ever assumed he had any to impugn. Though occasionally some superannuated toff from the House of Lords creaks out into the aisle to say how, with fifty Johnsons, he could turn this damn country of ours around. They always turn out to be in his pay. Our friend is a most assiduous corrupter, and not just of youth. He'll spend a small fortune corrupting the senile too. He certainly covers the waterfront, I'll grant him that.

'Put one and one together, and you might get eleven. But you'll never get two. The number one is not biodegradable; it resists fracture or multiplication. It is the one indivisible atom. That's what I reckon. We have to choose to be many. That's my politics. It's a choice Johnson has never made, and never will.

'Did you know, Robert, that in the first known image of a printing press in 1499, the bookseller is being carried off by Death. It is a *danse macabre*. And Death has returned to the world of printing: these days he travels under the name of Ernest Johnson, and he's as lethal as any medieval plague. His eyes, you may have noted, are lampblack.'

It was true that Johnson did have astonishingly dark eyes. Unlit coals in an unlit face. They matched his heavily dyed hair: Ernest Johnson carried his own darkness around with him.

'But what is he up to, Sam?'

'Search me. All his suggestions about changing the shifts around, having people on permanent call – well, they're off the wall, frankly. No printer in the land would put up with terms like that.'

The following week the letters started to arrive. Every employee, including me, received one. All signed personally by Ernest Johnson.

The old shift system was abolished. All weekly arrangements would now be provisional, and subject to alteration at twelve hours' notice. All employees would be required to make themselves available for two weekend shifts, to be notified by midnight on Friday. New contracts were being sent out at this moment. The old ones were now defunct. Any employee who did not wish to sign the new contract had better start seeking alternative employment elsewhere.

Then Sam worked it out. He took me for a walk outside.

What Johnson had realised, and the reason he had bought a print company of whose capacity he simply had no need, was this. Although the company had been sold as a going concern, with a proviso that it be kept trading, if the whole workforce could be laid off, rather than pensioned off, with a minimum outlay on the part of the business, merely minimal severance arrangements, then Owens Print could be rapidly closed down, and the net result would be a profit of twenty million pounds or more to the person left owning the asset of the fine building, and that asset was now owned by Samson Communications. Owens Print was an old building, on a most prestigious site. Hence the issuing of letters cancelling everyone's previous contract, and demanding impossible terms. Johnson knew they were impossible. He intended them to be.

The union at this time was already weak, almost supine. The Wapping Revolution had long before eviscerated it. Everybody at Owens started to squabble after the initial outrage. It began to occur to some that the new contract was maybe not so onerous really, not for those who knew that they would not be called upon for weekend printing work, since there wouldn't be any. Sam tried to harangue them.

'Don't you understand? You are all going to be sacked. He doesn't want this business, he wants this building. A quick buck, as usual: that's all Johnson wants. That's all he's ever wanted. He notices the holes in all contractual arrangements.'

Before long, much of the printing work started to be transferred to Samson's printing houses in London and Reading, which needed the work in any case.

'Clever,' Sam said. 'The business is beginning to engineer its own decline, so soon enough there'll be no alternative but to close it down anyway. He's put twenty per cent extra on all our quoted prices. Nobody's going to pay that for long. He drinks champagne in there, you know. Krugg. What else?'

'Can't you talk to him, Sam?'

'Talk to him? Have I not taught you anything at all, Robert? This is a man who has already answered any question before the question even gets asked. The only thing I can't work out is this: is it his own silence he must fill or ours? And he's already screwing Daisy.'

'Jacob's secretary?'

'Jacob's secretary. He's offered me terms. And I've accepted. He said if I didn't, the terms would be reduced. And he means it. I know him, and he means it.'

'I'll resign.'

'No you won't. You stay on. It's not your life, it's just a job. You'll be leaving before long anyway. Study him. Learn what we're up against. Learn how to fight. Not many do any more, you know – not many do.

'You can do one thing for me: see this book through the presses. The money is already paid – we had to make that a condition. We're just waiting for the final proof to come back.'

And he handed me a proof. *ISP: A New Form of Perception* by Dr Stewart Naseby.

'He's having it published himself, that's why we had to get the money up front. Been stung that way before by self-appointed authors. Though he seems like a distinguished enough fellow. Teaches at Oxford, I believe.'

'You met him?'

'Yes. Very nice man.'

'What's it about?' I said, leafing through the proof.

Sam seemed to hesitate.

'It claims to be about a deaf mute who has extraordinary powers of perception. He can't hear and he can't speak, but he can read minds. Put him in a room with a group of people and a few minutes later he'll know what all of them are thinking, and what they might have been thinking a long time ago.'

'Do you believe it?'

'I can't. My materialist principles won't let me. But it's a serious book, seriously written. It appears to be well-documented. We tend to forget how much we don't know. Newton discovered gravitation for us, but he was very sceptical, to the end of his life, about action at a distance, without which . . . it's hard to see how gravitation can work at all.

'Anyway, our man obviously couldn't get a publisher, so we're doing it for him, at his expense, and he's invented his own imprint for the purpose: Sioux Falls Press. And he's late getting that proof back. I could have run it off last week for him. The presses were idle. I phoned up and some hired hand informed me that Naseby was in the States, and that the final proof was now in the keeping of someone called Mr Tom. If necessary you might have to go and see Mr Tom. Johnson would be more than happy to keep the money and produce nothing. That's his idea of heaven. Mine of hell.'

5

Six months later Owens Print was no more. And the building was sold for a higher price than anyone had anticipated. The staff scattered. Ernest Johnson returned to his offices in London, taking Jacob Owen's youthful secretary with him.

I sat in Sam's tiny garden. We drank some wine he had bought from the off-licence. Summer was just beginning. If it hadn't been for everything that had recently happened to us, it might have been idyllic. Maybe it was anyway.

'A man I met in London, Robert. A middle-class, literate, affluent middle-aged man. Some service in the army behind him. Father and mother both doctors. Delightful people. Told me years ago how proud they were of their part in building the NHS. The sort of middle-class Brits who make you proud to be British. I tell Adam about the events that have unfolded here. And realise halfway through the explanation that our man has begun to gaze into the middle distance. Funny sort of smile on his face. Know what it is? He's smiling with admiration at Johnson, mogul, money-man, semi-legalised extortionist, bully, an exploding device of his own self-assurance. Young Adam, the child of so much post-war hope and expectation – not to mention honour and courage – admires him. "Can't help but admire him," he says. "Always turns everything round, wherever he goes." I realised at that point that I was looking at a dutiful fascist cadre, should it ever come to it. And it might, Robert. Believe me, it might. Just because we fought against them in the last big war doesn't mean we won't fight with them in the next.'

For a while neither of us spoke, then Sam, who had been examining the flowers around him, started to speak again, very softly.

'The veining of a leaf in the sun whenever you take it between your fingers and think: this is it, isn't it? Photosynthesis. Life on earth. You can feel it accepting the spectrum's energy, finding a form and expressing it . . . I'm going to die, Robert.'

Somehow I took this as part of his disquisition on the laws of process and design, and replied serenely, 'Well, I suppose we all are.'

'But it would seem that I'm obliged to do it rather soon. Will you accept my library? I'd like to bequeath it to you. The house comes only by way of its shelving. If I leave it to anyone else, they'll get rid of all the books and all the papers. You must promise me that you won't do that. My one condition.'

There was surely nothing more significant he could give. He had given me the books, with the house that stood around them. I couldn't speak. I nodded in silent assent.

And three months later he was dead. Two months after that I inherited his library, his papers, his house. Susan and I had already split by then. I had come back to the flat one day carrying a bag of second-hand books. 'You're not planning on keeping them here, are you?' She had stared at them. 'They're all spotty. They're not even new, Robert.' No, my love, but they are filled with intellectual content, which is more than could ever be said of you, however trim your acts of lovemaking. And now here I was, back in Jericho, in Sam's house but without Sam. I was working my way slowly through his papers. One notebook was entitled *The Decline of the West*. It began thus: 'We might as well start with Johnson, that emblem of our degradation. Grim as the prospect is, we might as well start there.' Somehow I was never able to read any further, but one day I will. One day. Johnson, needless to say, flourishes. Last I heard there was even talk of a place for him in the House of Lords. He is, after all, a great contributor to mighty causes. A man with deep pockets.

Oh, and I almost forgot. I did make that trip to Naseby House. So that we could get on finally and print what is surely one of the most curious books ever written. I'll tell you about this as soon as the other two have finished.

6

'That was a sad story, Mr Bones. I thought your nephew came out of it rather well. Except for his dealings with Susan. A lot of women find decomposing books unsettling. They've been brought up to be hygienic, which is why we so often value them as nurses, while they tend our flesh. The young man's undoubtedly at his worst with women, I'd have said. Must run in the family. Let's hope he never spends a night in Epping . . . '

'That will do, Harry.'

'Censorship, eh? Even in the afterlife. Old Sam must now be among us somewhere.'

'I believe he has an archival job. Apparitional. Subatomic.'

'That's enough about the dead for one day. What do you wish for the young, Mr Bones?'

'Terrible and appalling dreams.'

'*Pourquoi*?'

'What hope else is there for the future?'

'What hope else? There are times when you speak in a mode of antique precision normally associated with a dead language.'

'One of us died back there, Harry, but I don't think it was the English language.'

'One of us? Only one? Mind you, some of our finest writers have had what was effectively a posthumous style.'

'Not to mention a posthumous reputation.'

'We seem to have a posthumous career. Just look at the little boy out there grinning at me. He's got blue pants and a jacket too. Now, if we'd been estate agents, Mr Bones . . . '

'We'd have needed to specialise.'

'And what would our speciality have been?'

'Caverns measureless to man. They'd have trusted you. The wooden tragedian never lies.'

'Having no human sentiments to misguide him.'

'Except for the sound of the wind through the alder's branches.'

'By the side of the river.'

'Caverns measureless to man.'

'And yet we continue talking.'

'As they did in Homer's Underworld.'

'In Virgil's Hades.'

'In Dante's Inferno.'

'In London in the twenty-first century.'

'We continue talking.'

'Shall we have a flashback now?'

'We shall have a flashback. Flashbacks, fast-forwards – all the same to us now. Robert will travel to the Cotswolds, as requested by Sam Meadows, and there he will encounter Brother Tom.'

'And what has happened to our Brother at this stage?'

'The worst thing of all. He has discovered the dreadful power he can exert over his fellow humans. He, the maimed one. To become a dictator of other men's souls. Not to mention women's. As though he were Ernest Johnson plus ISP.'

'So what will he do? Tell me.'

'Let's watch it on the screen out there instead.'

A Cotswold Eden

1

I took the train to Gloucester, where I was collected by Mervyn who drove the ancient Wolseley which had remained in the family garage for forty years. I looked through the window at the greenery, the dry-stone walls, trying to see how many trees I could identify.

'Mr Meadows is anxious that we get the print run done as soon as possible. Given that the job is already paid for, and that a lot of re-scheduling is about to go on at the works, it seems a sensible time to print the job now. Sam – Mr Meadows, that is – couldn't understand the delay in sending back the proof. He'd supervised the setting himself, and was pretty confident that the text was clean. So he sent me over to see if we could finalise things today.'

Mervyn cleared his throat as he changed gear.

'You will need my help, possibly, in communicating. The work has been left in the hands of Mr Tom, Dr Naseby's protégé.'

'That's fine with me.'

'He's a deaf mute.'

'Ah.'

'But very bright. Yes, indeed. Remarkably bright.'

'Why won't he sign off on the proof?'

'He won't say. Dr Naseby has phoned several times from the United States enquiring about the matter. Mr Tom of course can't use a telephone, and I have been unable to elicit any relevant information from him. But now that you are here . . . we might finally resolve the matter. I do hope so.'

I was startled at the sight of him. Thin and tall with long whispy hair, a delicate beard and an ancient jacket from some craft fair. He had tattoos, and eyes that would surely have made him a fine interrogator.

Had he been able to speak, that is. Or hear. He could obviously lip-read with great skill. With a gesture so fluent it was almost balletic, he motioned towards his mouth and his ears, as if to convey the fact that neither of these organs worked in the expected manner. I nodded to show that I already knew. He had a sheet of paper laid out before him on the table and picked up a pen to write when he wanted to convey something to me. I asked him questions simply by speaking at my normal speed.

'Are there any corrections we need to make to the book before we can print?'

He wrote on one of the sheets the word No.

'Is there a problem with design, layout, typography, chapter headings?'

No again.

'Then can we proceed with the printing of the book?'

Mr Tom walked to the window and stared outside into the garden. Finally he came back to the table. In his fluent hand he wrote the following questions, and I answered by speaking.

'How many copies?'

'Dr Naseby requested a print-run of one hundred.'

'I want you to guarantee that all copies are delivered here.'

'We always keep one copy for reference. We do this with any book we print. For the library at Owens.'

'Not this time. All copies come here. It is a matter of security.'

'If those are the terms . . . '

'Those are the terms.'

'Then we will have to accept them.'

'When will the books be here?'

'A week to ten days.'

Then he turned to Mervyn, and wrote out his question.

'Would you be able to get one hundred copies in the car?'

'I suppose so. It's a big boot, and there's the back seat.'

'Then we will collect them ourselves. As soon as they are ready.'

And then he walked out, having nodded a farewell to me. We drove back to the station in silence until I finally spoke.

'Something extraordinary about that man.'

'Yes,' Mervyn said, 'yes there is.'

'He's the boy in the book, isn't he?'

Mervyn nodded.

'Why does he have to have every copy? Why can't we keep even one?'

'He has promised Dr Naseby that he will have them printed, as arranged, and it was so important to the doctor to have this book published. A sort of ritual event in his life. And Mr Tom has told me that once they have all been printed . . . '

'Yes.'

' . . . he intends to destroy them one by one.'

'Why?'

'He won't say. But I think I know. For a while a lot of people came here. I think they started to worship him.'

'That's a big word. *Worship?*'

'Worship, yes. Body and soul. He could have them in any way he wanted. And for a while he took them too, but then one day I saw the look in his eyes . . . '

'What was it?'

'I can't describe it. But I think if Jim Jones could have ever had that look in his eyes, if only for a few seconds, then all those people would not have died back in Guyana. He has asked me to tell Dr Naseby what will happen.'

'And have you?'

'No. I can't.'

'But we are still to print the books?'

'You are still to print the books. To fulfil some sort of contract.'

'Who with?'

'The future perhaps. Or maybe the past. I honestly couldn't say.'

So we printed the books and had them bound. No jacket. There was a look of austerity about it, like Gallimard books in France. I took one over to show Sam, still alive then.

'Utility war production. I like it. Makes such a pleasant change from all the three-for-two nonsense we are treated to these days. You say that he's the boy in the book?'

'It seems so.'

'Are you going over with him? In the car?'

'Wasn't going to.'

'I would. Not one single copy is to be preserved. Most odd. Don't you have any curiosity about all this?'

I took this as a rebuke. So when Mervyn came the next day I offered to help him load the books and said I was happy to accompany him back; I could help with the unloading. He seemed relieved. The books, and their fate, appeared to be making him nervous.

We drove back.

'Is he really going to burn them all?' Mervyn nodded. 'It seems a shame.'

'I really can't think what the doctor will say. And I haven't yet had the courage to tell him.'

'Does he know what went on back there?'

He shook his head. 'I still can't get the images out of my mind. One day I went into the big room and they were all cross-legged on the floor in silence, while Mr Tom sat at the front, not staring at them exactly . . . staring into them, somehow. I've never seen anything like it. And I never want to again.'

When we arrived we unloaded the books in the porch, and then Mervyn went off to find Tom. They came back a few minutes later. Tom stared at the books, then picked one up and opened it at random. Almost immediately he threw it back on top of the pile, took his little notebook from his pocket and wrote on it. He tore off the sheet and handed it to Mervyn, who read it, evidently with some distress. He now spoke to Tom.

'I can't do this without the doctor's permission. He made me promise that I would make sure these books were printed and kept safely.' In a gesture of seeming unconsciousness, Mervyn passed the sheet to me. In Tom's fluently calligraphic script were written the words: BURN THEM ALL.

Tom now stared hard into Mervyn's face. It was a curious moment. I felt as though Mervyn had no will left to act upon. Could Tom be taking over his mind? Then Tom once more took the notebook from his pocket and wrote some words on it. Then he handed it to Mervyn. After Mervyn had read it he sighed and nodded, put the notebook down on top of the books and turned to me: 'Could you please start helping Brother Tom prepare the fire outside?'

As he walked into the house I picked up the notebook and read:

Phone Dr Naseby. Tell him his books are about to be burnt. Tell him I do not wish anyone to read this story, or to try to find or create another Roentgen Reader, or to diagnose or employ ISP. Unless they are already cursed with it. And tell him I leave here next week to join him back in Sioux Falls, where I will devote the rest of my life to helping him in his work. Compensation for the conflagration.

3

And so we stood out there, thirty feet from the house, with the flames consuming the wood, as Tom threw the hundred copies of Stewart Naseby's book, one by one, into the fire, counting as he went. Mervyn might have been crying, or it could have been simply the smoke that had caught his eyes. It made a handsome little inferno, all the same. Books burn well, as the Nazis knew. For a second I seemed to see Blake's *Collected Works*, but that must have been some fiery illusion from somewhere. When he had thrown the last copy on to the pyre, Tom suddenly walked quickly back into the house. When he came out, I wondered if he could be playing games with my own mind. Because in his arms was now a figure I knew only too well. My uncle's dummy, Harry Sprite, the little alderman. Though looking cleaner than I had ever seen him look before. And just before he hurled him into the fire too, I managed to stop him.

'No. Please. How do you know about Harry? He was my uncle's dummy. I was the person who created the museum. Is that where you bought it? Please don't burn him. Give him to me. I'll look after him.'

Brother Tom stared into my eyes then and I had a sensation I've never had either before or since. My mind flashed. As though an electronic device in a camera had suddenly gone off at midnight in some ancient cellar. Everything lit up. More synapses than I had ever known possible. Things I didn't even know were there, like furniture you'd abandoned years ago and forgotten all about, suddenly vivid and bright. They say that the whole of your life goes through your mind in the few seconds before you drown. And it was like that. He handed me Harry and walked back indoors. And I was never to see him again.

So that was the end of *ISP: A New Form of Perception. Or the Oldest One of All*? Every single copy burnt. Except of course for one. I didn't print one hundred, but one hundred and one. And that final copy is open on the desk here before me now as I write. Otherwise, I'd never have made sense of all this, now would I?

4

'So many books made from so many trees. You nephew appears to have given himself over to art at last. To the study of Isaac Lenau and Rembrandt. I am only a piece of painted wood, Mr Bones, but then so is a Rembrandt.'

'Are you saying there's no difference between you and a Rembrandt?'

'We are both cultural artefacts, as any modern university will inform you.'

'Indeed.'

'I probably tell better jokes.'

'Granted.'

'Though he's often funnier, funnily enough.'

'QED.'

'And then there's the tricksy business of crucifixion.'

'With which he was much preoccupied.'

'A man dies fastened to the remnants of a tree.'

'Like a ventriloquist clutching the remains of his wooden dummy, beneath a window in Stepney.'

'Always remember: the tree died before the man.'

'Or the saviour.'

'Is there a place for trees in heaven?'

'They'll need to keep making those harps out of something, surely. And where are all the angels meant to settle, when they fold their wings, after those great interstellar journeys?'

Elephant Eyes

The invention of hell is the acknowledgement of nefas; *this means that* nefas *is always integral to human identity, even when its horror appears to contradict it.*

Isaac Lenau, Marginalia, F. 2001

1

We have arrived here at last. We have arrived where I am; where I have been from the beginning, of course. Only waiting for you to arrive. I am engaged in a curious task, which I will now describe. What beckoned me to perform it? Well, I was invited, if only through the pages of a journal.

One version of *The Doctrine of Signatures* became my highly acclaimed book, the other – much more toned down and dignified – having been my doctorate. So I am now Dr Robert Fowey, PhD. Not a real doctor then; I can't straighten your back or reset your fractured bones. I can't prescribe analgesics to fend off the pain you are enduring. I am a doctor of philosophy. Why, you might wonder, are there so many of us? Because philosophy is sick and sorely needs attention, since all its recent prescriptions have turned out to be no more than placebos? I don't know, but then I'm not really a philosopher either, despite my fancy title. I'm neither a real doctor nor a real philosopher. My particular area of expertise is art and its relation to literature; studying images, though, not creating them. Studying the way we situate images in psychology and language, and how language always figures images for itself, whether consciously or unconsciously. This began with what was once called the doctrine of signatures. And it was art and literature and their labyrinthine history that I was attempting to teach at the University of London when I saw this advertisement in the back pages of *Marsyas*:

Three-Year Fellowship

Scholar required to help complete the editing and annotation of the Lenau Papers in preparation for publication.

The applicant must have a good research degree in fine art and a firm command of German. London accommodation will be provided.

Salary: HEFCE equivalent.

Mmm. Not exactly a description of Robert Fowey as we know him, but one needs to be flexible, in a changing world. Even the oak tree bends, not to mention the alder, as Harry will doubtless confirm. Now I should explain a number of things here. Isaac Lenau was a figure of particular interest to me because we shared a fascination with the work of Rembrandt; in particular the way Rembrandt simultaneously enlivens and demolishes the motifs of antiquity. The Lenau Institute had published some, but by no means all, of the written work of this German refugee from Nazism. I had always wanted to read more. My thesis had referred to Lenau's fragmented writings more than to any other scholar; too much, in fact, according to one of the external examiners. The idea of sorting through his original papers certainly appealed to me. I was living alone (finally) in Sam's dilapidated little house in Oxford, and this proffered 'London accommodation' – which would certainly be a little grander than my present address – was welcome. But the idea of three years free of teaching and administrative responsibilities, three years of paid scholarship with no boxes to tick and no meetings to attend, and no wretched administrative documents to create: this part was irresistible, not least because my contract with the university was not a permanent one. As is the way with so many universities these days, even the ancient ones, my one-year contracts were renewed over and over, and I might well have had to end up posting application after application before the year was out. My success as a writer certainly did not guarantee my position at the university; on the contrary. There were those who simply resented it. And the cheques from the publisher had stopped arriving too, a phenomenon noted by many writers of books over the years. So I applied, being generally truthful in my self-description except in one notable respect: I was obliged to exaggerate my proficiency in German. I did know a certain amount by then, to be honest, but I was far from fluent, yet my wording somehow managed to give the impression that I was. I could remedy the deficiency soon enough: I am a fast learner. So I could say in my own defence that this was not so much a dereliction of duty as its zealous anticipation.

I was interviewed by an ancient lady named Henrietta von Baum. She had known Lenau personally. In fact, she had been his secretary for the last decade of his life, and had sorted, edited and published the first three volumes of the Lenau Papers after his death. As a result, she was known as Mother of the *Marginalia*.

'But there are at least another three to go. At least another three, and one of them is of particular importance.' She spoke with the fastidious precision of one who was not a native speaker of English. I wondered if she might slip into German. That would surely have been the end of the interview, since I could not have kept up, not even for two sentences, but she never did. Her face was a laid white paper delicately scored with the sharpest of blades. (For a moment I even remembered my Uncle Graham right at the end.) Her eyes were an unexpectedly milky blue, glazed bright as antique porcelain. Her hair, blonde once and now whitened gold, was pulled back severely from her forehead and tied up at the back in a red silk ribbon. Her ageing brocade dress was long, decorated with tiny motifs in white lace – butterflies, eagles, scarab beetles. She was a very beautiful old woman and must surely have been an astonishingly beautiful young one. I had a curious wish to reach out and touch her. I remembered that Lenau had never married. Had Henrietta von Baum, I wondered? When she moved her position on the chair she shifted her hips the way certain women do – those who know that every part of their body has always been closely observed by observant men.

We were sitting in the new annexe of the Lenau Institute in London. From high windows sunlight filtered through the ambient dust. I would be 'required to do this'; I would be 'expected to do that'. Then, as the interview progressed, she gradually dropped the conditional mood; she stopped saying 'should you be appointed' and started instead to say 'when you are appointed'. I wasn't sure whether this might be linguistic inadvertence; the unrelenting precision of her diction led me to hope not. By the end she was smiling at me with what seemed like genuine warmth.

'I admired your essay on Rembrandt in *Marsyas* and thought your references to Lenau's work in *The Doctrine of Signatures* both appropriate and exact. I would like to think that you can complete this work which I started so long ago. That would be good, *nicht wahr*?'

'*Ja*. I look forward to being able to show it to you.'

'Sadly, that will not be possible.'

Nor was it, for she died soon after, only two weeks after I had taken up my new position. She had sent me a note of congratulation on my appointment which had ended with the single word *Aufwiedersehen*.

'Henrietta decided she could trust you,' Gemma said to me later. 'Always went by her instincts, and her instincts told her that she could trust you. But was she right, I wonder?'

2

The final part of this narrative can have no coherence, at least not if Isaac Lenau is to be believed. The condition of modernity is fragmentation. The only coherence we have left here, in our mighty world of demolition and reconstruction, is to see the shifting shapes our ruins have bequeathed us. We are all of us Layard at Nineveh, on our knees in the past, staring hard to see what it is that time buried beneath us, and whether we might still make out its dusty runes.

And this is why the most recurrent motif in the whole of Lenau's work is the palimpsest. About this he was most insistent. Beneath the parchment on which the words of our culture are written lie other words; darker signs; ancient voices. This was in fact a standard technique a few centuries back. Parchment or vellum can have its inscriptions scraped away until the surface is apparently clean again; then a new text is inscribed, with the old one obliterated. It is not obliterated, though; it is still there, Lenau insisted. Always still there. Its potency remains, though hidden. In a remarkable augury he once declared: 'One day we will devise instruments that can read the ancient runes beneath the modern letters.' And it has come about finally, exactly as he predicted. For with our new magic lenses and our spectroscopic techniques we are finding those texts, the ancient pagan injunctions beneath the rubric of the missal. Parchment was always expensive; vellum even more so. The bona fide vellum favoured by the connoisseur could only be made from the hide of an unborn deer, such was the suppleness and milky texture of the embryo's skin. So if one narrative text had been remaindered in the great emporium of cultural fashion, and another had inevitably gained ascendancy in its place, why throw away the precious skins of the codices, or squander their elaborate bindings? Scrape away, my brothers and sisters; scrape away, then dip the nib in ink once more and scratch the new commandments into the page's clean flesh. Like finest blade marks on the face's ancient parchment.

But there was something else, something that is now beginning to keep me awake at night as it once did Isaac Lenau. Towards the end, after he had watched the construction of the Third Reich, and seen the human cargo that was needed to fuel its ovens, he also came to believe that the same figure of the palimpsest applied to the human psyche. That beneath the text which had over-written our new lives there was another, more ancient script, inscribed subcutaneously into the surface of our minds. Beneath the epidermis of civility we present to one another for the handshake and the brief caress, instructions remain regarding torture, annihilation, ritual sacrifice, the clearing of our crowded parish for some *lebensraum*. Whenever we find Apollo smiling, somewhere close by Marsyas will be having his skin cut away, inch by inch, to reveal the text written on his soul. *Dichtung und Wahrheit*. Only thus is the discordant music of our culture composed. Thus do we, like Oedipus, stare into the *nefas* – the dark thing we should never really have known, but we will have to come back to this theme. More than once, I suspect.

'So how are you getting on?'

Gemma had come upon me down in the cellar where the mighty files are boxed and shelved. I suppose she might have had a reason to go down there, or I might have been the reason: she certainly knew I was there. I'm there most days now. A reasonable table in the corner allows some light in from the stairwell leading up to the pavement outside.

She is slim; her dark hair is close-cropped. Her skin is as white as Henrietta von Baum's, but her face has nothing of that composed beauty. Her features are mobile, inquisitive. She flutters about like a small bird. Her eyes are the largest thing in her face: brown, almost black. Her nose turns up a little at the end. When she grimaces thoughtfully she could have stepped out of a Disney cartoon. She wears a dark-blue kaftan covered with symbols which I'm not in the mood to try to decipher. No scarab beetles, anyway.

'Not sure how long I can stick it down here, to be honest.'

'Why don't you take the papers up in bundles to that nice flat of yours on the fifth floor, and work there then?'

'I can do that, can I?' As I ask my question, she opens her arms in a great flourish and bows.

'You are the Lenau Scholar, appointed, even if posthumously, by Her Majesty Dr von Baum, and you can do whatever the fuck you like, sir.'

I start to laugh.

'Gather up what you want to take and I'll come down in an hour and help you carry it up.'

Two hours later we sit in the flat, my London flat for the duration of my scholarly activities. A residence in Oxford and one in London. How grand I'm becoming all of a sudden. And I didn't have to pay for either of them. What do you make of that? The kettle is boiling. Gemma stares through the window over the rooftops of London. She has a curious way of bending her right foot around the back of her left leg. On the windowsill is the son of Harry Sprite. On the table beside him is *Sacred Voices in Antiquity* by Graham Fowey and *ISP* by Stewart Naseby – the world's one remaining copy.

'Flamingo,' I say, making coffee.

'What?'

'You stand like a flamingo.'

She turns back to the window. 'You can almost see them from here. Pink freaks of evolution. Airborne anorexics with a surrealist streak. St James's Park. This is a nice flat.'

'Have you been here before?'

'Many times. Every day at one point. Then, when Henrietta started to . . . started to be ill, I used to bring the doctor up with me. A real doctor.' She gives me her cartoon grimace again. 'A real doctor to see another of these doctors of philosophy.'

'Ah. So she lived here.'

'Yes. First her. Then you.'

'And before either of us?'

'Sir Henry Flood. This was his home. You must have known that, surely?'

'Yes, I did know it. But I don't know much about it. Too preoccupied with Lenau and Rembrandt.' I had handed her the mug of coffee and we sat down, with her on the sofa, and me on a large armchair in the corner. 'Tell me the story of my new home.'

'All right.' She curled her feet up beneath her thighs, sipped at her coffee and started to talk. Much of the story I did already know, but I was happy to hear her speak. I liked the sound of her voice. Soft, hesitant, occasionally disintegrating into giggles when she realised she had said something which might appear odd or whimsical.

Lenau, a German Jewish refugee, brought his library to Britain in the 1930s so it might escape the lethal illiteracy of the Nazis: that was one palimpsest he did not wish to study. Not then anyway. The original bibliographic asylum was housed in Oxford, where it remains to this day, but a bequest from Sir Henry Flood brought the remainder of its precious stock to London, just in time for the millennium. Before his death Sir Henry, who had become a serious student of Lenau and the collected fragments we have come to call 'his work', had his five-storey London residence turned into a library, though a library containing at that point very few books. So completely had he accomplished this task, leaving only one section on the top floor for eating, cooking, socialising and sleeping, that some of his oldest acquaintances thought he had grown eccentric. Or, as the obituarist in the *Clarion* put it: 'Word soon went around that the old fellow was no longer in full possession of his faculties.' Sir Henry himself had introduced his last lecture at the British Academy by saying, 'Many of you are probably convinced by now that I'm a sandwich short of a picnic.' In fact, if anything, the old man had one sandwich extra, plus several proteinaceous rolls, and a spare box of dry biscuits. He had assessed the precise requirements of the Lenau collection in Oxford and decided to cater for its radical inadequacies. In consequence all the books which could not be racked and displayed in the old place were now racked and displayed in the new one. Gemma had been asked to become the librarian, having been for ten years assistant librarian in Oxford (how old was she, I wondered? She had an ageless, pixie look). She was provided with subsidised rooms in the Gough Building, an ancient bequest from another ancient member.

'Nothing like this, though. Nothing like these rooms.'

These rooms. My rooms. My home. For as long as I occupy my present position, which at this moment I have no intention of leaving.

Lenau's 'Collected Papers' were in fact still a chaos. The first person to attempt to collate and annotate them had, of course, been Henrietta von Baum herself, the principal librarian, first of the Oxford Institute and then of the London one. She had named volume one *Marginalia*. This name had somehow stuck and there were now three volumes: *Marginalia One, Two* and *Three*. I was now engaged on *Marginalia Four*. An oddity had struck me quite early on: what was the text, of which these writings constituted the margins? I asked Gemma and she smiled.

'You know what Henrietta said, don't you?'

'No.'

'That the more she studied, edited and collated these writings, the more their contents became indistinguishable from her own thought. She could no longer separate her mind from Lenau's.'

'So the *Marginalia* are annotations to . . . '

'The original text of the palimpsest.'

'And that only emerges through . . . '

'The *Marginalia*.'

'The labyrinth is circular then. There's something else I find odd. The boxes containing the papers I'm working on, they don't seem ever to have been opened. Surely she would have wanted to look inside?'

'That's exactly what she didn't want to do.'

'Why not?'

'Because she knew very well what was there. She was Lenau's lover for the last ten years of his life. She knew what happened to his mind. She'd already read everything.'

'Didn't he go . . . '

'He went insane and was institutionalised. That might have been the easy part. It was the period leading up to that, the Oxford war years, when he wrote his papers. Henrietta was only twenty-one. And he decided to explore from the inside what the world was exploring only too brutally outside. Degradation. Torture. The flaying of Marsyas. You will find that some of the explorations of these themes involve Henrietta. It's one of the reasons she told me not to apply for your post.'

'You were going to apply?'

'Yes, I'm qualified. Perhaps more qualified than you, *mein Freund*. But she didn't want my mind getting stained. She was . . . very fond of me. Which is why I was made librarian after her death. All the same, I made her a promise before she died that I'd help with your work. Give you necessary guidance. Even encourage you towards the kind of ruthlessness which she thought might not come naturally, but I wonder about that. I think you might be an intellectual survivalist. I remember Henrietta saying, "What a curious way to think you can perfect your German. Following it through the nine circles of the inferno." '

'She knew then?'

'She was no fool. My German's perfect. Though you're about to find that you won't be needing much German anyway: the writings are in Lenau's curious English. But don't imagine that will make them any less painful for you.'

4

I suppose Marsyas was too obvious a mythic precursor for Lenau to ignore.

Here is the story in short: Athena invents a flute, but finds that the distortion of the face required to play it was making a palimpsest of her beauty. She throws it away. Marsyas, a satyr, finds it; teaches himself to play and flutes away to the birds and the animals, enchanting the whole forest. So exalted does he become with the music swelling inside him that he challenges Apollo to a musical duel. The god of light and serenity is angered by this hairy upstart, this deformed outgrowth of nature, this thing of darkness, and outplays him with his lyre. His victorious manoeuvre is to turn the lyre upside down and still play it perfectly. Marsyas cannot do that with a flute. Note the lethal inhumanity of symmetry here: a theme that was greatly to preoccupy Lenau throughout his life. The gods in their judgement are all agreed that Marsyas has lost. And since this is victor's justice, Apollo is given his choice of punishments. He will have Marsyas flayed alive, inch by inch, so that his cries will fill the forest, just as his flautist's notes once did. According to the testimony of the spectators, since there are always spectators at an execution, avidly consuming their picnic packs, sandwich by sandwich, Apollo smiled a smile of infinite satisfaction as the cries were extracted and the blades began to scrape away.

There was a great vogue in the seventeenth and eighteenth centuries for *ecorché* figures, sculptures, engravings, etchings. They showed a human body, male or female, with much of the skin, the musculature, the arteries stripped away, or pulled aside, so that one can peer in. In Rembrandt's *Anatomy Lesson of Doctor Tulp*, the same process is going on while the studious gather round to look. An executed criminal is laid out on a table and turned inside out so as to facilitate the new anatomy, the new medicine, expensive new cures for those who are not to be executed. If we are to find out what goes on in there then we must have some warm examples laid before us so that we may make our incisions. It is, after all, a condition of modernity: knowledge requires entry by the eye, the blade, the recording machine. Our telescopes and particle accelerators grow bigger and bigger; we will enter all nature, including our own. We must get inside the nucleus. We murder to dissect, said Wordsworth. Though with Tulp's anatomy lesson, we execute first and then dissect. *Yesterday*, Jonathan Swift wrote, *I saw a woman flay'd, and you will hardly believe how much it altered her person for the worse.*

5

In the mirror I sometimes seem coherent. There is an image there which looks as though it knows what it's about. Not at four o'clock in the morning though, obviously. The ghost face floats on quicksilver in darkness and it's no more substantial than I normally feel these days. Come the morning, the bathing, the shaving, the dressing, the composition of the expression on the face – once all that self-composition is done – I seem to confront my own image as one who would say, 'Right then, we're ready for you now, evidently.' Who though? Of late, when I have looked in the mirror, I have seen Gemma peering in there too, looking at such a composed image and grimacing. Why should her ghost have joined me here? Might her words have begun to unnerve me a little? It starts to seem possible. All the same, there is six-foot-something of me there, slim, blue-eyed (if not so vividly as Henrietta), my blond hair falling whimsically about my high forehead. Women often seem to like me. Henrietta did. But how much does this apply to Gemma? She seems happy enough to join me in my flat, where she now comes every day, just as she once did when it was occupied by Henrietta von Baum.

'There was only one other serious candidate for the post. Apparently serious, anyway. Henrietta thought not. She did not trust her at all. You she did trust. Though we both found it intriguing that you had to lie so much about your prowess in German.'

My face reddens.

'But we never actually spoke German.'

'No. But she dropped in a little test. You failed it miserably. Don't you remember?' I shake my head. 'She said at one point, "I suppose we should have to translate *Gleichschaltung* in Lenau as equality." It was a ludicrous mistranslation, but you did not demur.'

'Maybe I was just being polite.'

Gemma now curls her right leg a little more fluently around her left calf. The fabric of her black trousers pulls tight against the flesh. Her thighs are a little heavier than I had imagined, and I have imagined them many times already.

'Would you like me to set you an unseen German translation here? You could redeem your honour *instanter*.'

I shake my head.

'So what was my qualification then?'

'*Nefas*.'

'*Nefas*?'

'Oh dear. Deficient in the languages of antiquity too. *Nefas*: the darkness into which Oedipus peered a little too intently. That was his real crime, according to Hölderlin, whom Lenau revered, as you will doubtless recall. The finest madmen often bond, in my experience. I'll be keeping an eye out for you on this score. Henrietta thought it might well be there in me, but she didn't want my little well of *nefas* to be either plumbed or deepened. She loved me by the end, you see. She had undergone her own terror with Lenau, and then had it to do all over again when she read the wartime papers. He was writing them in the night while she lay in the bed. Then she locked them up for fifty years. Oedipus can only answer the Sphinx because he sees *nefas* where others see merely obscurity. He made out the dark places of the gods, heard their hideous laughter ricocheting off the walls of Piranesi's prisons. His own dark deeds are nothing compared to what he sees in the gods' mirror. He seems to understand the heart of Apollo, even as Marsyas is flayed, and that is *verboten*. For humankind it is *verboten*. And you're about to start looking in that mirror with him, my friend. Box 18.'

'What?'

'Cut to the chase, Robert. Box 18. That should fill up your three years here nicely. If you can endure it without suffering Lenau's fate. Then you can decide.'

'Decide what?'

'Whether or not to destroy his international reputation.'

'How would I do that?'

'Possibly by publishing what you are about to read.'

I am standing at the window looking out over the grand rooftops south of Piccadilly. The mighty city – I've been in love with it ever since I arrived here. Like so many loves, it is mixed – almost equally – with hatred.

'There's still something I don't understand.' Gemma has come to stand beside me. There are only inches between us.

'And what's that, Robert?'

'Why was my weak German not a disqualification?'

'I thought I'd already explained. Because almost everything you're about to work on was written in English. A very curious English sometimes. And a very potent one.' I stare into her face. She is smiling, but it is a distracted smile. 'In 1940, Isaac Lenau renounced his mother tongue. He did what Paul Celan never could do, and said farewell to German. Kurt Weill I seem to recall did something similar. The language in which the Reich had been conceived was one he no longer wished to speak. So he bade it farewell. Said he would speak only English from now on. Speak English. Write English. Think English. Dream English. But given that his study was the cultural palimpsest, which is another way of saying how, under all civilisation, lies an original trace of savage arousal, he had inevitably to seek in English the same force of evil that had emerged in German. So he began his study: the etymologies of slaughter, how savagery is rooted beneath the veneer of our civility. And his two subjects were: the modern state as sacrificing priest, and man's relationship with his sexual mate, his specific object of study here being Henrietta von Baum herself. Two starting-points for authority and oppression. The nearest and the dearest. How we use them as mirrors to find out who we really are.' Gemma now for the first time placed her hand on my hand. I was surprised how tiny her fingers seemed, and how delicate the touch. 'She said that she almost went mad herself, but she never abandoned him. He the Jew and she the Gentile. Do you normally sleep well?'

'Up to now.'

'Let's hope it continues then.'

And that is why I stand here, examining the figure in the mirror before first light, wondering if I have ever had any real notion who that person actually is, was or might come to be. My mother always insisted that there was a strain of insanity in the Fowey male. I am alone in this building. It will be hours before the others arrive. But I may as well go down into the cellar and bring up some more of the contents of Box 18. I have started, you see. I have already started. And another statement that Gemma made once more echoes in my mind.

'Whoever is to sort through these fragments had to have one thing in common with Lenau, that's what Henrietta said. He too must me a *noli-me-tangere*. One whom other human beings only touch by accident, and then only briefly. He has to get back to his *nefas*, you see. The dark reflections there transcend the daily goings-on of mere mortals.'

(Did this mean, I wonder now, that the well of *nefas* is a mirror too?)

'Am I a *noli-me-tangere*?' I can still feel her fingers on my hand, even though they are no longer there.

'Oh yes. Didn't you know? Someone must have bestowed that special blessing on you. You must tell me about your childhood one day. Mummy, daddy, the whole caboodle. And isn't there something odd about your uncle? There's even a museum, isn't there? Puppets. You are far harder to touch than you seem to imagine. Sometimes you seem to me almost . . . wooden.'

6

I am making my way up from the basement with another bundle of papers from Box 18. At the Admissions Desk, Gemma is being attentive to a very elderly gentleman with a freakish cloud of white hair; one of our ancient Lenau devotees. His grandfather invented a famous aeroplane.

'I think someone's spilt some white soap in the gents; I suppose it could be semen. Either way, the floor's slippy.'

'I'll go through in a minute and mop it up.'

'Might be better if a gentleman went, I think.'

'I'm sorry?' Gemma says.

'Just in case it *is* semen. Don't want you getting impregnated, my dear. Though it's probably chilled beyond any effective use by now. Nothing to do with me, by the way. Long since stopped scattering my seed, though I certainly feel as old as Onan on some of these cold mornings.' She looks across at me and smiles. The Lenau: a curious institution. There seems to be an element of madness not merely in the man but also in the tradition he founded. She told me one day about the deaf mute who'd come in bearing Stewart Naseby's card.

'That's Mr Tom,' I said. 'I have a book about him here. The only copy that still exists. Might let you read it one day.'

'The madness could be starting already, I see.'

Up in my apartment, I examine the papers. They begin in 1940 and are almost entirely in English, though the very first words are French: *L'enfer s'enrichit*. Hell is enriching itself. Now where would that be from? My computer is turned on, so I click through to Google and ask. The phrase is not recognised. Did Lenau invent it then? I turn back to the papers on the desk. It is 1940. There is no reason for anyone in Europe to suppose at this moment that Germany and her allies will not be victorious. Lenau has just renounced his beloved mother tongue, the *Muttersprache*. And he sees hell enriching itself.

Why does Apollo smile so calmly? Why does the skin peeling off Marsyas, and the satyr's screams, give the god such serene satisfaction?

In the representations, the god smiles unrelentingly. Is he smiling once more? The state is Apollo. The sacrificing god, the sacrificing priest, has become the state. But the necessity for the victim's sacrifice has never left us. Not knives now, bombs. Flesh torn away still – blades, flames. Still, like Apollo, they listen to music. Schubert, I believe, is a great favourite.

So this is Box 18. The handwriting looks heavier than an English hand would have been at the time. The black ink still carried a memory of the gothic script of the *Vaterland*. If the writing started in 1940, then when did it end? I set off down the stairs to the basement once more. Down five flights; no lift. Over in the far corner is the box. I pull out bundles until I can reach the papers right at the bottom. And they are dated: 1945. Five dark years then; this is Box 18. 1940 to 1945. I lift out the last fascicle of papers and head back upstairs. I walk quickly through the entrance hall to avoid catching anyone's eye. I want to see the last words written. The first words and the last: then I shall make my way through all that was written in between. And here are the last words Isaac Lenau ever wrote in Box 18:

December. Finally managed to see the Wilder film. *Buchenwald*.
Human trophies on Kommandant's table. Including skin. Fragments of human skin, and a lampshade made from the same.
Skin is cut away from the satyr, the dissident, the Jew, while Apollo smiles his endless smile of reason. Reason. Who can live inside it now? Look what reason did to Marsyas; is still doing to this day. Reason has declared: I am god. Now you must suffer for your song.

1945. The year of Lenau's hospitalisation: the year that he was declared once more insane. Reason: the domicile he could no longer inhabit. He died five years later, before he might re-enter it. He never came out of his institution.

And Henrietta?

7

'Have you realised yet why Rembrandt was so important to him?'

'I once thought I knew. Tell me, in case I didn't actually understand anything. I do wonder some days.'

Gemma, as ever, is sitting on my sofa with her legs curled up beneath her haunches. She is caressing her mug of coffee as though it were a favourite creature, come back once more to nestle in her hands. Her fingers describe little caresses all over it, as if they had never before encountered such warmth. As though the ceramic object had a heartbeat.

'Because he declared war on Apollo, the god of reason. Rembrandt believed perfect form was a sacrifice to pagan gods. It was the murder of actuality. Apollonian symmetry necessitated genocide; humanity is just too untidy to survive. The only time we ever see Jesus entirely symmetrical, remember, he is on a cross; splayed; symmetry is torture.'

Images are passing through my mind: the modernist lines of the utility buildings at Auschwitz; the use of Occam's Razor that led to the development of Zyklon-B. I'm no longer sure I want to be thinking about this. Gemma seems able to hear my words, even though I never actually uttered them.

'Now would be the time to abandon it all, you realise that?'

'Abandon it all?'

'You are on the edge of the well of *nefas*, my friend. But you don't necessarily have to fall in. Henrietta never wanted me down there.'

'Give up my post, you mean?'

'In a month's time, you won't be able to make the choice. Your probationary period will be over.'

'But I want to find out more.'

'You do and you don't. You look different. Even today. Your eyes are less . . . blue.'

'Less like Apollo's then?'

'More like those of Marsyas, maybe, before he starts screaming. Or even Henrietta, with that curiously glazed look her own eyes took on. A blue-eyed Marsyas; I suppose that's progress, of a kind. Redemption through miscegenation. Have you found the diary?'

'I didn't know he'd written one.'

'Not his. Henrietta's. It's in there somewhere. It became more of a notebook than a diary. She had me put it in there, at the end. Told me not to open it up again until after her death.'

'And now she's dead.'

'Must be time to open it then, Robert, mustn't it?'

I found it later that day, pushed firmly into the middle of one of the fascicles. An old leather-bound diary, a large one with a page for each day of the year. And the year was 1945. Compared to Lenau's hand, Henrietta's was delicate and spidery. All her letters were fastidiously formed. I opened it at random and read the entry.

Monday: I asked him what the purpose was of his entering the same darkness, as though he were of their number; he, whom they would have slaughtered, whose mind is as finely sharpened as theirs is lethally blunt. To understand, he said. It is all I am here for. Otherwise I should die. Your mind might die anyway, I told him. There isn't enough space, even in your mind, for so much darkness. He held up his hands to me. He is growing his nails. The flaying. I have bought more cream. I put it by the bed each night. How long can this go on? *Nefas*. Darkness. Unfathomable darkness. *Nefas*.

'So she wrote in English too then?'

'They shared the pact. Renunciation of the *Muttersprache*.'

'How well did you know Henrietta von Baum?'

And now Gemma looks at me, head on one side, with a smile I've never seen before on her face. A smile that seems to announce some kind of advantage.

'Well enough to see the scars he'd left on her back. Some of them never healed entirely.' The flaying, presumably.

'Where did it come from, the word *nefas*? Do you know?'

'I think he got it from the *Thebaid* of Statius. Coroebus shouts at Apollo, calling the monster the god has sent *tuum mortale nefas*. Your mortal thing of darkness. Remember Prospero on Caliban: "This thing of darkness I acknowledge mine." But Lenau was his own thing of darkness; he became his own *nefas*. And you are entering that space, Robert. I look at you as closely as I do because I'm curious. How deep is that well inside you, I wonder? And what images will you discover inside it underneath the floating moon?'

8

Sometimes a whole fascicle would be devoted to his thoughts on art. It could seem like a reprieve then, simply to follow Lenau's brooding mind as it considered the history of representation in the West. Did it represent a reprieve for him too, I wondered? Though these thoughts were also dark; Lenau was never far from darkness, even before he disappeared into the ultimate one. His own *nefas*.

I have begun to classify, following the von Baum principle.

Marginalia, N. 21046, F. 204
Exemplary texts often appear to overcome entirely, or even exclude, the raggedness of life, its incoherence. R. took all such texts and reinserted enough raggedness to require another redemption. Vide *Samaritan*.

It took me a while to understand his characteristic abbreviations and ellipses. I have already been at this task for four months now. Let me try to elucidate for you.

Lenau often spoke of the Kingdom of Causality as that place where randomness is 'redeemed' everywhere into pattern, coherence and symmetry. It had been part of the effort of all the great artists of modernity to put contingency back into the picture. The conventional dating of the artists of modernity usually begins with Manet or Courbet, or just possibly Turner. But Lenau's first two great exemplars of modernity in art and literature were instead Shakespeare and Rembrandt, those near-contemporaries, whose scandalous talent consisted of demolishing the boundaries between genres, between ancient and modern, comedy and tragedy, the sacred and the profane, the classical and the documentary. Take, for example,

190

Rembrandt's etching *The Good Samaritan* – to which the Lenau fragment above is referring. The poor beaten fellow is being taken to an inn by the friendly and charitable alien. In the foreground a hound is hunkering down and excreting. Why? Why should such a thing be happening at all, let alone in the foreground of the Gospel story? And why is a man who looks suspiciously like Rembrandt staring over the horse's saddle at this spectacle while lifting up the wounded pilgrim at the centre of the parable? Because, says Lenau, the obligations of modernity leave him no choice, since one implication of living in modernity is the random feculence of life, its malodorous intrusion into all activities. Its shittiness. This fact could never be negated, since the refusal of modernity, in a kind of antiquarian reverse manoeuvre, meant for Lenau the abandonment of thought itself. And this was his great puzzle in regard to the Nazis and the Reich: the combination of modernity with a nostalgia, amounting to lethal kitsch, for primitive slaughter.

All images, Lenau says, are a relationship between a text and a performance. They are translations. With Rembrandt, this is often straightforward enough: the text is often antiquity or the Bible, and in performance the artist reinserts contingencies the text left out, like the defecating dog in the Samaritan etching. After all, even as Jesus was preaching, a dog must have been defecating somewhere. Even as God speaks, some bowel is being emptied. God made the bowels, along with the speech, and so is hardly in a position to complain regarding their evacuation. No redemption without dross; no perfection which does not have refuse somewhere in the frame. But it applies to all his other images too: even the landscapes are translations, conversions of nature and technological makings into these marks on a sheet.

According to Lenau, Rembrandt's art was exemplary for its constant act of translation: the perfect text, the exquisite tradition, translated into the street, the market, the bedroom. Apollo found himself con- stantly translated into Marsyas. The bemused, the bewildered and the frankly indifferent look on, as the divine miracle is effected. Those who stone St Stephen to death are pleased with their strength. It is a pleasure for them to see how their well-aimed blows draw blood and take life. These are surely the disciples of Apollo. Or could they even be the devotees of Dionysus, Apollo's opposite? The delirium of the Bacchae has to fit in here somewhere. Lenau sometimes appears confused about this.

Where was Rembrandt? In a town where Descartes was often busily separating mind from body, at the same time that Rembrandt was realising their indissolubility. Spinoza had been there too, grinding lenses for microscopes and telescopes, excommunicated by the Jewish community for daring to say that angels might be hallucinations; not that he ever said the truth couldn't arrive in the form of a hallucination. Suddenly, Lenau has a paragraph that could be about Rembrandt, but it could just as well be about himself:

When he was young he had been afraid of the things outside his body that might kill him; now he is old and afraid of things inside that will do the same. He listens to the knocking and the creaking and the siphoning of blood, and he hears death's stealthy progress, its daily encroachment. Nothing ever improves. He looks in the mirror and death mocks him from inside the contours of his own flesh. Did Rembrandt ever meet Spinoza in Amsterdam? Or Descartes? A mind immune from prejudice; he had many contacts among the Jews of the time.

And then he is suddenly comparing Rembrandt's fate with Shakespeare's:

Here is the list of his dead. In comparison the author of *Hamlet* had a charmed life, surely – only one son gone at eleven; that still left two daughters and a wife. And how many lovers in London, how many Henriettas behind closed doors? And unlike his father, the alderman, never a bankrupt either. He just grew richer. Closer and closer to the crown that eluded Rembrandt. Now what did the painter lose? Whatever money he had. Possibly from speculating on the Bourse. Both his daughters dead within months of entering the world. One son lost in infancy too. Then Saskia, the beloved bride. Her smile sceptical and knowing, but her thighs opening to him all the same. After her, Hendrickje Stoffels, the housekeeper, the one his Calvinist brothers in Christ called the painter's whore. And finally even Titus, the beloved boy, taken away from him at twenty-six by plague. In those late self-portraits you are witnessing a man who has seen more than he ever wished to see. Even a painter can see more than he wishes, to end up looking at his own eyes in the mirror, waiting for them to close at last. You look out upon a world as on a graveyard. Behind the flesh, the bone. Open up the criminal's body so as to see if he might have left his soul in there. All the heat of the sun could not warm what's been frozen. The dead. Saskia. Titus. Even the self-portraits finally become wells of *nefas*.

9

'So you're staying then?'

'It's been almost five months, so it looks like it. Sorry to disappoint you.'

'You don't disappoint me. Does your hair go like that naturally at the front? The way it just springs out in a little yellow spray?'

'As far as I know. Never noticed anyone coming up and squirting anything at me.'

'Women sometimes pay a lot for that sort of effect.'

'You don't.'

Dark hair cropped and forgotten. Gemma's erotic charge had nothing to do with vanity.

'That's true.'

'I don't suppose you fancy dinner, do you? Out of the Lenau Scholar's fabulous salary? It's just that I'm . . . '

'Lonely.'

I wasn't going to say that, but it was in fact true. She's good at truth, Gemma. It can be unnerving sometimes.

'It can get a little quiet around here.'

'You don't have to stay in the Lenau every night. Lots of places in these parts with all sorts of exciting things going on.'

'I'll take that as a no then, shall I?'

'No. Take it as a yes. But I'll pay my own way, thank you. I don't

193

want to start being indebted to anyone at the Lenau. I always paid my own way.'

'Even with Henrietta?'

'Particularly with Henrietta.'

At the bottom of one of the streets that runs down into Piccadilly, there is a basement, converted into a wine-bar and a restaurant. Gemma specified the location. It was dark. I seemed to be specialising in dark basements these days. But then *nefas* is after all my subject. That's merely another way of saying 'concentrated darkness'. So we might as well blow the candles out and get on with it.

I had already ordered a bottle of wine by the time she arrived. I had been listening to the conversation between the man and the woman at the next table.

'What was the first thing that struck you about me?'

'The fact that you were stark bollock-naked, standing outside my door.'

'Was that all?'

'It was more than enough at the time, Jack; more than enough, believe me. And while I think of it, flashing doesn't become any less illegal because you happen to be doing it from the inside of a Santa Claus outfit. Can you try to bear that in mind this Christmas? Particularly while you're giving my mother her pressies.'

Gemma was suddenly standing beside me.

'How did you know I liked Colombard?'

'I didn't, but I like it. Maybe we like the same things.'

'Maybe. I shouldn't necessarily count on it, though.'

The noise was the low growling hubbub of any London bar, enhanced a little by the stone floor. We ordered food. Soups. Salads. Rice. Vegetables. We had to lean across to one another sometimes to hear what was being said. My knee found hers during one of these manoeuvres. She did not flinch away, but after a few minutes the knee was no longer touching. Mine had stayed in place. The wine, so cold to begin with, soon grew warm inside. By the time I ordered the second bottle, anything seemed possible. Anything and everything.

'What drew you to the work of Lenau?'

'Mickey.'

'Mickey,' I repeated witlessly. A boyfriend? A teacher? I was embarrassed it might be a foreign scholar whose name I should know but didn't: Michi, Mekea, McKee. 'Give me a clue. One of your mentors?'

'No. My mouse.'

'Your mouse.'

'Don't keep repeating my last phrase, Robert, or I'll start to sulk and drink this nice Colombard in silence.'

'So explain.'

'I'd always wanted a pet, but my parents wouldn't let me have one. Said they all smelt, even fishes. Then *Mouselife* was launched. Ever see it?'

'No.'

'Software package. Your own mouse. You nourished it, fed it each day, watched it grow, weighed it. It made tiny noises. Adorable little noises. Often slept. Infinitesimal snores. Played with its toys. My Christmas present. My parents could cope with that; the one thing Mickey couldn't do was smell.' She stopped and took a long sip of wine.

'Can't see the connection with Lenau.'

'One day Mickey died. Part of the realism the product boasted. And I cried for a whole evening. Wouldn't eat. Lost the one thing in the house I unconditionally loved.' She seemed to be grieving again momentarily.

'And Lenau?'

'It was months later. Came across a quote. Still remember it: *Once the representations all came from the gods. Now they are the gods. Our representations rule our reality.* That's what had happened with Mickey: a representation had come to rule my reality. I started to study Lenau; and here I am these days to prove it. And you?'

'My parents were Plymouth Brethren. At least my father was. My mother was just my father's wife. The last time I looked they'd switched to the Exclusive Brethren.'

'Is that better or worse?'

'Worse. They won't let anyone into heaven at all. I think my father

195

was worried that with the other lot it was already getting into double figures, and there'd be nowhere to park up there.'

'Almost as far from this to Lenau as from Mickey.'

'One day he came back with a book. Something about representations of divinity. And I was looking through it. There was one line that caught my eye. And I still remember it: *In portraying God we project into the darkness outside and the deeper dark within the morphology of our pain.*'

'*Marginalia Two.*'

'I asked my father about him.'

'Did he know?'

'No. Said he sounded Jewish.'

'Was he an anti-Semite then? Was that a necessary part of being in the Plymouth Brethren?'

Now I start laughing. It's a long smooth laugh, lubricated with dry white wine. I think I might have practised it in front of a mirror once; it might even have been intended to make me attractive to women. Not sure it works, to be honest.

'You could put whatever category of human being you like behind the word "anti" with my old man and it's almost bound to fit. They're not planning on having more than fifteen or sixteen up there, remember, plus the Trinity; and for the rest of us, it's eternal damnation.'

'So not many Jews bound for Paradise then?'

'One must assume that Jesus got in . . . I had a mouse once.'

'A *Mouselife* mouse?' Gemma seemed genuinely excited at the prospect, and I was sorry to have to shake my head and disappoint her.

'No, the old style. Soft and furry. I used to take it in my hand and run a finger across the fine hairs. So delicate. It used to quiver. It felt like . . . '

Gemma was looking at me, and had it not been so dark I think she might have seen another blush.

'Like a *sooterkin*.'

'What's that?'

'In the eighteenth century Dutch women were said to place stoves

196

under their petticoats. Which led to the breeding of a tiny creature in there, exactly the size of a mouse. You need a friend, Robert. A man going down into Lenau's *nefas* needs a companion, something a little bigger than a mouse, even if she does keep a *sooterkin* under her petticoat. Even Lenau had Henrietta.'

'Do you need a friend too?'

'Maybe. Maybe not. Maybe my affections do not that way tend.'

It was only later, walking home alone, the long way round through the park, that I asked myself a question I should have asked before: how did Gemma get to see Henrietta's unhealed scars? The ones Lenau had left in her flesh with his nails? And what exactly did she mean about her affections and the way they tended?

10

The tears of the grieving satyrs and nymphs at Marsyas' torture and death formed a river, known as the Marsyas to this day. Lenau had always planned to visit it before he died, but he ended up in the asylum instead. Maybe he visited it in his own way. Maybe his thoughts flowed into his own River Marsyas. The satyr was a shepherd; he had presumably flayed sheep in his time, so as to make his shoes and clothes. But not alive. Marsyas had shown the dumb animals a kindness the god of reason would not in turn show him. In his notes Lenau wondered how long the flaying had taken. As long as a normal crucifixion? The two measures of torture: intensity and duration.

I had to get out for air and light. I had been working since dawn and I needed air and light. There was precious little of either in Lenau's papers. Gemma was standing at the Admissions Desk, signing out a book. The young bearded man was staring unrelentingly at her. I had seen him often in the Reading Room. He was perennially unsmiling. Bespectacled, bearded, unsmiling. I stared after him as he left, then turned back to look at Gemma.

'Melancholy Malcolm,' she said. 'Imagines he's in love with me.'

'Why so melancholy?' I reckoned I could guess, if he was in love with Gemma.

'He thinks if he'd just learnt one more chord, he could have been a rock star by now. Instead he's ended up as Charles Friend's research assistant. Friend's writing Lenau's authorised biography, but you already know that, presumably; you should meet him, by the way, when he gets back from the States – Charles, I mean. Malcolm, despite his own self-estimation, is not intellectually distinguished. I went for a drink with him one night, and if his mind were a car you'd have to conclude it was two write-offs welded together.'

'And on top of all his other troubles, he's in love with you.'

'I said he imagines he's in love with me. He hasn't the faintest idea what that "me" is, so how could he love it?' How indeed? 'Has his own band.'

'What's it called?'

'Mongolian Warthog.'

'Why?'

'Why were the Beatles called the Beatles? I went to a gig one night. He gave me a ticket.'

'And?'

'Malcolm thinks terminal sadness represents some kind of qualification in life. He's wrong, sadly. He's also in search of chemical enlightenment. But he seems to be just too moderate to find it, somehow. Too thrifty with the molecules.'

I step out into the square and start walking.

According to the great philologist Lachmann, there are three main ways in which a text is corrupted on its journey downwards through history. The first is contamination, when the source text is mixed up with other variants and mongrelised; the second is scribal conjecture, when the copyist deliberately alters the text he has been given to copy because he believes he can improve it; and the third is polygenesis, when the same errors occur in entirely different places, perpetrated by unrelated hands and for reasons that must frequently remain inexplicable.

I'm about to recount a curious variant: human polygenesis. The text to be copied in this case was the Book of Life, and the form it took was a human being, or rather, two of them. Two human beings both inscribed with an identical, if polygenetic, flaw. To one you have already been introduced, since it is myself. Much of my business in life concerns books: their authority; their provenance; their deceptions; their histories. All books have histories, just as we do. As the Lenau Scholar, I spend most of my days querying sundry volumes, trying to understand their interrelationships. It is a characteristic of the Lenau that books are given precedence. People must wait to consult them, and then remain silent while doing so. Imagine if the world beyond the library were always like that – then I might wish to visit it more often. Fortunately, most of the world is not permitted ingress to our library except on the most stringent terms of visitation.

I must try from time to time to summarise Lenau for you. Or could it be for me? Such a summary is in fact impossible, but I suppose I must attempt it none the less.

Underlying so many of our words are images, and underlying those images are the primeval conflicts with nature and our fellow creatures from which our species was so painfully born; this is the teaching of Lenau, as I presently understand it. And who could disagree? Yet Lenau had pursued this unexceptional perception in some unlikely places, and with a vigour and virtuosity which can still astonish. I am as you know presently collating his scattered remarks on Rembrandt, and were the Lenau not a dedicated place of silence, I might occasionally murmur or even laugh out loud down in the stacks. Lenau has a way of bringing you to a perception at which you would never have arrived alone, and then presenting it to you in a manner that seems incontrovertible, as though the illumination had been your own all along. That's probably what Henrietta meant when she said her own thoughts had become indistinguishable from his. When the light shines brightly enough from a certain direction, shadows vanish.

Just before Bloomsbury loses the last rags of its Georgian exquisiteness and abandons itself to the vulgarity of Oxford Street and Centre Point, there is a bookshop. It is a hybrid, but its main identity comes from the sale of academic remainders. I like it in there. I never know what I will find. What I see this day I have seen before in catalogues, but could never afford. It is a book of Rembrandt's etchings, each one reproduced actual size; for some reason the Lenau has never acquired a copy. My hand reaches out and I touch it, and at that very moment another hand reaches out and touches it too. Polygenesis. Two texts emerge from different places bearing the same flaws; or two human beings bring identical flaws to the same place.

'I saw it first.' She is beautiful. We are both holding the book. She smiles. Shorter than Gemma, no more than five foot two, blonde to Gemma's brunette, face sunwashed and freckled. Gemma is right: I do need a friend. Warmth beneath a petticoat where the *sooterkin* brushes its downy hair and longs to escape.

'Let's go halves.'

'Then how would we share it?'

'Over a coffee, to start with?'

'I'll have a cappuccino.'

'Anything to eat?' She shakes her head. She has blue eyes too. The pair of us: blond(e) and blue-eyed. Had Lenau seen us together he would surely have thought Hitler's children had arrived in his new homeland to mock him posthumously. When I return to the table with the coffees, she is immersed in the Rembrandt. Evidently a passion with her too. The saucers tinkle on the table.

'I'm Robert.'

'Louise.'

'Professor, maybe?'

'Doctor.'

'Philosophy, is it?'

She smiles and nods.

'Two of us then.' Enhanced with a doctorate apiece. Who could ask for anything more?

'Now about this book . . . '

'I need it this afternoon. I really do. I'm writing something I just have to finish. This has the illustrations I need.'

Shall we be trusting, then? Without trust there can never be love, my friends, we must surely all know that. Even a *noli-me-tangere* understands this much.

'Well, I need it this evening. For something *I'm* writing.' Louise has a smile that twists one side of her face asymmetrically. Rembrandt would have liked that. I certainly do. 'Which means, I suppose, that we'll just have to meet for dinner, and do a deal.'

11

The book of Rembrandt etchings lies open on the table before us. We have dined lightly on pasta and salad. We are on the second bottle of wine. We are even sitting at the same table where I sat three weeks before with Gemma. And my knee is pressed against Louise's as it once pressed against my companion's from the Lenau. But the knee has been there for half an hour now, and Louise's has remained just as firmly pressed against mine as mine is insistently pressed against hers. Maybe I have found my friend at last. Will Gemma be pleased for me, I wonder? Why shouldn't she be, after all? She would appear to have no interest in me herself.

Louise's hands are turning the pages. There is a candle in a bottle on the table. Almost upright, it weeps wax tears. Beneath its swerving light, the images pass. We have stopped speaking and simply stare instead: at the naked woman seated on a mound, as unerotic a nude as an artist has ever created. It could only produce desire in a necrophiliac. Adam and Eve are a pair of Yahoos. This is a paradise only for ravening beasts. But then there was the one called *Lit à la Française* with the girl's contented eyes as the boy enters her, and *The Monk in the Cornfield*, where the monk is performing his devotions between the legs of a local farmgirl. My knee pressed a little harder.

'So what do you actually do, Robert?'

'I'm the Lenau Research Scholar.'

Her knee pulls away suddenly, and her face twitches.

'Then you must be Robert Fowey.'

'How did you know that?'

'Because I applied for the post too. I was curious to know who finally got it. So . . . ' the knee has returned very gently to its position against mine ' . . . what special gifts did you have to end up in such a prestigious position? What have you got that I haven't, Robert?'

'A singular lack of German and a certain expertise in *nefas*.'

'You'll have to explain.'

'Have another glass of wine first.'

I don't know whether Louise's curiosity was greater about me or my rooms in the Lenau. Anyway, she came back that night. And stayed. When we weren't making love or sleeping, we talked of Lenau. I spoke about the papers of 1940 to 1945, and how they were revealing aspects of the scholar I'd never before imagined, aspects which were now entering my dreams nightly. When I woke in the morning, Louise was not in the bed. I wondered for a moment if I might have dreamed her too. But when I stepped out of the bedroom, she was there sitting at my table, dressed only in the shirt I'd given her the evening before. Makeshift nightclothes. She was so absorbed in the Lenau Papers that she didn't even register my presence at first. Finally she looked up.

'I hope you don't mind. My curiosity got the better of me.'

I made her toast and coffee. Once again our knees met under the table.

'So where are you off to today?' I asked finally.

'Here,' she said. 'This is where I was heading. I'm a Lenau Associate Member. This was my next port of call. But now I've started reading what you have here, I just want to carry on. Can I? Do you mind?'

I didn't mind anything at all about Louise that morning. She could have whatever she wanted. And so when I went downstairs, she stayed up in my rooms. And it must have been while I was out walking in the park, counting my possibilities, that Gemma turned up for her late-morning coffee. She often came unannounced these days. I simply hadn't thought about it. I arrived back to find them both eyeing one another across the room.

'I didn't realise you knew Lou,' Gemma said, as I walked in.

'You two have met then?'

'At the Iconology Conference two years ago. You weren't there, were you, Robert?'

'No. Couldn't make it.'

'Immersed in your German studies, probably.'

Mmm. What does that remark signify, I wonder? Maybe Gemma isn't so pleased for me after all.

'I see Lou has been helping you with the Lenau Papers. She shouldn't really, you know. They're for your eyes only at this stage – until you resolve the matter of publication. It's part of the wording in your contract, if you ever take the trouble to read it.'

'I'm just having a quick look,' Louise said and smiled a little blankly.

'Quite a slow quick look, I'd have said.' And then Gemma left.

Louise came over to me, took my hand and placed it on her breast. 'I think she's jealous.'

'She's gay.'

'Well she wasn't very gay at the Iconology Conference. She and Tim Everett were in and out of one another's rooms more often than the cleaners. The pair of them looked positively pink with satisfaction the whole weekend.'

'But she had some sort of affair with Henrietta von Baum.'

'Did she, by God? That's a new one on me. That's really interesting.'

I had in fact already started to feel uneasy.

'I suppose she does have a point. About the papers, I mean. I probably shouldn't be showing them to you at this stage.' But by now my fingers were pressing, caressing the flesh beneath them, and Louise was letting her fingers tiptoe down below my waist. A minute later we were on the bed. And when it was all over and I came out of the bedroom once again, she was already sitting before her laptop with the papers around her.

I went down to the cellar, to do some more rummaging.

Evening. Tickety-tickety-tick. The keys on Louise's laptop. Her face aglow from the light of the screen, the only light in the apartment. Her fingers jive over the keyboard letters; the laptop hums its deep dark buzz of satisfaction. I had come in quietly and she hadn't even noticed. Tickety-tickety-tick. The sound of a thousand soft-bodied insects colliding against a lighted lamp. The Lenau Papers were scattered over the desk. Louise was staring at one and typing quickly.

Tickety-tick. What a lot of notes my new love was taking. Finally she looked up.

'Who's the other person writing notes here?'

'Henrietta von Baum.'

'God. That's amazing. Is there anything else she wrote about . . . about all this?'

'A notebook.'

'Do you have it?'

'Yes.'

'Can I see it?'

'Listen, Louise, I think you'd better tell me something, you know: what are you planning on doing with this stuff?'

By then she is already moving towards me, smile in place, her fingers ready for action. And before I can ask another question, it's beginning all over again. Which was exactly what I wanted it to do. I'm not pleading innocent to any charges here. What I gave, I gave; and what I took, I took. And the same, I think it fair to say, was true of Louise. Ring any bells? So I gave her the notebook. She bought some cream and put it by the side of the bed.

'Do it like he did?'

'What?'

'Your nails in my back like Lenau did with Henrietta. Here in this temple dedicated to his mind and work.'

And I did. I often do as I am told when I find myself with women. I certainly did with Louise. She cried out so loudly that I was glad we were the only ones there in that building that night. If I were so associated in her mind with Isaac Lenau that she could no longer distinguish between us, I decided I didn't care. And whenever I woke up she was not in the bed beside me, but there at the table, tapping into her laptop, transcribing from the papers or the notebook with undistractable zeal. Isaac Lenau and Robert Fowey: she can't seem to tell the difference between us, so why should I?

When I woke up finally on Friday morning, she was gone. She had packed up and gone. A note informed me that she needed to get away. It had all been 'wonderful', but now she was 'confused'. There was someone else; she should have told me about him before. That would have been sensible; but common sense hadn't really come into it, had it, with either of us? Where was Apollo, the god of rationality, when you really needed him? Elsewhere, supervising the flaying of Marsyas, presumably.

12

Marginalia, 2176.

Layard on his knees in the dust, as though at prayer. Scraping away at the surface of time's palimpsest; finding Nineveh. Underneath the top layer we discover the earlier deposits. Scrape away the mind's skin. Who are you then? Apollo or Marsyas? The tranquil god hearing the cries of torture, and silently applauding their propriety, or the satyr, half-beast, half-man, who tried to play sublime music as though he were a god?

One who could smile like a god while the creatures of the earth screamed on.

And that phrase: *scrape away the mind's skin.* Last week I saw a woman flay'd, and you will hardly believe how much it altered her person for the worse, said Swift. Ah, but I will, I will.

The cormorant and the bittern lodged in the lintels of that city. Nineveh: a desolation and dry like a wilderness. So much we were told by Zephaniah. Those idols cursed by Noah before the flood. The winged lions and bulls.

Some days now I feel as though my own mind has Lenau's blade pressed against it, scraping away the top layer of words, the biblical injunctions of my father, and his Father, to find the Ur-text that lies beneath all this contemporary confusion. How vivid every image became for Lenau, as though the words themselves had been cut into the parchment of his skin with blades.

Gemma has taken to interrogating me.

'Do you love your father?'

'I don't know. I don't think I can separate him from the idea of God.'

'Do you believe in his big book then, his Bible?'

'I believe it when it's true – the same way I believe Shakespeare when it's true, or Isaac Lenau for that matter.'

'That's not the way he would have wanted you to believe though, is it, your father I mean?'

'No, it isn't. He wanted me to put away my intelligence before reading. And you, Gemma, what about your parents? Where do you come from in the great genealogical line?'

She is sitting on my sofa, her foot curled beneath her thigh, sipping at the mug of coffee I have given her.

'My mother is Pamela, the concert pianist, who renounced her life in music so as to be my father's wife and the mother of his children. And my father is Doug, the waste-disposal consultant. Any jokes coming, Robert, let them arrive now.'

I shake my head. 'What is a waste-disposal consultant?'

'Someone who gets rid of other people's shit for them. Takes shit away from the rich folks and dumps it a lot nearer the poor ones; they don't seem to mind so much. They're already used to the smell. Dougsie the Dogshit Demon, we always called him. The feculent Pharaoh. He was good at his job. Very successful. And he had three daughters. But how he wanted a son. Another little shit-shoveller to follow in the old man's footsteps.'

'Why did your mother give up music?'

'To dedicate herself to her true vocation in life: providing the chips for her husband Dougie to piss on. She shopped for them, scissored open the plastic bags, laid them out on a grey metal tray, pushed them into the oven, gloved them out again thirty minutes later, distributed them on terracotta plates alongside fish, meat or whatever, and her dear husband, my beloved father, would then begin. That's the way it was: cooking for her, micturition for him. A division of labour, a sexual apportionment if you like. If a man is to spend his life pissing on someone else's chips, so that the vinegar of his acidity might be lengthily appreciated, then someone must supply those chips in the first place. And this was what my mother did for over twenty-five years. Until last year. When she finally resolved that if old Douglas wished to carry on pissing on chips, then he had better start supplying the items himself. Treat someone else to the lofty and ruinous tang of his acerbity. She seemed to realise, suddenly, that she'd always preferred rice.'

'And the music?'

'She has taken to playing in public once more.'

'So the story has a happy ending then?'

'If you regard two and a half decades of wasted life as a happy ending.'

'Not entirely wasted, surely. There's you, for a start.'

There was a pause then. I had a bad feeling I knew what was coming.

'How much did you show her?'

'Box 18.'

'All of it?'

'The whole manuscript and Henrietta's notebook.'

She stared at me in silence for a moment.

'The notebook as well. So desperate for a fuck, eh?'

'It wasn't just a fuck.'

'No, but it wasn't less than one, was it?'

'No.'

'Been in touch has she, since making such liberal use of our library facilities?'

'No.'

'Spent a lot of time taking notes, I reckon.'

'Yes.'

'Your taste in women, Robert, is not inspiring.'

'I liked you.'

'Can't help noting the past tense in that statement.'

13

Naked, ithyphallic, I intrude upon my own dream, coming from the opposite direction in the dark. There is an explosion, the usual kind, and I wake like a candle flaring, dripping my own warm wax tears, turning inside out. Louise. Gemma. Anybody really. Anyone at all. Somewhere there must be an emergency number you're meant to call at times like this. Does anyone out there know it? All that's left for me here is to turn to Harry, as vivid as ever, perched on my pillow.

'What's to become of us, little man?'

His grin as ever is unanswerable and answers nothing. Where are wave-form cerebretonics when you need them?

14

Long after the Reformation, benefit of clergy still had a hangover. It was called the neck-verse. If you could recite Psalm 51 (the one about the Lord's tender mercies) then you could avoid being hanged after a murder. This was a throwback to the time when the simple ability to read at all meant you must be either something to do with the king or something to do with the church: no one else was getting any reading lessons. This loophole saved Ben Jonson's life after he had killed Gabriel Spencer in a duel. And I was trying the same gambit now. I wasn't about to read the psalm (which, as it happens, I know by heart – thanks, dad, for all your tender mercies) but I was going to find passages in Lenau and in Henrietta's diary so urgent in their significance that Gemma might stop looking at me as though Lou was still lying on the bed draped in my shirt with her thighs peeping out. I didn't want to think about those thighs, or the inches of mouse-hair between them. Little *sooterkin* with its mousey life. Mickey. However assiduous she had been in pressing her body against mine, she had been at least as assiduous in taking notes from the MS and the notebook. Ten hours a day for six days. Even lover-boy here marvelled at her concentration. She'd had time enough to transcribe every single passage she needed. What was she going to use it all for, though? I only hoped it was for what academics normally call research: i.e. an article of such obscurity that only five other human beings will ever be likely to read it in fifty years. And they will only scan it in the hope that you might have fumbled one of your distant references so that they can pounce, and thereby prove their mettle.

I even counted all the MS pages, and went through the notebook to make sure no section had been razored out. It's a wonderful thing, love, banishing all fear and suspicion as it does. I had phoned fifteen times. Answering machine. When I contacted the university they said they thought Dr Knowles might have gone abroad for a while. To Venice, no doubt. Stolen documents; flights overseas. We were in a Jacobean drama. Or possibly by some fetid waterside with the late Henry James.

And so I hunted for my neck-verse. What might save me from the gallows of Gemma's disapproval? She was there for her coffee, as usual, at eleven.

'Who's the bloke in shorts and sandals?' I asked her. Another one hovering around in the Accessions Hall, needlessly extending his conversations with Gemma.

'Donald. He's an artist you won't have heard of. He even did some drawings of me once.'

'What sort of drawings?'

'Nudes.'

'Can I see them?'

'Why?'

I hesitated. 'I suppose I'd like to see you naked.'

'But you wouldn't see me naked, Robert. You'd see representations of me naked. Surely you've read enough of Lenau's work to know the difference by now. No one can make love to a nude.'

'Well, beggars can't be choosers, can they, Gemma? A nude representation of you is at least one step up from no you at all. Be fair.'

Anyway, I spent the whole of my adolescence making love to nudes; first introduction to the glories of Western art.

At this point Gemma put down her coffee, stood up and started laughing. She raised her black T-shirt to her neck, revealing what had been evident to me for some time: she does not usually wear a bra. I stared at her breasts. They seemed (seem) perfect, dark-nippled, touchable. Smaller than Louise's, designed somehow to fit into the palms of your hands. Or mine anyway. Yes, let's say mine. Then the T-shirt is pulled back down, and Gemma spins round and is gone through the door. I hear another brief laugh as she makes for the stairs. Wax is slowly hardening on a candle somewhere inside somebody's dark well. Someone's *nefas*. Could this be the waxing before the waning, or might it be the other way round?

Later that day I stand in the Accessions Hall until the man has gone; the last man. The Lenau's final creature of the day. Closing-time. The door is locked behind him.

'So who's the bloke with the beard growing round his frown?' I ask her.

'Oh Dolley. He's nuts. A megalomaniac. Told me once that, if he wanted, he could make that beard of his grow on other people's faces. Reckons he can alter the weather when he's really concentrating.'

'What's his subject?'

'Psychology.'

A pause. 'I've got something you should see.'

'Sure you wouldn't rather show it to the district nurse? I mean, is the swelling painful?'

'It's a passage from Henrietta's notebook. And a parallel text from Lenau. And I think you should see it.'

Have I found the neck-verse? We will soon know. Gemma and I are walking upstairs together. Pray for me now, my brothers and sisters. I am in need of your prayers.

She sits on my sofa. Feet curled beneath her thighs, as ever. She does not have a coffee in her hand, but a glass of wine. I took the precaution of going out and buying a bottle of Colombard, which I chilled in the fridge. She sips. She stares. And I begin to read from Henrietta's notes:

He has convinced himself that Cro-Magnon man created the 'species alienation' that later displaced itself to racial alienation. The collective enemy, according to him, can then be identified, assessed, attacked, exterminated. This facility for abstraction, the abstraction of one type of human being from another, followed by pre-emptive annihilation – is this the beginning of the human imagination? This is his question. I can't answer it. The origin of Dante's *Inferno*, Michelangelo's ceiling, the technicolour hell on that judgemental wall at Pisa? The guillotined dissident, Armenians marched to death? Reich Number Three. When his alienist looked into his eyes (Leipzig, 1934) did he see another race, another species, an inhabitant of the Kingdom of the Mad, the other world to which the mass of undesirables was despatched? Jew lunacy, the little schlepper from the shtetl, who has lost his ruined mind at last? He who should never have been given any rights to it in the first place.

I look up. Gemma is expressionless.

'Lenau had been institutionalised and treated in an asylum by an alienist during the 1930s, when he had undergone his first mental collapse. But then, you already knew this?'

'Yes, Robert, of course I did. Now carry on.'

He says humanity grows thrifty with imagination. One people's glory perfectly balances another's annihilation. The symmetry of nature which Rembrandt rightly saw as the torturing into shape of humanity. Apollo is smiling as the flesh of Marsyas is cut away. And the answer Oedipus gives to the Sphinx, remember, is Man. That is the answer to the riddle. Which means that inside that little word 'Man' all riddles must be contained. Euripides. The *Bacchae*. The corpse of Pentheus, with the head missing; but then, Agave, his mother, had been dancing with it. And so the god disguises himself as a man. Travelling incognito in the humdrum flesh. And the Maenads beat the tightened skin of their drums; they vaunt and ululate, sing litanies, blessings, invocations. They entice, and draw us after them.

Again I looked over at Gemma. I had expected some reaction by now, but there was none. I switched from Henrietta's notebook to the MS of Lenau of a corresponding date.

'He quotes Hamlet. "O God, I could be bounded in a nutshell and count myself a king of infinite space – were it not that I have bad dreams." And then Lenau continues:

You did not invent your dreams, Hamlet, and I did not invent mine. They are species dreams we have inherited. As we scrape away the protective flesh around the mind we find the hidden writing of the palimpsest. We find ourselves, so securely disguised beneath the text of the present. So imagine it then. The primal scene. The true primal scene. Aurignacian crowds coming down the valley. Dim-eyed Neanderthals watching, waiting. Eyes so much bigger than their brains. Homo sapiens, so much better at killing, already entirely modern in this respect, slaughters the men and ravishes the women. That, after all, is what he is there for. But no offspring. Noah survives, with his family. The rest are genocidally wiped out. He had been tempted to do something similar in Abraham's time, but the old man talked him out of it. Noah doesn't bother. He's too busy preparing the seafaring gear. Carving the gopher wood. Can't be too sentimental. Plenty of salt in tears, and he will doubtless be weeping for himself up there. And the endless theme of mis-cegenation in Nazi propaganda has surely been prepared for by that business with the angels and the daughters of men. The Jew as the poisoner of Aryan potency. And the mighty God ever ready to exterminate his own verminous brood.

There is silence. I look across at Gemma, who stares into the bowl of her wine-glass as though Lenau might have refashioned himself in there as a minute, vinicultural fish. And then she looks up finally, unsmiling.

'You have been growing your nails, Robert.'

I stare at them for a moment and grow flustered.

'One of my odder duties in this place is to organise the laundry. A complete set of sheets had to be thrown away. Couldn't get the bloodstains out, you see.'

'It was her idea.'

'Lovely Lou?'

'She bought cream.'

'Reliving the bedtime stories of Isaac Lenau and Henrietta von Baum, is that it? What you can't do with Lenau himself, time-travel being problematical, you might as well do with the Lenau Scholar instead. How quaint Lou-Lou is. And how very pliant of you. Did you like it, out of interest?' I say nothing. I look through the window. Brief clouds skid across a darkening blue sky. I wish I were someone else. 'Did you like it, Robert? You see, I heard something similar went on with Tim Everett.'

'But she said you were the one who . . . '

Gemma looks at me and slowly starts to nod.

'So that was what she told you, was it? That it was me at the Iconology Conference, fucking like a Duracell Bunny with our London professor? No, it was your devoted companion, I'm afraid. Who, I gather, will not be a mere lecturer at York for much longer. She's about to take a post as Reader in Everett's department. That will give her more time for research, evidently, not to mention arranging her publications. And she'll doubtless be helping the prof to grow his nails again, and keep them sharp. She does make the best of her liaisons, I'll give her that much. You are an idiot, you know.'

'I know. Are you gay?'

'What?'

'Are you gay? I just want to know. You told me about the scars on Henrietta's back. How did you come to see them?'

'Because I was her friend. Her nurse. Her companion. I helped soothe her pain. Is that permitted? Oh, for God's sake.' She is looking at me and shaking her head. 'Go and cut your nails, Robert.'

'What?'

'Go and cut your fucking nails, now. Whatever the Lovely Louise's tastes might be, they're not mine.'

15

We lay on the bed together afterwards. Halfway through making love it had struck me why she had said nothing as I went through the words of Lenau and Henrietta.

'You'd already read it all, hadn't you?'

'Yes.'

'Why didn't you tell me?'

'Because you had to find it all out for yourself.'

'What's Everett like?'

'Oily enough to float on water. Oleaginous. The sort of man who walks into a room carrying another man's jock for him. Got to the top by kissing the right arses. Constantly greasing his inside leg, to slide the more fluently up the academic pole of preferment. Invited me to his thirty-ninth party three years running. Obviously can't face the prospect of being forty, though I can't see how it can be much worse than what he was before. The intellectual life of Britain today. Could make you proud to be illiterate.'

We fell silent for a while.

'What did Henrietta tell you?'

'Oh, he was on to something, she knew that. We behave as though knowledge has displaced the symbol, the symbol that was our terrified attempt to capture or resist so much power in the first place; but is it so, Lenau came to ask more and more – is it really so? Knowledge is such a thin and treacherous covering, there to overlay the terror, and all its symbolic expressions. They are never far beneath the surface, these terrors. They are full of energy and can be released with a certain amount of slick manipulation. The great public Nazi processions and ceremonies were to prove that, and with so little resistance. At Nuremburg everything was symbol, preternatural power; the fierce emotions simply inspirited the ancient forms. Murder was on the move again, across the face of the earth. Lenau looked on from a distance, horrified. He managed to stay out of the asylum for a while in his Oxford fastness, but only just. And only because he had another kind of asylum to harbour him: the Lenau Institute. A library with its face set against the whole of modern reality. And Henrietta, who permitted him his experiments on her body and her mind. So as to keep him from the Kingdom of the Mad. But she couldn't keep him from it for ever.'

My hand is gently caressing Gemma's breast. Her back is pressed into my midriff. She is staring away from me, up towards the window. We can see the last clouds before the light fails.

'The trance into which reason is always tempted to put itself, so as to resolve the agony of its troubled logic: that's what he said. Reason, should it accept the invitation, will then use all its considerable resources for purposes of oppression and murder. He had become convinced that murder, genocide, was coded inside us. That was the palimpsest. Our art and our religion and our music were not attempts to find out the ultimate truth about ourselves, but our most energetic attempts to evade it. That is why great art costs so much – it has to travel so desperately away from our true inclinations. And it's why Apollo was the god of music.'

Gemma's body was in my hands. I still couldn't believe that.

'Was he right?'

'No. Henrietta explained that to me.'

'How did she explain it?'

Gemma moved gently, and my hand slipped down her thigh.

'Henrietta was the most courteous human being I ever met. She seemed to have lived through the whole of her life with a sort of smiling *gravitas*, a sceptical attentiveness to the demands either of romance or resentment, quizzical, half-amused; she always kept her equanimity, interrupted only at the end by what she called death's brief and vulgar discourtesy. You saw how she always pulled her hair back from her forehead with such stringency, as though it might be better if it pulled her face right off. Then she'd have been honestly blank to each unwanted request for concern or interest in Lenau. His mind. His work. His madness. As though she'd never existed except when she was attached to him.' She fell silent for a moment now.

'Unhappiness, if it is severe enough, leads to untruth. That's what she told me. And that's what happened to Lenau. His unhappiness became so severe that it led to untruth. He convinced himself that all the expressions of cruelty were expressions of a primordial truth. She thought otherwise. And she was right. We escaped, she said, both Lenau and I. We didn't have to die, consumed by another's dream of order. We came here and lived. If he'd got well again, she believed he would have come to see it too. Instead he wrote those fascicles, and she wrote her notebook. And presented by themselves they tell an untruth. If they could be put in the context of the two lives, they could tell a truth instead.'

I stood at the window in the evening light. A peregrine falcon had found a pigeon's nest, with its hatched young, and it was harrying.

'How I wish I could be that falcon, just for thirty seconds,' I said. 'To understand how it feels to rest on the wind like that. To see what it sees when it looks down on the young pigeons or the rubbish bag.'

'Henrietta would have had a very simple answer to that. You'd see nothing if you were only a peregrine falcon for thirty seconds. It would be like having a bucket of red paint thrown in your face. You'd have had to have been a falcon all your life to have their eyes. Otherwise they'd blind you. Either the little man grinning away on your pillow goes or I do.'

'Give him another week. You'll get used to him.'

'What's he called?'

'Harry. Just like his old man. Not much good at harrying, though.'

16

Lenau had been much preoccupied with light. It took two forms in his work. When God in the opening passage of Genesis says, Let there be light, the phrase translated into Latin was *Fiat Lux*, not *Fiat Lumen*. *Lux* was that light associated with divine power; *lumen* the material traces such heavenly light might leave. And so, over the centuries, *lumen* came to have the meaning more and more of the object of scientific enquiry. It is *lumen* that Newton was investigating in his *Opticks*, not *lux*. And *lumen* then comes to carry a further significance: it is the light that penetrates the observing being, ourselves for example, rather than the light which shines from within us outwards. We perceive *lumen*, where we might possibly have communicated with *lux*. The prismatic contraptions of Newton's work are designed to track the path of a force through material bodies, not to fathom the behaviour of the Almighty Spirit in its visible form.

But in Rembrandt's nativity pictures, whatever the science of his day, the light that shines out of the cradle is evidently the divine light as described by John: 'And the light shineth in darkness; and the darkness comprehended it not.' This light transcends its material circumstances, but it does not override them; otherwise there could be no crucifixion. The divine illumination cannot be baffled and contained by the shadow of the world's chiaroscuro. The shadows represent the foil by which the light displays itself.

Rembrandt the non-denominational Protestant, though with a

leaning towards the Mennonites, saw light as originating with God and warming the spirit. The light that comes from the Child in the cradle, or the forgiving Saviour, or the risen Lord, is *lux*. A *lux* that comforts the humble in heart, and blinds the mighty like Belshazzar. And Lenau believed there was a survival of this ancient notion of generative light in the form of genius, and its iconography. Here once more is the mystery of transmitted light. The sense of a source of energy that cannot be tracked beyond its unexplained source in an individual psyche. Genius. Einstein with the electrodes in his head. Picasso painting with light.

I looked up at the night sky. Despite London's light pollution, I could still see enough stars. What would Lenau have made of those Hubble images? A keyhole into the distance is also a telescope into the past; that much he already knew. So what we see is what has already been. Fifteen hundred galaxies have left their traces, and we have arrived belatedly with our instruments to try to fathom what the traces mean. A single bright supernova is as bright as ten billion stars. The brightness would be incommensurable with both our eyes and our understanding, should we ever come close enough. Beauty, said Rilke in the *Duino Elegies*, in lines Lenau knew by heart, is nothing but the beginning of Terror we're still just able to bear. This is where the heavy elements are born. Without such burn-outs, we wouldn't exist. Antennae Galaxies. The swirling capes of blue and orange are a firestorm, a cosmic Dresden of destruction, in which hydrogen collides with more hydrogen. From such internecine warfare, new stars and planets are forged. Lenau was fascinated by astrology, since for us, patterns must always represent coherence, even the coherence of death. Stars may give life, but they have their own lives too. Sometimes we seem to be attendants at a cosmic funeral. The gases are flung away and form a halo, leaving the burnt-out case of a white dwarf. I had to come back from the stars.

What exactly was I going to do?

17

I wake empty. For once I'm glad to be empty. I've been full of so much lately – Gemma, Louise, Lenau, Marsyas. I'm happy to feel nothing. I want to walk out into the day and feel nothing. My mind flayed, all its skin taken off at last. Gemma isn't here. Perhaps she's downstairs, opening up the Institute. Her last words to me, before we fell asleep last night: 'What are you going to do?'

'If I could work out the problem then I might know the answer.'

On the table was a sheet of paper covered with Gemma's tiny and immaculate handwriting.

> This is the problem, Robert. These last papers of Lenau, and the notebook of Henrietta, read by themselves, tell a lie. They show a mind shaken by grief and unbalanced by it. They can be presented as sensational – they could even by serialised in the *Mail on Sunday*. They probably will be. 'Genius of Sado-Masochism'. All the usual palaver. Placed in context, they could help to elucidate Lenau's life and thought. Out of context, they will overshadow everything else he ever did. It would be better that they should be destroyed rather than highlighted. That is the problem then. I'll repeat it: it would be better that they should be destroyed rather than published by themselves.

Destroyed. Could she really be serious?

In the Accessions Hall there's another one hovering about her. Some scholastic loser. There is no end of them. I look at his blinking brown eyes, brown hair, brown beard, mouth hanging half-open, features a-quiver, and I think of a giant rodent sniffing the wind nervously. What would Rembrandt have made of him? As the lever to Archimedes, so was decaying flesh to Rembrandt. He marvelled at the squalid domiciles in which the inveterate soul was prepared to reside.

Gemma contrives to avoid my eyes. She is going about her professional business; she is also a little wary of her new position as lover of the Lenau Scholar. I can understand that. I had suggested we resolve the matter immediately through marriage.

'Do I have to?'

That had been her answer. Not the most melting answer a woman ever made to a man who's gone a-wooing. On the other hand, it's not actually a no, now is it?

'Who's that?' I ask as the bearded man leaves.

'My dad.' My look must register incredulity.

'I know: he looks so nondescript for one who has capitalised with such panache on the world's excreta. But there you are. That was old Dogshit Doug, to whom I owe my life. Or the first squirt of it anyway.'

I walk the London streets. What to do with this stuff of Lenau's? My head is full of the manuscript now, and Henrietta's responses to it. Race is the modern tyrant's dark apothecary, that's what he said: all sensitivities can be dulled or heightened by the injection of *xenon*, that hideous narcotic. A nose one inch longer invites slaughter from the latest Roman proconsul (but surely no Roman ever expected such homogeneity across his conquered terra firma?). And so obsessed with it all had he become that his mind had gone astray. And this last time it never came right again. Henrietta:

> He had so attuned himself to receiving and calibrating slights that he had become in effect a resentment machine. Nietzsche's automaton. His psyche duly kicked against the pricks, even when there were no actual pricks to kick against.

That's what she'd written. What was I supposed to do with all this? I remembered Gemma's remark to me right at the beginning: whether or not I would choose to destroy Lenau's international reputation. By publishing his thoughts from 1940 to 1945. *By themselves.*

By the time I got back Gemma had already let herself into the apartment with the spare key I had given her. She was standing at the window with a mug of coffee in her hand. She didn't turn round to greet me, but started to speak straight away.

'Do you know Harry Phelps? The editor of *Marsyas*?'

'Never met him, no. We corresponded. He published my piece on Lenau and Rembrandt, of course.'

'Yes, I remember. Henrietta was impressed. That's why you're here. He's just received a long essay. About Lenau. Entitled "The Long Descent to the Inferno". Written by one Dr Louise Knowles, presently of York University, soon to be a Reader at London University.'

I sat down on the sofa where Gemma normally curled up.

'He felt he had to check with me regarding the authenticity of the quotes. The source for them is given as the Lenau Institute, London. Particular thanks are due, I gather, to the Lenau Scholar, for his generosity with unpublished manuscripts. Doesn't mention the Lenau Librarian – which strikes me as a trifle impertinent.' Gemma walked across to the table and picked up the manuscript, which she had stacked into a neat pile, and Henrietta's leather-backed note-book. She lifted the sheets up and then dropped them down on the table.

'So there we are, Dr Fowey. Over to you. It's your call. You'd better make up your mind, sharpish.' And then she walked out.

18

The brain is so physically tiny, said Lenau, and yet capable of containing the vastness of the universe; in our physical specificity we are infinitesimal, yet our minds are illimitable. In the gap between the infinitesimal and the infinite we create art; that's also where madness gets started. That was Lenau's take on himself, and the rest of us too.

I spent the day turning the pages of the manuscript and going once more through Henrietta's notebook. Some of Lenau's insights were extraordinary, even if none were entirely reliable. His companion's notebook was her attempt to map the parts of his mind still worth exploring. By the end she too had given up. *He has led himself into the darkness – I don't believe this time he even wants to come back.* That was what she wrote. And of course, that last time he didn't return. And now my Louise, whose face had glowed so avidly in the light from her laptop, was about to make all this public knowledge. Clickety-clickety-click. And I have a terrible confession to make. What I felt worst about was not the damage to Lenau's intellectual reputation, nor the impropriety of making available these unedited and unpublished texts by Lenau, but Gemma's attitude to it all. I wanted her; all this was coming between us. I feared that she was beginning to hold me in contempt.

I made a decision, right there and then: I would leave it up to her. Whatever she decided to do, I would accept. Whatever.

It was evening and the last of the stragglers were leaving. I went down into the Accessions Hall. Gemma busied herself with her cards.

'Can we have a talk about it?'

'Have you made a decision?'

'Sort of.'

'I'll come up in a minute.'

And she did.

'So what's the decision?'

'Whatever you decide.' I have a feeling she was expecting this.

'Right. Then we must either let her publish, which will cost you your job, by the way, or we have to deny the validity of the documents she's quoting from.'

'And how would we do that?'

'Who has actually seen them? You, me, Henrietta, a very dead Lenau, and of course . . . '

'So, it would be her word against ours.'

'Against yours, Robert. You are the Lenau Scholar.'

'And yours. You are the librarian. Tell me what to do.'

It seemed to take Gemma only a few seconds to make up her mind.

'Go out and have a drink somewhere. Leave me alone here. Come back in an hour.'

So I did.

When I arrived back there was neither manuscript paper nor notebook on the table. There were two parcels wrapped in brown paper, one large, the other small. I looked at each parcel in turn, then I looked at Gemma.

'What are we going to do with them?'

'Did you mean it? When you said that, whatever I decided, you'd agree.'

'Yes.'

'You'd better mean it, Robert. Or one of us will be moving out of the Lenau. And I'll be moving out of your life.'

'So what are we going to do?'

'Burn them.' I stared in silence. 'Don't you see: that's preferable to the alternative. We are going to destroy them, and then notify both *Marsyas* and Dr Knowles that, as we suspected, the documents have all turned out to be forgeries, and have been put away while legal enquiries are pursued. Any scholarly writing produced on the basis of them will be shown to be ill-judged if not fraudulent, and will probably destroy the reputation of the person perpetrating it. And will do no good at all to the publication.'

'You're sure?'

'I'm sure.' So, that's the woman I love then. *Nefas*. A dark well you must sometimes dive into. And whatever she says, I'll do it. That was my promise, and I'm keeping it. You don't have to look at me like that.

Beyond the back door of the Institute, which is seldom opened, there is a small yard. It is paved and surrounded by walls. That's where we lit the fire with old newspapers from the Reading Room and threw the manuscript bundle on to the flames. The second thing to join the flames was the little parcel containing Henrietta's notebook, which Gemma had been holding. She kissed the brown paper before finally tossing it on the bonfire. I thought that was it, and that seemed bad enough. But then she reached into her canvas bag and took out Harry. As she lifted him up, I said, 'No.' The second time I'd seen him heading for the flames.

'You said, whatever I decided, you'd go along with it. So decide.'

And I turned around. My back to the little inferno. When I spun round again, Harry had lit up like a diminutive Guy Fawkes. Then, when it was all over, we brushed away the ashes and went back inside.

'I bought some wine,' Gemma said.

'Are we celebrating then?'

'I don't know what we're doing.'

We sipped at our glasses in silence, and she lifted up this typescript from the table, the same one you are now reading.

'What an interesting family history, Bob. Now I see why you're always going over at lunchtime to stand outside that puppet museum. There's a handwritten note here explaining that fiction can sometimes be a form of non-psychotic paranoia, but I'm far from sure about that.'

'You didn't ask if you could read it.'

'It was lying here on the table. I sleep with you each night. You wanted me to read it.' She was right. I need her to understand all that has been written here. If she can't, then who will?

'One thing I don't understand,' I said finally. I kept thinking about everything I'd read in that manuscript – the other one, I mean. The one by Lenau. Often unsound it might have been, but it was fascinating. 'That phrase "elephant eyes".'

'What didn't you understand?'

'It's normally ascribed to Picasso, isn't it?'

'Rembrandt's elephant eye, is what he said. The way the flesh decays even around the most penetrating eye that ever existed. Lenau and Henrietta visited him in his studio in Paris, you know. There's a photograph somewhere by Brassaï. So who knows which one of them said it first? Does it matter anyway?'

'I suppose not.'

'She would have been pleased.'

'Who?'

'Henrietta. That's what she was hoping you'd do.'

'Destroy it all?'

'No. Not permit it to be published in a sensational way. She didn't believe it could add anything to his genuine reputation, not done that way. Our age is in love with sensation, degradation, madness. She was in no doubt that it would have been of interest. Even made money. For all the wrong types, all the wrong reasons. Now, I'm going to phone up the editor of *Marsyas* and tell him why he can't publish that article by the lady in York, and when I'm through, you're going to phone her.'

'She won't be there.'

'Yes, she will. Back in harness since last Saturday. I've already checked.'

So I sat listening as Gemma spoke on the phone.

'At this moment, Harry, the question of authenticity is paramount.

223

First tests on the paper show it was manufactured in 1960, ten years after Lenau died. In which case it's a fake. Don't ask me why. No idea. Maybe Henrietta did it herself, to bring him back to life. She had a complete breakdown after he died. Went on for some years . . . What I'm saying, Harry, is if you were to publish it, there would have to be a statement from the Lenau, which would inevitably bring your editorial judgement into serious question . . . The matter's been put in the hands of the police. That's what I thought you'd say . . . No, don't worry, we'll contact Louise directly. Only courteous, after all. The papers concerned are now out of circulation, so they can't do any more damage.'

Then she rang off and handed the phone to me.

'Your turn, Robert. You can inform Loulou that her project terminates here. But you can also tell her that we've actually destroyed the documents. Otherwise she'll keep banging on. I know her, and she will.'

'So I tell her that we burned the stuff?'

'Say I showed you definitive evidence that the documents were forgeries. Bogus ageing of the paper and so on. Evidence only just came through. And we made the decision together – that's you and me, remember – that we had better destroy the lot before any further mischief could come of it. Before vulgar little minds came sniffing around these parts – again. The story about the cops is just a ruse, obviously.'

'She must have put quite a bit of work in, preparing that paper . . . '

'Yes, she put quite a bit of work in preparing you as well. Come-uppance time. Phone, Robert.'

So I did.

I held the phone away from my ear, but her voice was still coming through.

'It's that cow Gemma, isn't it? Jealous little twat. You'd never have had the balls to do that by yourself. She put you up to it. I suppose she's supplying your bedside needs these days. I hope you both get thrown out on your fucking ears.'

With that, she put the phone down.

'What did she say?' Gemma was sipping her wine and smiling.

'She said it was possible we might have acted a little rashly, but that didn't necessarily make us bad people. Scholarship is all.'

'What did she really say?'

'That you were a jealous little twat, and that I'd never have had the balls to do it alone.'

'She might have a point, Robert. Or even two.'

She came over to me then, opened my mouth with a kiss, and then let the wine from her mouth seep into mine. We both still smelt a little of smoke.

'I do wonder if all this might create a problem with that new Readership of hers.'

'That would break your heart, obviously, Gemma.'

19

That night I had Lenau's dreams, not mine. I had read the details of so many of them that they felt like mine anyway. The one with the child in the glass case, perfectly still, expressionless and wearing a white suit, even as the oxygen is sucked out. The delta filled with primordial creatures, each one mimicking the others until the slaughter begins. Acres of ocean turning red. And the ceremony with the captured Neanderthal woman, as *Homo sapiens* finds out if she can perform the same acts as his own female creatures. They couldn't understand any of her cries, though she understood well enough what they were doing to her.

I woke alone and reached out for Harry, but he'd already passed over to the other side, hadn't he? Just like his father. Blades and flames. Flames and blades. They all go into the dark. When I came out of the bathroom, Gemma was back, sipping her coffee at the window. Standing on one flamingo leg. I walked across and put my hand on her shoulder.

'We shouldn't have done it, you know.'

'You showed an admirable devotion to me, Robert, but a little less responsibility in your other role as Lenau Scholar, I must say. How are you planning on making up for it?'

'I've started having his dreams. I'm Lenau's Posthumous Dreamer. We shouldn't have done it.'

'Maybe we didn't.'

'What?'

'Heard about Charlie Friend, have you?'

'No.'

'You're so unworldly, my darling. Died in his little love nest in New York. His young man phoned for an ambulance but by the time they got there, he was already a stiff. Poor old ticker couldn't take all the excitement. His wife will be upset, down in Surrey with the boys. But it does leave an unfinished biography of Isaac Lenau, all the same. Which you, being the obvious candidate, are going to finish. Using material old Charlie had never even seen.'

'And which we've just destroyed.'

She shook her head at me then, and gave me a sorry look. 'You don't really think I'd have let you send up those precious documents in flames, do you?'

'Then . . . what?'

Gemma walked over to the cupboard in the corner where I dumped old magazines and papers, and opened the drawer. She took out the Lenau manuscript and Henrietta's notebook. Whatever had been inside the brown paper wrappings destined for the flames, it hadn't been them.

'So what did we burn then?'

'Ten copies of *Marsyas*. The issue with your essay on Lenau and Rembrandt. *Ten* copies, Robert?'

'They sent them to me.'

'All of them?'

'One. I bought the other nine.'

'What a vain man I seem to have partnered. Anyway, they all went up in flames, tragically. Meaning that we still have Lenau and von Baum to ourselves, after all.'

'So why the charade? Why the charade with me?' I felt a certain anger beginning now. Which I was entitled to, surely?

'Because you would never have been so convincing with that old flame of yours otherwise. Now would you? And we really did have to convince her, you know. Or she would not have backed off. Not if I know Lou. And I do know Lou.' She did have a point there, I have to admit. 'And I don't think she'd have believed you unless you were telling the truth. So I helped you to mean it, because you really believed it was true. And now we can get on with our work, can't we? You have a biography to write. That will put the late material in context, the way Henrietta had always intended, but we couldn't have known at the time that Charlie would so conveniently die. He was the wrong person entirely to be writing about Lenau. No *nefas* in him at all. Just murk. All appetite, deceit and self-congratulation. I'll help you with the chapters on Henrietta.'

'We could co-write it.'

'We'll see. Anyway, we've just made a dead old lady very happy.'

'And a living young one very mad.'

'Good. Come here.'

And I went. Couldn't resist Gemma for long.

'Am I still a *noli-me-tangere* then?'

'Oh, I haven't even started to touch you. Not even started.'

'And what about my *nefas*?'

'Like most people's dark well, it will probably remain unplumbed, until you finally drown in it.'

Gemma put her arms around my shoulders and started smiling. Then, among the caresses I'd grown used to, I felt a cut like a blade going into my neck. Something as sharp as a razor making its entry. I jerked back and took hold of her hand. I stared at it as she began to laugh.

'You've been growing your nails.'

A tiny fleck of blood on the index finger.

One Last Posthumous Dialogue

'Astronomy was originally a form of time-keeping, you know, Mr Bones.'

'A celestial wristwatch.'

'More of a sundial really, with the solid earth we walk on as the gnomon.'

'The years go by . . . '

'The rivers rise and fall . . . '

'Deltas are made fertile . . . '

'Cities are inundated . . . '

'The midwinter shadow is longest of all. Any conclusions to be drawn here, Harry?'

'I'm a dead piece of wood, Mr Bones. Like the paper on which these words are written. And I have recently lost a son. I'm in mourning.'

'Shall we go back to the beginning and start again?'

'In search of further clarification, you mean?'

'Or merely to while away the time.'

'Look at London out there on the street. The endlessness of it. Like elementary particles rushing hither and yon. We have all the time in the world.'

'How much time is that?'

'It's both a very big number and a very small one.'

'I think we had better leave my nephew and Gemma alone for a while.'

'Yes, I got that impression too. I have loved my own kind you know, Mr Bones. One vent had me on one knee and Tamara on the other. A little Hawaiian girl with a chain of live caterpillars draped around her neck. Tiny undulations they made. Always made me think of pollinated flowers, furry, rainbow-coloured. I would reach out a finger sometimes and one of the tiny bodies would curl around it. I tell you, Bones, if I hadn't been a tree . . . '

'Are you making this up, Harry?'

'I can't remember. Can you? Could it be, Mr Bones, that my ultimate function was to bring out the primeval murderer in you once more? That seems to have been Isaac Lenau's argument anyway.'

'I think it might also have been mine. We remember the prehistoric catastrophe, the early slaughter. We both remember it and don't. Jacob steals Esau's birthright. The hairy one, the Neanderthal, is bested by his lethal, intellectual brother. Apollo, the smooth-faced god, has hairy Marsyas flayed to death. We're revisiting the earliest site.'

'These are elegies for the people we killed?'

'The people we killed to get history going.'

'Are we scheduled to do it all again?'

'I don't know.'

'Anyway, our physics is posthumous now. There is no chronology. Sometimes it was your breath providing the life, but my words that uttered it.'

'That's ventriloquism for you. Once the word leaves one body and enters another . . . you could be abrasive sometimes.'

'And also abraded, as I recall. By the adze. I still hear them sometimes, you know, crying out in the night as the saw goes through them.'

'A Caesarean operation.'

'So that man may flourish. All flora and fauna across the planet must ensure man's flourishing. I no longer grow. I sit here in this puppetmaster's shrine, but I no longer look like the tree I was. No leaves; no branches. I have been made over in the image of he who made me. Only my painted cheeks appear to blossom.'

'Then you are an idol.'

'But we already knew that, Mr Bones. A wooden tragedian. A fetish. Like Queequeg's little god in *Moby-Dick*.'

'And look at the crowds of them out there.'

'You can hardly see the wood for the trees. We want magic, Bones. Oh, how we crave it. We want those dry old bones to resurrect before us, enfleshed once more, telling us tales of the grave and the hereafter that will make us quiver. A porcupine on the back of every neck. What happens if you call a man, Bones?'

'He will surely have to die.'

'Clairvoyance, at long last.'

'We see so clearly now, do we not?'

'Is it a comfort?'

'It is not a comfort.'

'Last night I thought I felt your fingers running round my face. Round and round the circles went. Back into the past and back into the future.'

'Dendrochronology.'

'I woke in tears.'

'But we don't sleep . . . '

' . . . and we don't cry.'

'Have you noticed these days . . . '

' . . . how often we end one another's sentences.'

'We've said this before. We've surely said all this before . . . '

'Well, a tear found its way into our little glass shrine, all the same.'

'The precipitation of sorrow. A little condensation from the fading heat of our lives together.'

'Fading?'

'Faded, then. *Faded*.'

'You still burned, all the same, when they put you in your own wooden box.'

'One night I dreamed, whether I was awake or not. And I thought I saw the earth itself, the blue globe, silently weeping. One vast salty tear was starting to drown the world. Already in Bangladesh, homes made of corrugated iron are swamped as the rivers rise and the waves increase.'

'If only you had filmed my dreams, Mr Bones, we could both have been rich. You should have brought in Francis Ford Coppola – he could have directed it for you.'

'Is Harry dreaming any different from Harry waking then?'

'The carbon atoms, Mr Bones, do they see or feel? My eyes, as you have presumably noticed by now, are painted.'

'We sometimes seem self-created. I believe there is a spider that self-generates.'

'Arachnoid parthenogenesis.'

'Wouldn't put it past the eight-legged little bastards. All silk and poison. Sounds like you in your heyday, Harry.'

'The only heyday I ever had was when I was a tree, Mr Bones. Swaying in a breeze by the river. Before you came along and cut me down.'

'Maybe it's your heyday now.'

'Now there are no days, whether heydays or dog-days. Merely the alternation of light with darkness. Was I really a maker of mischief, Mr Bones?'

'You were undoubtedly a malcontent. You cackled at the fall of cities.'

'Which cities fell, then?'

'During your time as a puppet, more than I care to count.'

'And I cackled?'

'You cackled.'

'Continously?'

'I don't think *continuously* would be too strong a term. You said, Now they know what it's like to be cut down in your prime. Now they can carry my burden for a while.'

'Are we concluding?'

'It certainly feels as though we are concluding.'

'Take a bow. You deserve one. The audience has appreciated your performance. Last night, Mr Bones, I went fishing in a dead canal.'

'A dead canal?'

'How well you chorus me.'

'And you caught?'

'My hook snagged repeatedly. On decommissioned wheels, drowned dolls, the odd boot discarded by a strolling merman, and a skull illuminated by night-lights . . . '

'Hard to believe you found a skull, Harry, particularly an illuminated one.'

'The skull (like these dialogues) was posthumous, obviously, so everything is possible, with respect, sir. The skull glowed underwater like the eyes of eels on their amphibious journeys through waterway and field. Maybe it had an eel coiled inside it.'

'*Memento mori quia pulvis est.* Dust would be pretty soggy, believe me, down at the bottom of that canal.'

231

'Posthumously, I always think of canals as lachrymatories.'

'Absolutely. Channels of tears over which the barges glide.'

'Even when a canal flows, it flows to no purpose.'

'The water goes nowhere.'

'And the cargoes on the barges' backs . . . '

'Are covered over with tarpaulins.'

'How mysterious. Is it possible I'm more useful than you, Bones?'

'How so?'

'You leave behind one set of bones, which is either laid in the earth or incinerated. From the tree you expect far more. Chairs and tables, altars, sculpted saints and spearshafts, boxes and handles and still – astonishing as it may seem – the chassis of the Morgan sports car. Trees branch out, even in death; but humans, unless they donate their organs, go to extinction unused.'

'We are undoubtedly concluding. Brother Tom?'

'Is sitting with an Indian boy even as we speak. Dr Naseby wept when he saw him walk through the door. He feels that both their lives have now found meaning once more.'

'So the secrets of ISP and wave-form cerebretonics must probably die with us then.'

'In which case they've already died. Except that we can't die.'

'And Robert Fowey and Gemma have just conceived a child.'

'Even as we speak?'

'Even as we speak. Just as well we left them to their own devices for the last half hour. In fact, no wait, they have conceived twins.'

'Isaac and Henrietta?'

'Henrietta and Isaac. It's the waves that keep arriving at the shore.'

'Not the sea.'

'Never the sea.'

'Without the sea staying where it is . . . '

' . . . there is no shore for the waves to arrive at . . . '

' . . . and no waves either.'

'So let's start again.'

'Shall we?'

'Yes. Let's.'